A PERFECT STORM

A
PERFECT
STORM

MIKE MARTIN

OTTAWA
PRESS AND
PUBLISHING

OTTAWA
PRESS AND
PUBLISHING

ottawapressandpublishing.com

Copyright © Mike Martin 2020

ISBN 978-1-988437-49-1 (pbk.)
ISBN 978-1-988437-51-4 (EPUB)
ISBN 978-1-988437-50-7 (MOBI)

Printed and bound in Canada

Design and composition: Magdalene Carson at New Leaf Publication Design
Cover after photograph kindly provided by Kurt Sampson.

Library and Archives Canada Cataloguing in Publication

Title: A perfect storm / Mike Martin.
Names: Martin, Mike, 1954- author.
Description: Series statement: A Sgt. Windflower mystery
Identifiers: Canadiana (print) 20200323652 | Canadiana (ebook) 20200323660 |
ISBN 9781988437491
(softcover) | ISBN 9781988437507 (Kindle) | ISBN 9781988437514 (EPUB)
Classification: LCC PS8626.A77255 P47 2020 | DDC C813/.6—dc23

This is a work of fiction. All of the characters, names, incidents, organizations,
and dialogue in this novel are either products of the author's imagination
or are used fictitiously.

To Joan. Thank you for your ongoing love and support in helping to create another Windflower adventure.

ACKNOWLEDGEMENTS

I would like to thank a number of people for their help in getting this book out of my head and onto these pages. These include beta readers and advisers Mike Macdonald, Barb Stewart, Robert Way, Lynn Tyler, Denise Zendel and Karen Nortman; Bernadette Cox for her excellent support and copy editing, and Cassie Doubleday for the proofreading at the end.

A PERFECT STORM

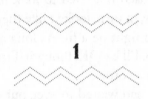

Eddie Tizzard passed his card over the sensor and pushed the door open. He flicked on the light. "Holy jumpins," he said when he saw what was on the bed in his hotel room—thousands of dollars strewn around like confetti. When he looked closer, he saw something else. There, right in the middle of the bed, was a very red, very large bloodstain.

His first instinct was to run. But his years as an RCMP officer got the best of him, and he had another look around. Soon the source of the blood became obvious. It was a man in a suit lying face down in the bathroom with a visible hole in the back of his head. Tizzard should have trusted his first instinct because when he did decide to leave the room, he walked directly into the path of who he would later find out was the head of hotel security.

He was remembering all of this as he sat in a holding cell with a dozen other men in the Las Vegas jail. Tizzard had gone to Vegas for private detective training, having decided on a new career path after leaving the Royal Canadian Mounted Police, or the Mounties. Technically, he was on leave for the rest of the year, but he doubted he'd ever return to his old job. He'd applied for and received his firearms licence, but he wanted a certificate to put on the walls of his new office, that is when he got an office. That seemed very far away right now, about as far as he could get from his home in Newfoundland on the eastern tip of Canada.

He'd watched enough police shows on TV to know that he could make one phone call. But nobody had said when he could do that. The duty officer kind of smirked when he pushed him into the lock-up with his dozen new friends and told him, "Yeah, yeah, coming right up."

Tizzard was confused but tried to look like he fit in with his fellow cell mates. They, in turn, looked like they were measuring his clothes to see if they might be a fit. As long as they don't find out that I used to be a cop, I'll be OK, thought Tizzard as he backed up as far as he could into a corner.

It seemed like he had waited forever, but as several of his new friends came in for a closer look, he heard his name called, "Tizzard, Tizzard."

"That's me," he said and pushed by the two large men who had got the closest.

The duty cop opened the door, and Tizzard walked along the hallway to an interview room. He was pushed inside, and the door clicked shut behind him. It was a small, windowless room with a camera in the ceiling, a mirror on the wall, a single chair on one side of a table and two on the other. Tizzard knew the drill and took a seat on the one-chair side. Then he waited, again. Feels like home, he thought. Just not my home.

On the other side of the continent Mayor Sheila Hillier was wrapping up her town council meeting and was on her way to meet Moira Stoodley who was babysitting her daughter, Amelia Louise. The meeting had been made unpleasant by a couple of contentious issues, including whether the older buildings in the downtown core of Grand Bank should be modernized or restored to maintain their historic character. But Sheila also realized that most of the tension was really about who would replace her as mayor in the election only a couple of weeks away.

Jacqueline Wilson was Sheila's preference, but there was another candidate, Phil Bennett, who was leading the anti-tax faction of council. Every meeting, Bennett would try to disrupt things to show how influential he thought he could be, but Sheila would have none of it and would put him back in line. Bennett's behaviour in itself was more than enough reason for her to want to leave, she thought.

Sheila had decided to go back to school part-time, eventually do an MBA once she had cleared up her scholastic records and completed the course load for an old degree program she had started several years earlier. Politics had never really been her thing, even though she was very good at it. She had only taken the mayor's job to try to improve the town's economy. And she had succeeded, mostly. The Town of Grand Bank's fish plant was now operating on a regular basis with a quota for crab and the sea urchins considered a delicacy in Japan and China. The town also had a recycling factory and a solar panel fabrication plant.

Half of the town's people wanted to not just preserve the past but to live in it. The other half wanted to blow it all up and start over. They had no use for the old and wanted everything to be modern, like the way it was in St. John's or even nearby Marystown. It seemed there was no middle ground for the residents of Grand Bank, yet Sheila was sure you could have the best of both worlds. Getting others to agree with her, though, seemed impossible.

Sheila gathered up her things and drove to the Mug-Up, which was known through much of the province to be the best little café there was in Grand Bank. That it was the only café in Grand Bank was usually not mentioned. Sheila had owned the place years ago but gave it up after a horrific car accident left her with a slight limp and no desire to stand all day. Moira and her husband, Herb, had taken it over, and it was there that she found Amelia Louise sitting at a table with her Poppy Herb.

"Mama, mama," she shrieked as Sheila's heart melted. "Ook, ook."

"I think she's got talent," said Herb Stoodley.

Sheila examined the crayon scrawls on the paper and murmured her approval. "It's so nice," she said. "Is it Lady, your doggie?" she asked, making a leap of faith based on the fact that there was one small circle on top of a large mass of scratches.

Amelia Louise smiled and nodded her head up and down emphatically. She had always been able to somehow say no, but now the 20-month-old toddler was happy to signify yes with a grand gesture.

"Well, thank you," said Sheila. "And thank you, Herb. And here's Moira, too. Thank you, Moira, for looking after her."

"It's our pleasure," said Moira, wiping her hands on her apron. "I was just finishing off some baking."

"Em," said Amelia Louise. "Ook, ook."

"I can see," said Moira. "Has Poppy Herb been nice to you?"

"She's like our baby, too," said Herb. "It's easy to be nice to her. 'Those that do teach young babes, do it with gentle means and easy tasks.'"

"Okay, my soon-to-be-famous artist, let's go," said Sheila as she put on Amelia Louise's jacket. Once outside again, Sheila noticed the November air had lost any tinge of summer warmth, and the wind was picking up, making it a bit of an adventure to walk the short distance to their house. Sheila tried to carry her daughter, but Amelia Louise was determined to walk on her own while examining every leaf that blew their way.

When they got home, Molly the cat watched them carefully as they came up the walkway. The dog, Lady, was more directly affectionate and showed how much she had missed them both by almost knocking them over in the hall. The only one missing from the happy family was Sheila's husband and the father of Amelia Louise, Sergeant Winston Windflower of the RCMP Grand Bank Detachment. He was at work, but Sheila expected to hear from him soon because his stomach would be rumbling any minute now, and he'd want to know what was on for dinner.

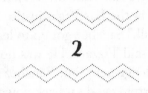

2

Back in Las Vegas, Eddie Tizzard was still waiting in the interview room. That gave him a bit of time to think about how he had got to this point in his life. The last six months had been a whirlwind. He used to be Corporal Eddie Tizzard of the RCMP. Now, at least in his mind, he was E. Tizzard, Private Eye. That's what he envisioned would be on the plaque on his desk. That's if he ever got a desk. Or an office!

He'd had a few problems at work, he told himself. But when he thought about it more, he knew he had to scratch that idea. He'd actually had many problems and even had physically attacked a superior officer. The guy was a jackass and an abuser and an all-around bad apple, but they couldn't just let Tizzard get away with that. They did go easy on him, he had to admit. They offered to suspend him for three months and bust him back to constable. He didn't mind the three months. Might have even been able to go moose hunting with his dad. But give up his stripe? No, he just couldn't agree to that.

Plus, he'd been thinking about getting out of the Mounties ever since he got shot by a deranged coke user a few years back. Maybe go back to school and be a lawyer. He might still do that, assuming he was getting out of the Las Vegas jail. But that was all the time he had for pondering his life as the heavy door swung open and a massive man in a loose, ill-fitting suit walked in and sat in front of him.

"I'm Detective Julio Sanchez," said the large man. "I have some questions for you."

"I did ask to make a phone call," said Tizzard, more than a little intimidated.

"If you cooperate, we can make this easy. If not, then sometimes things go very slowly in the Las Vegas justice system," said Detective Sanchez. "Your call." Sanchez got up to leave.

"Faster is better," said Tizzard. He was hoping for a smile and maybe some acknowledgement, but Sanchez casually opened the folder he had been carrying and sat back down.

"You from Canada?" he asked. "New Found Land? Where's that?"

Tizzard thought about giving the detective the correct pronunciation, as in NewFinLand, but wisely resisted.

"Yes, sir. I'm a former RCMP officer, a Mountie," he said, hoping that would gain him some favour with the LVPD. But it didn't work out that way.

"But you're not anymore?" Sanchez opened the door to a longer discussion about why Tizzard was no longer a cop, a discussion Tizzard was hoping to avoid, under the circumstances. Tizzard tried to shift gears.

"I'm on a leave of absence. Thinking about going into the private detective business."

"That's why you were in that hotel room with the dead guy?"

This was not going the way Tizzard had hoped. Time to try and come clean and hope for the best.

"Listen, Detective Sanchez, I'm in town to do my training and get a certificate so I can set up shop back home. I walk into my hotel room and find the guy and all that money just lying there. I don't even know who he is, was."

"He was Martin Joseph Spurrell. Says here he was also from Canada, that New Found Land place. Are you sure you don't know him from back home?"

"I don't know him."

"Well, we're going to have to do some digging around. This is going to take some time. Sit tight. I'll be back."

Tizzard thought again about asking for his phone call. But who would he call? He couldn't call Carrie, his fiancée. She'd freak, for sure. He could call his dad, but he'd been having heart trouble. Windflower, that's who he'd call, his friend and former boss, Sergeant Winston Windflower. But what would Windflower say?

Probably a quote from Shakespeare to start, one like, 'Love all, trust a few, do wrong to none.' Tizzard did try and practice that in his life. And one of the few people he absolutely trusted was Windflower. He made up his mind to ask Sanchez for that call when he came back, if he ever came back.

Sergeant Windflower had his own problems at the moment. He'd been out to investigate a report that some kids had been playing around an abandoned mine between Fortune and Lamaline. Someone saw a fire and called it in, but Windflower had nothing more than that to go on. Just before he got to Lamaline, he saw the rotting old sign for the Finlay Mine. Word was that the mine had never really opened. There was a sizable silver deposit, but when the price of silver had dropped suddenly, the owners walked away before moving to full production. He drove down the gravel road and found the remnants of a bonfire and pieces of old cars and appliances that tend to accumulate in temporary dump sites or abandoned premises.

There wasn't much left to pick over after the fire, but Windflower decided to investigate the building around the top of the mine shaft. It was mostly metal, and that meant it was nearly indestructible, or at least reasonably safe from both the weather and vandals. But the lock had been broken off, and the door was swaying in the wind. That wasn't good and was probably the most dangerous thing that Windflower had seen all day. He pulled out his phone to call in before he remembered there was no service in the area.

So he decided to take a closer look himself. That was his first mistake. He got his large flashlight out of the trunk of his RCMP Jeep and walked carefully inside the metal shack. The floor creaked as he stepped inside, and most would have taken that as a sign to not go any further. But Windflower ignored the message. That was an even bigger mistake because, while the housing cover was metal, the floor was wood, and everyone knows that wood rots over time. That is, everyone except for Windflower, apparently, who was great until he hit about step six into his foray.

He felt the floor fading away underneath him a piece at a time in slow motion. He reached out to try to grab the sides, but they were too far away. Within seconds he fell. How far he couldn't tell, but luckily, he'd hung onto the flashlight. Unluckily, it felt like he'd broken something in his left arm on the way down, and the ankle on that side had buckled too. Shocked, in pain and with the wind knocked out of him, Windflower struggled but was able to get his breath back in a few minutes. He shone his flashlight all around. There was dust, dirt, debris and all kinds of garbage, but not a lot of anything else. There was no way out but up. And the pain told him that getting out on his own wasn't an option.

He tried to calm his mind and think. He was quite a way up a deserted road and almost literally in the middle of nowhere when it came to cell phone reception. There were only a dozen or so cars that normally passed this way on a daily basis, and he was not visible from the highway anyway.

But somebody would be looking for him, right?

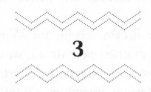

3

Windflower knew Sheila would certainly miss him if he didn't call before the end of the day and show up for supper. He never missed a meal if he could help it. But he hadn't told Sheila where he was going. He'd had no reason to because he was expecting a regular, ordinary day like almost every other in little Grand Bank. Then he remembered that Betsy, his administrative assistant, knew where he was going. He had told her before he left his office.

But he also remembered having sent her home sick. She was coughing and hacking and looked so miserable that he told her to go home and take care of her cold. He saw her leaving as he pulled out of the parking lot to follow up on the report of children at the mine.

So, here he was, down a mine shaft hole, aching with bruised and maybe broken bones, and absolutely no one would think of him as missing until much later today. He glanced at the time on his phone. Three in the afternoon. Windflower was not a swearing man, usually. But it felt right to let loose with as many oaths as he could remember and as loudly as his pain would allow. Somehow that calmed him enough so that with the strange mixture of pain and aftershock, he drifted off into some kind of trance. He wasn't sleeping, but it was certainly something that allowed him to release himself from his broken body.

It was like he simply floated up from his body lying on the ground and hovered for a few moments looking down at himself. Then he was no longer there. He was back in Pink Lake as a young boy trying to catch up to his grandfather who he could hear tramping in the woods in front of him. "Grandfather, wait for me," he called. His grandfather either didn't hear him or ignored him.

Windflower pushed on through the dense bush until he came to a clearing.

This was familiar dream terrain for Windflower. His whole family, led by his grandfather, were dream weavers. This wasn't just because they were Cree from Northern Alberta. Not all Indigenous people were able to interpret dreams even though many had a strong sense that the dream world might be as real as the one they walked in. But Windflower's family was able to, and he had spent many months with two master dream weavers, his Auntie Marie and Uncle Frank. Of the two, Auntie Marie was the most powerful by far, and Windflower knew that this dream or vision was special because there she was, sitting on a log around a roaring fire in the clearing.

"Come, Nephew, have some stew," said Auntie Marie.

"Auntie Marie, what are you doing here?"

"I'm having some stew. Do you want some or not?"

Windflower sat on the ground beside his aunt and took the bowl she offered.

"Why are you here?" he asked as he smelled the fragrant aroma of the stew filling up his nostrils.

"I am old," said Auntie Marie. "I have not been well for a long time. This is the only place where I can find peace and comfort right now. Soon it will be time to live here."

"You are not so old," said Windflower.

His aunt cackled. "Thank you, Nephew, but I have lived a good life, and I am happy to move over to this side. They tell me that this is the second-best place of all, this transition place where we can still see our people and our old lives; it's just that we're not in them anymore."

Windflower had a lot more questions after that, but his aunt kept talking.

"The question is not why I am here," she said, "but why you are here, Winston."

Windflower paused and took a forkful of the stew. It tasted as good as it smelled. "I fell down a hole," he said finally.

"That's how you got here," said his aunt. "Go on," she prompted.

"I don't know why I am here. Maybe it is to have some stew and visit with you."

"That's what you'd like to believe. Do you want to know why you're here?"

"Yes," said Windflower.

His aunt smiled. "You are here as you always are and always will be, to ask for help." She spooned up another helping of stew for herself and offered more to Windflower. "It's fat-free," she said. "No calories over here."

Windflower laughed.

"You don't like to ask for help, do you?" she asked.

Windflower shook his head.

"That's a male thing," said his aunt. "Get over it. That's something the world over there has taught you. It doesn't work for you and keeps you stuck. It's like an extra layer of skin that women have learned to shed but men stubbornly want to hang on to. You're stubborn, too, Winston."

Windflower started to protest but then decided to stay silent.

"Good," said Auntie Marie. "There may be some hope for you yet," and she started to laugh. And laugh and laugh.

Windflower didn't find it all that funny, especially when he felt himself waken from his trance and come back to life and to great pain in his arm and ankle. "Well, I could certainly use some help right now," he said out loud. He thought about yelling but realized that was futile. Might as well save his strength. He tried to make himself as comfortable as he could lying at the bottom of the mine shaft. Then he waited and waited some more.

Back home, Sheila decided it was time for Amelia Louise to have a nap. With the baby securely in her crib, Sheila went back downstairs and checked her phone for messages, but there was nothing from her husband. She texted him to ask what he wanted for supper and started rummaging around the freezer to see what was there in case he had no suggestions. She found a package of frozen halibut steaks and put them in the sink to thaw. She had no doubt that her hungry husband would like them, maybe with a green salad and some roasted vegetables. She was getting hungry herself.

She made herself a cup of tea and sat to take advantage of the calm that her daughter's nap provided. With Molly the cat curled up on her lap and Lady, their collie, at her feet, she picked up her book and started to read. It was the latest Michael Crummey book, The Innocents, about two orphaned children left alone in a desolate outport community in Northern Newfoundland. It was tragic and sad but absolutely riveting, and Sheila passed a wonderful hour immersed between its covers.

When she heard Amelia Louise stirring on the monitor, she came back to reality. She checked her phone, but there was no response from Windflower. Maybe she should call Betsy and see where he was. But for now she had a more pressing assignment. She could hear Amelia Louise singing. One of the best times of the day was right after the baby woke from her nap, and Sheila didn't want to risk missing any of it. She ran upstairs and completely forgot about her husband.

4

Someone who was still thinking about Windflower, however, was Eddie Tizzard. He'd been brought back to the holding cell and given a cup of soup and a slice of bread for lunch. He started to drink his soup quickly, partly because he was hungry and didn't know when he'd eat again. But, also, several of his new friends had been eyeing his lunch along with his relatively nice-looking clothes. He gulped the chicken rice soup as fast as he could and offered up his bread in sacrifice.

The bread was accepted, but it didn't seem like enough according to the look from the brute who snatched it from Tizzard's hand. As things started to turn a little bleaker, Tizzard heard his name called and stood to walk out of the cell. He smiled at the big man who stood between him and the doorway and managed to squeak by after the man snarled and moved over an inch. "Thank you," murmured Tizzard, as a polite Canadian boy would do, but otherwise he held his breath and thanked the heavens for the narrow escape.

Once again, he was taken to an interview room, this one a bit larger than the other, with a table and a desk and six chairs. The first person he saw was not Detective Sanchez, but a short, black woman with intense blue eyes. Tizzard hadn't seen many black people with blue eyes—there really weren't that many black people at all in Newfoundland, except for his colleague Yvette Jones, and he had only seen one with blue eyes before on television. It was almost like her eyes were glowing, and Tizzard was mesmerized.

He was brought back to reality when he saw Sanchez, followed by a tall thin man in a dark blue suit.

"I'm Detective Sergeant Clarice Rutherford," the black officer said. "And this is Special Agent Thomas Hillebrand from the FBI."

That got Tizzard's attention. He knew the FBI didn't get involved unless it was really serious and a federal matter. He didn't have much time to focus on that before Rutherford started peppering him with questions. "Who are you and why were you there? Are you sure you don't know Spurrell?"

"Never heard of him," said Tizzard.

"Then how do you explain the fact that your name was found on a note in his pocket?"

"I have no idea," said Tizzard. "How do you know it's me?"

"How many Eddie Tizzards do you think there are in Las Vegas?" asked Sanchez wryly. "It's right here," he said, holding up a piece of paper. "Eddie Tizzard and somebody named Sergeant Wildflower. You know him?"

"It's Windflower, Sergeant Winston Windflower. He used to be my boss back at the RCMP. He's still there in Grand Bank."

That got the FBI guy's attention. "You used to be a cop, right?"

"Yes," said Tizzard. "On leave, thinking about trying the private detective route. That's why I'm here, as I told Detective Sanchez."

"Did you check that out?" Hillebrand asked Sanchez.

"I got a call into RCMP Headquarters in Ottawa, Canada. I'm waiting on a call back," said Sanchez.

"Listen," said Tizzard, seeing an opening. "Let me call Sergeant Windflower and see if he knows anything about that Spurrell guy. He might have some information to provide."

The three other cops looked at each other. "Sit tight. We'll be back," said Rutherford.

Tizzard started to breathe again once the other police officers had left the room. He could hear them talking outside. After a few minutes Sanchez came back in. "We'll let you make a call now," he said. "You can call that friend of yours, Wildflower, or your lawyer, or whomever you want. Then you're going back in the tank until we find out who you really are."

Sanchez led Tizzard to a room with a bank of phones. "Go ahead," he said.

Tizzard picked up a pay phone on the wall. He'd never used a phone like this before. He'd seen them sometimes at airports but wasn't sure how they worked. He also didn't have any coins to put in the machine. He looked back at Sanchez who was sitting on a bench.

"I'm assuming you're calling long distance," said Sanchez. "You don't need money. Just follow the directions and call collect."

Tizzard checked the directions and then keyed in the number for the Grand Bank RCMP Detachment. If he couldn't get Windflower, he would leave a message with Betsy. The phone rang and rang with no answer. Finally, the machine came on. He heard Betsy's voice, but no Betsy to talk to. He hung up and saw Sanchez looking at him. He quickly pressed the buttons to redial. This time the phone rang and rang and just when Tizzard was about to give up, a man's voice came on the line.

"Grand Bank RCMP, how can I help you?"

"Collect call from Eddie Tizzard, do you accept?" asked the operator.

"I guess so," said a surprised Constable Rick Smithson.

"Smithson, am I ever glad to hear your voice," said Tizzard.

"Eddie, is that you? Where are you, and why are you calling collect? I don't even know what that means. Are you in trouble?"

"Don't talk," said Tizzard. "Just write down what I tell you and get it to Sergeant Windflower as soon as you can. Got it?"

"Got it," said Smithson. "But he's not here right now. Should I call Inspector Quigley?"

"Yes, OK, but call Windflower as soon as you can, too, please."

Constable Smithson was the only one in the office. He was a wizard with technology and a good cop, but he knew that he was a poor substitute for Betsy, as she ran the detachment office with machine-like precision. Without her, they were lost, and today, Smithson was at sea. It was Yvette Jones's day off, and Carrie Evanchuk was dropping off a prisoner in Marystown. Sergeant Windflower had been in earlier, but Smithson had no idea where Windflower was now. Betsy might know but she was gone. He'd been trying to manage the phones, and now Tizzard was in trouble and needed help.

Smithson tried not to panic but was losing that battle. Just as he hung up his call with Tizzard, the phone rang again. He almost didn't answer it. He was glad he did once he heard the voice on the other end of the line.

"Mayor Hillier, how are you today?" said Smithson.

"I'm well, thank you, Constable. Is my husband around?"

"No, ma'am. I haven't seen him for several hours. I will try and raise him on the radio if you give me a minute." Smithson went to Betsy's desk and called Windflower on his car radio. But there was no response.

"Sorry, ma'am, no answer on his radio. Have you tried his cell phone?"

"Several times," said Sheila. "Phone and text and no answer. It's strange of him not to call back."

"Is there anything I can help with?"

"No thank you, Constable, but if you hear from him, please have him call me."

5

After Sheila hung up, she felt the worry hit her in the bottom of her stomach. Women's intuition told her something was wrong. She didn't know what, but things didn't feel right. Then she told herself worry came with the territory, and it was just part of being a police officer's wife. It was frightening and maddening at the same time, always worrying and never knowing. Though she tried to convince herself worrying was useless and she needed to stop, she soon found herself saying a little prayer. She wasn't super religious and didn't know if the prayer could help her husband, but somehow it helped her. She felt better, that is until she saw the living room.

In the few minutes Sheila had been on the call, Amelia Louise had taken all of Sheila's wool out of the knitting basket and with the help of Molly and Lady was redecorating the room. Fortunately, Sheila had childproofed the basket and put her needles out of reach. Not as fortunately, she'd left her nearly completed afghan on the floor, and Amelia Louise had managed to unravel most of what she'd done and was wrapping Lady in the remnants.

Sheila almost screamed and then decided there was little point in doing that. So instead, she sat on the floor and laughed. Soon, Amelia Louise was laughing, too, and not to be left out, Lady started her 'running around the room I'm so excited to be alive' routine. Molly didn't show her emotions that freely, as that would be uncatlike. She was very content to purr along as she sat on the top of the couch overseeing the proceedings.

Sheila gathered up her knitting supplies as best she could. "Let's go outside for a walk," she said to Amelia Louise who screamed in delight. "Side, side, side," she warbled. Lady knew that word, too, and showed her enthusiasm by nearly knocking over a lamp. Sheila put on her coat and Amelia Louise's, grabbed Lady's leash and led them outside. For the next hour she thought about nothing else but enjoying the fresh air and the pleasant company.

They meandered around the small coastal community of Grand Bank, greeting neighbours and friends. Amelia Louise gurgled at almost everything she saw while riding in the stroller, and Lady enjoyed the affections of everyone who stopped to say hello to the mayor and her daughter. They walked down towards the beach where Sheila let both her dog and her little girl roam freely. Lady was particularly excited by all of the scents down near the water while Amelia Louise tried to pick up every beach rock, no matter how large, to pass to her mother. Sheila had played this game before, so when she got handed one rock, she laid the previous one down, knowing her daughter's attention span wouldn't last.

With the salty air in their lungs, and a stiff breeze coming in off the water turning their cheeks a rosy red, Sheila led her party back home where Molly was sitting in the window observing them with more than a little disdain. Probably peeved she got left behind, thought Sheila. As if to prove that point, Molly went directly to her basket in the kitchen rather than greet the family who had so clearly deserted her. Sheila got everyone cleaned up and settled away and checked her phone.

Now she was getting really worried. It was close to 6 p.m. and still no word from her husband. She called the RCMP offices and got Smithson again.

Windflower was getting worried, too. He wasn't in any immediate danger despite his injuries, and it would take days for him to dehydrate to a harmful point. He could stand to lose a few pounds, so he wasn't worried about food either. What really bothered him was that he hadn't informed more people about where he was going. With a useless cell phone and Betsy at home in bed, he was really trapped in the hole. He shone his flashlight around again, but nothing more than dust and dirt was revealed. Just after he turned the flashlight off to save its energy, he thought he heard something rustling around.

Great, he thought. I have visitors. No, make it I have neighbours. He realized that the mice, voles or rats that were scampering around had lived in the mine shaft long before he had arrived on

the scene uninvited. He hoped there weren't any rats. But he had
to admit, there probably were. They could live anywhere, and they
were likely renting a room nearby. That didn't cheer him much, so
he racked his brain for a Shakespeare quote to help him. All he
could come up with was 'the best safety lies in fear,' and he resolved
to stay vigilant and, if possible, not fall asleep.

One way to do that was to pray. Like his wife, Windflower
wasn't a big religious guy, but he did try to connect with his native
spirituality. He found peace and some comfort in smudging and
prayer. Smudging was something he tried to do on a regular basis.
Simply put, smudging was the act of burning sacred herbs and then
passing the smoke over your body. It was and is a common practice
among many Indigenous and religious people all over the world.

Almost daily, Windflower practiced smudging. He put a very
small amount of herbs such as cedar, sage, sweetgrass and tobacco—
all universally recognized as sacred smudging medicines—in an
abalone shell. After lighting the herbs using a wooden match, he
used a fan or large feather to waft the smoke from the medicines
over all parts of his body. He spread the smoke over his eyes and
head to help him see and think clearly, over his heart to keep his
thoughts pure, and even under his feet to help him walk a straight
and honest path. He allowed the smoke to linger around his head
and body for as long as he could. Then, when finished, he laid the
ashes on bare ground so all negative thoughts and feelings were
absorbed by Mother Earth. Lastly, he prayed.

Prayer was another useful tool for Windflower, especially
prayers of gratitude. His grandfather had taught him early on that
the best prayer was simply to say thank you. If you were grateful for
all the things you had, you would likely receive more. Windflower
sometimes read from a book of Ojibway meditations by Richard
Wagamese. One of his sayings was that if you pray for more, all the
universe hears is the wanting and you may never receive what you
need. But if you give thanks, the universe will hear your gratitude
for what you have and always, always send more.

Given his predicament, Windflower couldn't smudge. But he
could pray. First, he gave thanks for his family, Sheila and Amelia
Louise in equal measure and then a nod to his four-legged family
members who gave him much more pleasure than he felt he

contributed or deserved. Then he prayed for Auntie Marie and Uncle Frank, as his parents were long gone and he had no siblings. He said a special prayer for his Auntie, and while he really wished that he would see her again, he knew that might not be possible. He prayed that she not suffer too much as she made the transition to the other side.

He thought about his friends and co-workers. Ron Quigley was both, although technically he was Windflower's boss. Inspector Quigley had been his friend even before Windflower got to Grand Bank, having first met him in Nova Scotia. Windflower had been in Newfoundland almost nine years now, something he found hard to believe, and Ron had also been in Newfoundland that whole time. Soon Ron would be leaving not just the province but the Atlantic region, having won a promotion with the Mounties in Ottawa. He'd be relocating next month and had asked Windflower to apply for his job.

Windflower was still mulling that one over. It would mean a move to Marystown, about an hour away. That wasn't the biggest issue, although Sheila was a Grand Bank girl and would prefer to stay. It wasn't even the fact that he and Sheila had bought and restored the historic B & B overlooking the harbour. They had thought about selling that many times and had finally found someone they trusted to look after the place whenever they went away. Levi Parsons was still a teenager, but he had grown from night clerk to day manager and was taking hotel management courses at college in St. John's.

It was more whether or not Windflower wanted to continue being a police officer, a Mountie. He'd struggled with that for a few years now, putting off the decision and getting a break on redeployment because his friend was the inspector. That would change with a new boss, and it was time to recommit or get off the pot. Something like that.

He thought about his friend and confidant Herb Stoodley. Herb was a friend for all seasons and all weather. For the few hot, sticky days of summer and the stormy nights of winter, Herb always had a cup of tea and an ear to listen to Windflower's issues, concerns and complaints. As close to a father as he'd had for many years since the early death of his own, Herb was a former Crown Attorney with a love of the law and classical music, and he schooled Windflower in both. He also shared his time and secret fishing holes with him, and many quiet and peaceful hours were spent with their lines in the water and a smile on both their faces.

There was also Doctor Vijay Sanjay, one of Windflower's first friends in this part of the world. Sanjay was what the locals would call a character. He'd been here when Windflower arrived and was one of the few brown faces in a sea of white in Grand Bank and surroundings. He joked with Windflower that they were the only two Indians in the area, and he liked to practice Newfoundland sayings with his Cree brother. 'How's she goin' b'y?' was one of his favourites whenever he saw him.

He also welcomed Windflower into his home for chess and to sample his single malts and Bengali cuisine. Sanjay was no longer the official coroner for the area but was still one of the few who knew so much about forensic medicine that he was often the first called to any suspicious death scene. Even without the title, he still had an office at the clinic in town and would provide preliminary examinations of any sudden or unexpected deaths in the community.

Windflower was starting to feel grateful despite his current predicament and let his mind turn to the RCMP officers under his command. Young Rick Smithson was a fine constable with an expertise in technology that made him invaluable to Windflower, but Smithson was likely to be transferred out soon. Yvette Jones was a capable and reliable officer who Windflower thought should be promoted to corporal. He would need another second-in-command since Tizzard had taken his leave of absence. And there was Carrie Evanchuk, a firecracker police officer who could be counted on for anything. She and Tizzard had got engaged last year, and that meant she would likely try to stay around Grand Bank for a little while longer.

That brought him back to Betsy. Why hadn't he followed her simple instructions to write where he was going on the handy whiteboard that she had put up on the wall near the entrance? All the other RCMP officers were doing it, but Windflower thought he didn't need to because he always told Betsy where he was going.

Now, he wished he had done what she had asked. If he had, they'd all know where he was right now.

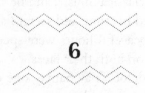

6

Eddie Tizzard was thinking about Betsy, too. She was never away from the office when anybody called. Mrs. Reliability he would call her. But not today, when he needed her the most. Instead, he'd have to rely on Smithson getting hold of somebody to help him. And he didn't even know where Windflower was. At least Smithson was going to call Inspector Quigley in Marystown. Ron would know what to do. At least, he hoped Ron would. Otherwise, he was in trouble. Big trouble.

That was totally confirmed when he was put back into the holding cell where some of his new friends were waiting for him.

Smithson meanwhile had just tried Inspector Quigley but had to leave a message as he wasn't picking up. Smithson was barely finished his message when Sheila called again.

"No news, I'm afraid, Mayor Hillier."

"You don't know where your boss is?" asked Sheila, showing her anxiety and frustration more than she wanted to.

"Not at the moment, ma'am," said Smithson. "I'm all by myself and doing the best I can." He sounded a bit more helpless and hopeless than he wanted to as well. "Jones is off today, and Evanchuk is out on the highway."

Sheila paused, and realizing she would only make things worse by getting upset with Smithson, she decided to take another approach. "Okay, I know you're busy and working late, but I don't think that Sergeant Windflower would normally be out of touch for this long, either with me or your office, do you, Constable?"

"No, ma'am," said Smithson. As he was speaking, he noticed Evanchuk's car pulling up. "Evanchuk's back, ma'am. I'll get her to hold the fort here while I check around town."

"Thank you, Constable. Let me know as soon as you can."

Smithson hung up the phone and looked at Evanchuk as she walked in.

"What's wrong with you?" she asked Smithson.

Smithson sighed. "Sit down," he said. "This may take a while."

"Let's call Jones and get her in," said Evanchuk as soon as she heard the news. "I'll call the inspector, too, and get him to see if he can find out anything about Eddie."

Smithson called Yvette Jones, and she was there within 15 minutes. One of the advantages of living in a small community is you can get anywhere really quickly. Jones arrived in jeans and an RCMP sweatshirt. Smithson was surprised by how beautiful and elegant she looked, even in casual dress. The young black officer deliberately tried to hide that part of her at work.

"What are you looking at?" snapped Jones. "I thought there was a crisis around here."

Smithson stammered and started to speak when the phone rang.

"No, Mayor Hillier, nothing yet. But we've got another situation we're dealing with, too," said Smithson. He could hear a pause on the other end of the line, and it felt like an explosion was coming. Smithson was smart, but he wasn't particularly brave. "Here's Constable Jones. She's going to look after this now."

Jones had a 'what the heck' look on her face, but she took the phone from Smithson and scowled in his direction.

"Yes, Mayor Hillier. It's Yvette Jones. How can I best help you?"

"You can find my husband," said Sheila with as much control as she could muster. "Your boss hasn't been heard from all day and I'm worried. You should be, too."

"Absolutely," said Jones. "We'll start the search right now. I'll call you back in an hour with a report."

"Thank you," said Sheila, hanging up the phone. Then, speaking to no one in particular she said, "I'll give them one more hour, and then I'm starting my own investigation."

Not surprisingly, no one responded, although Lady did wag her tail hopefully.

The police officers understood that Sheila was concerned, but they knew their boss was highly trained and very familiar with the region. He was probably okay and not in any kind of serious trouble. And they were doing their very best under a bad set of circumstances. Smithson filled Jones in on how bad the situation really was.

"Tizzard is in jail in Las Vegas," said Smithson. "Something about him being found in a hotel room with a dead man."

"What?" asked Jones.

"Yeah," said Smithson. "Evanchuk's trying to get Quigley to help him."

"I talked to the inspector," piped in Evanchuk. "He's going to make some calls."

"Okay," said Jones. "So while he's doing that, let's try to find the sarge. Anybody know what he was doing today or where he was going?"

Smithson and Evanchuk shook their heads.

"I saw him this morning talking to Betsy when I left," said Evanchuk. "No idea where he was going."

"Betsy's gone home sick," said Smithson. "She left me in charge of the phones."

"I'll do the tour around town, pop into the café and run around the perimeter. Carrie, why don't you start at the other end and run the back way through town?" asked Jones.

"Sure," said Evanchuk. "Once I'm done that, I'll start out on the road past Fortune. I just came back from Marystown and didn't see anything along the way from that end."

The two female officers started to leave. "What about me?" asked Smithson.

"You stay and answer the phones," said Evanchuk. "You look like you're pretty good at it."

Smithson gave her a half-smile, half-spite look.

"Go through the incident reports we received over the last 24 hours," said Jones. "See if there are any we haven't followed up on."

Smithson brightened a little at that suggestion. That he could do.

While Smithson was busying himself with incident reports, Sheila decided she simply couldn't wait another hour to hear back from the Mounties. She was going to call Betsy. Yes, she was sick. But if anybody knew where Windflower was, it would be Betsy.

Sheila looked up Betsy's number in the phonebook and called. Betsy's husband answered.

"Hi, Bob. It's Sheila Hillier. Sorry to bother you, but I need to ask Betsy a question. I'm trying to find Winston and thought she might be able to help."

"Betsy's in bed, ma'am. She's got an awful cold. She was shivering and shaking when I covered her up."

"I'm really sorry, Bob, but this is important. Could you please ask her if she knew where he was going today?"

"I knows she'd want to help the sergeant anyways she could," said Betsy's husband. "Let me see what I can find out."

7

Sheila glanced down at the call display and instantly answered the phone.

"She sez he was going to take a look at an old mine site somewhere past Fortune. Said there was a complaint about some kids starting a fire and he wanted to check it out."

"Thank you so much, Bob. And please pass along my thanks to Betsy. Hope she's feeling better soon."

"She was very happy to help. I'm warming up some soup for her now. I'm sure she'll be fine in a few days."

"Thanks again, Bob."

Sheila hung up the phone and called the RCMP office.

"I think he's at an old mine site somewhere past Fortune," said Sheila.

"I just saw a report that came in earlier about kids setting fires in a mine between Fortune and Lamaline," said Smithson. "Evanchuk is heading over that way now. I'll call her." Smithson hung up and ran over to Betsy's desk to grab the radio so he could reach both of the other officers.

Jones answered first. "I know where it is. It's right before you hit Lamaline. There's part of a sign left."

"I know it," said Evanchuk, chiming in. "I'm passing Point May now. Should be there in less than 10 minutes."

"Great," said Jones over the radio. "I'm leaving town and will be there as fast as I can."

Smithson then called Sheila. "Evanchuk is on her way towards the mine site, and Jones is right behind her."

Sheila felt a moment of relief. At least someone was out looking for her husband now. "Call me when you know anything. Anything," she said.

Ten minutes later, Evanchuk saw the sign and turned up the gravel road. Windflower's Jeep was at the end of the road, but there was no sign of Windflower himself. She stopped and jumped out.

Windflower was starting to wonder if he'd be spending the night in the mine shaft. He certainly hoped not. The critters down here could see much better than he could in the dark, and they could move faster, too. Then he heard a rumble above him. Could that be a car? Then he heard a woman's voice yelling. It took him a few seconds to recognize that she was calling his name.

He tried to yell but only managed to croak a little. He tried shining his light up through the shaft. That seemed to work better since the person above shone a light back at him.

"Sarge, is that you? Are you okay?"

Windflower recognized the voice as Evanchuk's and thanked his lucky stars. "I'm okay," he said as loud as he could.

"Okay, Sarge," said Evanchuk. "I'm going to call in for help."

Evanchuk radioed in the information that Windflower had been found, and by the time she was back at the top of the mine shaft, Jones was driving up the dirt road. She got out of her cruiser and ran to Evanchuk.

"I've got a rope in the back," said Jones. "You or me?"

"I'm smaller," said Evanchuk.

Soon Evanchuk, tightly secured to her vehicle, was slowly lowering herself down into the mine shaft. Windflower shone his flashlight to guide her down.

"You okay?" she asked again when she finally got to the bottom.

"I hurt my arm and my ankle on the way down," said Windflower. "I'm really glad you're here."

"He's got some injuries," said Evanchuk as she called up to Jones. "Doesn't look too serious. But I don't think he can climb out on his own."

Windflower started to say something, but Evanchuk kept talking. "Let's get the paramedics and the fire department."

"It's not an emergency," said Windflower.

"It is to your wife," said Evanchuk.

"Can somebody call her, tell her I'm okay?"

"Consider it done, sir," said Evanchuk.

She stayed down with Windflower until they heard the siren

of the paramedics and, a few minutes later, the louder siren of the Grand Bank Volunteer Fire Department.

"It's a bit too much drama," said Windflower just after Evanchuk called to Jones to help pull her up. "This is the most excitement people around here have had all year," said Evanchuk back at him.

And all they would talk about for the next one, thought Windflower. But he was certainly happy not to have to spend the night in the hole.

Back home Sheila was dancing around the living room with Amelia Louise. Lady and Molly were trying to keep up. None of them except Sheila knew the cause of the celebration, but they were all happy to be part of it. Sheila realized she was hungry—really hungry. She had completely forgotten about supper. Fortunately, an earlier fruit cup had tied Amelia Louise over, but she was starting to look grumpy. Sheila decided she would make herself and Amelia Louise a grilled cheese with soup. She didn't have an appetite for the halibut and put it back in the fridge. Maybe tomorrow, she thought, when Winston's home.

"Daddy's coming home. Daddy's coming home," she sang to Amelia Louise, and that started a whole new round of dancing with all the pets joining in again. "Dada, dada, dada cumming ome. Dada cumming ome," sang Amelia Louise for one of the first times she put more than one word together. Sheila was happy to sing along.

Windflower was happy, too. He was looking at the firefighter coming down with the mesh basket that would bring him to the top. He recognized him as one of the people who worked in the butcher shop at the back of Warrens.

"Hi, Frankie," he said.

"Hi, Sergeant," said Frank Simmonds. "Are ye well enough to come up in this here contrapshun, or should we git a stretcher?"

"That will do," said Windflower, already more embarrassed than he'd been in some time.

He became, however, even more embarrassed when he got to the top of the shaft and heard the cheers from all the assembled paramedics and firefighters. He waved sheepishly to everyone as the paramedics put him on a gurney and wheeled him to their vehicle. He called Sheila when the ambulance got into a cell phone service area.

"Are you sure you're okay?" asked Sheila.

"I'm fine, a little beat up, but good. I have to go to the clinic and get patched up, and hopefully they'll let me go home," said Windflower.

Sheila didn't say anything, but based on what Smithson had told her, her husband was going to need x-rays and who knew what else after that. But she didn't want to put a damper on his or her spirits. "I'll come over to the clinic once I get Amelia Louise straightened away," she said. "I've got Marian from next door coming to babysit."

"Okay," said Windflower. "I'll see you soon. I love you."

"I love you, too," said Sheila. "I have to admit, I was getting worried."

"I'm fine," said Windflower. "Just fine."

8

Eddie Tizzard was anxiously waiting in the holding cell. Now he knew why they called it a holding cell. You had to hold onto everything you had for dear life. If you didn't, your stuff and you could disappear really quickly. He also noticed that there were definite groupings among his new acquaintances. There was a large group of brown-skinned men in one corner and an even bigger crew of black men in another. They didn't seem to pay much attention to him. But there was a third pack of white guys with shaved heads that kept eyeing him up. That was the group that scared him the most.

One from that group came over, and Tizzard could see he wore a large crucifix around his neck but had a tattoo that looked almost like a Nazi symbol. He was thinking that he did not want to find out any more about this guy or his friends when he heard his name called again. Breathing a sigh of relief, he walked to the door to meet Sanchez.

"You got a visitor," he said.

That was quite a surprise to Tizzard. He didn't know more than four or five people in Las Vegas, most of them cops. But he knew exactly what the visitor was as soon as he saw him. He was a little ruffled looking with a tie that had been thrown on hastily and a briefcase opened on the desk in another small windowless room. This one didn't have a mirror.

"You're my lawyer," he said.

"That would be correct, Lesley J. Coombs. Here's my card."

Tizzard looked at the card and then back at Coombs. "I'm hoping you're getting me out of here."

"We'll see," said Coombs. "That inspector of yours up in Canada seems like a persuasive enough guy. I hope he can help because you haven't got many cards to play."

"Other than I'm innocent?" said Tizzard sarcastically.

Coombs didn't even raise an eyebrow at that remark. "Let's get your story down while we wait for your inspector to do his magic. You didn't know the dead man, Spurrell?"

"Nope."

"But he's from around the same area as you. No connection at all? What about his family. Know any of them?"

"Nope," said Tizzard again. Then a light bulb went on. "I don't know him, but my fiancée, she's a cop, she had a prisoner who she was taking to another jail. I think he had the same last name—Spurrell. Can I call her and get some more information?"

"Probably not right away," said Coombs. "But that's interesting, and it might be a connection, although I'm not sure that you should share that with the locals here."

"Why not? Oh yeah, it links me to the dead guy." Tizzard slumped in his chair. "This is hopeless," he said.

"It's not good. But hopeless is when they lock the door behind you for the night. We're not there yet. 'There is nothing either good or bad but thinking makes it so.'"

"Shakespeare?" asked Tizzard. "I'm stuck in a Las Vegas jail, and my lawyer is quoting Shakespeare?"

"English major," said Coombs. "Switched to law after that didn't work out."

"You'd like my old sergeant. Walks around quoting it all the time."

"Sounds like an interesting guy."

"Very interesting," said Tizzard, thinking about his friend Windflower.

Windflower, at that very moment, was being wheeled in through the emergency door of the Grand Bank Clinic. Minutes later he was in an examination room waiting for the doctor when Sheila arrived. She tried not to cry but couldn't hold back. Windflower was in quite a bit of pain by this point, but he, too, felt a little weepy and more than a little grateful.

The couple didn't have long to wait until the on-call doctor arrived.

"I'll see you in a few minutes," said Sheila as she nodded hello to the doctor and left the examination area. Part of her wanted to stay with her husband, but the other part wasn't sure she could bear seeing him in pain much longer.

Windflower managed to smile at Doctor Danette White despite the throbbing in his arm and leg. She was a friendly and familiar face that he had dealt with many times since she arrived in Grand Bank.

"Okay, let's see what we have," said the doctor. "This may hurt."

That did hurt Windflower, a lot, when she started poking around his arm and almost as much when she examined his ankle. He tried not to scream and managed to make it through the physical examination with only a minimum of moaning. He felt almost proud of himself and definitely relieved when she pronounced that part over.

"I'm going to get x-rays on your arm and ankle, but I think there's at least one, maybe two breaks in your arm," said Doctor White.

"And the ankle?" asked Windflower.

"Certainly a bad sprain, but we'll know more after the x-rays."

"Can I go home after that?"

"No," said the doctor firmly. "We will need to reset the bones in your arm, and you will need a cast. We'll see about your ankle once we have the x-rays. You are here at least overnight and maybe longer depending on what we find. I'm also writing you a note for a week off work. I know you won't take it, but you should."

Windflower struggled to smile, again. "Can I have a few Tylenol or something?"

Doctor White laughed. "Absolutely. Let's get your x-rays done, and we'll have something ready for you here once you're back. You will sleep well tonight. I guarantee it."

That prescription worked perfectly. After the x-rays Doctor White confirmed her earlier diagnosis and gave him his painkiller. He remembered saying good night to Sheila but nothing else when he woke in the morning with his left arm in a cast and his left leg wrapped up. He didn't feel much pain, which made sense once he saw the drip above him, but he was nauseous, and his mouth and throat felt like he'd walked through a sandstorm.

He realized quickly that he was in a hospital but only foggily remembered getting there or anything else. The first person he saw when he woke up wasn't a doctor, or even a nurse. It was Inspector Ron Quigley.

"Morning, Sergeant," said Quigley.

"Wa, wa, wa," stammered Windflower.

"They said you'd be thirsty. They left you these ice chips. Just suck on them." He placed some chips on Windflower's lips, and he hungrily sucked on them.

"Easy," said Quigley. "Don't try to talk. You've been through the wringer a bit. But not too bad for falling down a 20-foot hole. Broken arm and a sprained ankle, they tell me. You're tough, Windflower."

Windflower offered a faint smile as the nurse came into his room.

"Good morning, Sergeant. How are you this morning?" asked the nurse.

Windflower started to speak but only croaked a little more.

"The doctor will be by to see you in a bit. I see your friend gave you some ice. Are you hungry yet?"

Windflower shook his head no. His stomach was growling, but he didn't think he could hold anything down.

"I'm going to unhook this IV," said the nurse. "You won't need this anymore."

Windflower thought about protesting. He wasn't looking forward to the pain, but he didn't really want to beg for painkillers with Quigley sitting right next to him.

The nurse noticed, though. "I can give you some Tylenol if you want after you have something to eat. You don't want to be taking anything more on an empty stomach."

When the nurse left, Windflower started to wake up and feel more alive. There was a lot of pain, but certainly he was more alert. After a few more spoonfuls of ice chips, his voice came back, too.

"So, I assume you didn't come over just to visit, but thank you," he said to Quigley.

"Can't I come to check on the troops?" asked his boss.

Windflower groaned. "Spill it," he said.

"You're not the only one who's been in a hard spot. Tizzard is in a jackpot in Las Vegas."

9

"asn't he out there to do some training for his new career?" asked Windflower about Eddie Tizzard.

"Yeah, but I guess he walked in on a crime scene with a dead guy and tons of cash," said Inspector Quigley.

"Wow. He isn't involved in anything, is he?"

"It's Tizzard."

Windflower nodded. There were few men he knew that were as innocent or good-hearted as Eddie.

"But they're holding him as a witness until they can get a handle on the situation," continued Quigley. "I got him a lawyer and will talk to the investigator later. Here's the real interesting part. The dead guy is Martin Spurrell. That name ring a bell?"

"Spurrell? Spurrell? I don't think so," said Windflower. "Hey, wasn't the guy we sent over to Marystown named Spurrell?"

"Yes indeed, Paul Spurrell. They're brothers. But I don't know anything more than that. That's what I came over to chat with you and your people about."

"Check with Evanchuk and Jones. They were the ones who picked him up. But I think they only had him on a breach. I don't think he's from around here though."

"No, he's from Placentia," said Quigley. "That's one of the things I want your folks to check out. What was Paul Spurrell doing in Grand Bank, and was there any connection to his dead brother?"

"You've been doing some digging."

"Not really, Sergeant. A lot of the info is from headquarters. Rumour is it came from the FBI."

"Interesting." Windflower decided to change the subject for a moment. "Listen, Ron. I've been thinking about recommending

Jones for corporal. We need a 2IC here, and she's the most logical choice."

"Okay by me," said the inspector. "Why don't you talk to her and let me know? But remember that I'm only here for another month or so. Ultimately, you'll have to deal with the new guy on this, unless that person is you."

"I don't think so," said Windflower. "I've thought about it, but moving to Marystown is not right for me or any of us right now. I'm not going to apply."

"Fair enough. You've always preferred the simple things in life and haven't been driven by ambition."

"'The very substance of the ambitious is merely the shadow of a dream,'" said Windflower, quoting from Hamlet.

"Well, your brain still works," said Quigley. "But, remember, 'The fool doth think he is wise, but the wise man knows himself to be a fool.'"

Windflower tried to think of a smart retort, but that was the end of their conversation as Doctor White came into the room.

Quigley said good morning and waved goodbye to Windflower.

"So how are you feeling this morning?" asked the doctor.

"I'm a little stiff but feeling better, thank you," said Windflower. "I think I'm ready to go home."

Doctor White stifled a laugh. "I don't think so," she said firmly. "At least one more day to see if everything starts healing properly and to make sure there are no complications. I know you won't take the week off, but I insist you stay quiet for the day at least. We'll see where we are at the end of the day."

The doctor finished her examination and ordered him some dry toast for breakfast along with water. Not even coffee, thought Windflower as he nibbled on his tasteless toast. He drank his glass of water and took the two painkillers the nurse had left him. The one thing that cheered him was finding his phone on the bedside table. But before he could call anybody, he had two very special visitors, Sheila and Amelia Louise.

"Dada, dada, dada," screamed Amelia Louise, and she ran to her father.

"Hello, gorgeous," said Windflower as Sheila tried to keep

Amelia Louise from climbing up into the bed.

"Easy, easy," said Sheila. "Be gentle. Daddy's got a sore arm and a sore leg." She lifted the little girl up and sat her gently on the bed. After the two gave Windflower kisses, the little girl made a full inspection of the cast on her father's arm.

"Ish hard," she said as she tapped her hand on the cast and gave her daddy yet another hug. Windflower gladly gave her the last piece of his toast, which she ate while singing and looking all around the room.

"How are you this morning?" asked Sheila. "You were pretty out of it last night."

"I'm good, groggy but good. I thought I could go home, but Doctor White wants me to stay for the day."

"She knows you," said Sheila. "You won't slow down unless you're forced to."

"Unlike you, of course, Madam Mayor and all-around super-woman," said Windflower. "You just missed Ron Quigley."

"That's too bad. I would have liked him to have seen Amelia Louise. When does he leave for Ottawa?"

"Another month. I told him I'm not going to Marystown. We're not going to Marystown."

"Good. Make any other big decisions while you were in a near coma?"

"Only that I'm staying with you."

"That's good," said Sheila as she lifted Amelia Louise off the bed. "We'll pop by to check on you later." She led the toddler out by the hand, but once near the door, the little girl ran back to the bed.

"Ug, ug," she screeched. Sheila lifted her again for a final hug goodbye. Windflower held onto her as long as possible until she squirmed, a signal for her mother to help her down. Sheila blew Windflower an air kiss and Amelia Louise followed suit. She was probably still doing that in the car as her mother strapped her into her car seat, thought Windflower. With that happy vision in his head, the toast and Tylenol did their trick, and despite his best efforts, he soon fell asleep.

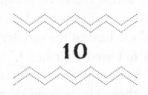

10

Windflower drifted into a very deep sleep, the kind where dreams are born. He had been here many times before. He had learned from his Auntie Marie to look for his hands when he was dreaming. That would allow him to be fully alert during the dream and to be able to better interpret and understand any messages that were being delivered. He found his hands and started to look around. One thing that he'd also learned was that the dream world might seem the same, but it was really different.

Sometimes things, people, animals and events were presented in a straightforward manner. But most times what appeared in the dream world was symbolic of something else. And dream weavers like his aunt and uncle had learned the art of deciphering those messages. Windflower had also learned to pay particular attention to dreams that involved members of his family, especially Auntie Marie and Uncle Frank.

So he was very excited to see that when he 'opened' his eyes in his dream that Uncle Frank was waving to him in the distance. His uncle was in a clearing, as he had often found him before, but in this dream he was calling Windflower to follow past the meadow into the forest. Windflower followed along after him and could hear animals moving around in the forest as well. The brush started to clear, and soon Windflower heard running water. When he emerged, he saw a rapidly running river, and Uncle Frank was sitting by a large fire on the opposite side.

His uncle called out to him to come over. At first, Windflower hesitated, but then he started walking into the river. The river deepened, and he felt a powerful current underneath him. He almost turned back but resisted the urge, and with a few powerful strokes, he was almost halfway across the river. He pushed on, and before long he was sitting on a rock next to Uncle Frank, feeling the warmth of the fire and the heat of the sun drying him off.

"That's good. You followed your heart," said his uncle. "Even though you were afraid, you still crossed the river."

"Because you were there, Uncle," said Windflower.

"That was a motivator. But you were always brave. Foolhardy, sometimes, but courageous, too," said Uncle Frank with a laugh. "We can do many things for other people, but sometimes we have to do them for ourselves as well."

"Why are you here?" Windflower knew that one way to get answers from a dream was to ask questions.

"I am just visiting. I want to see what life is like over on this side. I may be here soon."

"No, Uncle. You have many more years with us yet."

"Our time is passing. Your aunt is closer than I am, but we are nearer this world than the other. But anyway, why are you here? I heard you had a fall."

"That was nothing. But you know, Uncle, I'm not even sure I know the questions to ask."

"Are you willing to ask for help?"

"Sometimes," said Windflower, trying to be honest. There didn't seem to be much point in lying to yourself in a dream.

"Then just ask," said his Uncle. "I may not always be with you, but your allies will be. If you need courage, ask the bear. If you need love, ask the eagle. If you need truth, ask the turtle. If you need humility, and we all need humility, ask the wolf. And if you need wisdom, ask the beaver. Here he is now."

With that, a very large, furry and wet beaver rose out of the water and came near the two men. It shook its fur and flapped his tail very loudly, spraying water over all of them. "It's cold down there," said the beaver. "Good to be in the sun and by this fire."

Windflower had ceased being surprised when animals spoke in his dreams. It happened almost every time, and in his culture four-legged animals could be his allies and friends, just as well as his brothers or sisters. The beaver symbolized a lot for his people. Beaver was a keeper of wisdom, but there also were many old stories about the power of Beaver, including how one giant beaver had flooded the earth after some humans had betrayed its trust.

Windflower didn't know what to ask the beaver so he just sat there admiring its sleek black coat. Finally, the beaver spoke. "The young one is very quiet, Frank. Unlike you," it said with a hearty laugh. "So, let me give you some advice," said the beaver, turning towards Windflower. Windflower tried to look as attentive as he could. He stared at the beaver.

"We learn from our mistakes. So don't fall down any more holes," was the beaver's wisdom for the day.

Windflower looked at the beaver and then at his uncle. Both Uncle Frank and the beaver started laughing so hard, they were soon rolling around on the ground.

"Don't take yourself too seriously," said the beaver, barely getting the words out through his laughter as he slid back into the water. Windflower could still hear Uncle Frank's laughter as he started to wake up.

"Somebody's in a good mood," he heard a voice say. When he opened his eyes, he saw Jones and Evanchuk standing in front of him.

"Funny dream," he said. "Must be the meds."

"You don't look too bad," said Jones.

"I'll take that as a compliment," said Windflower. "I'm ready to go home."

"Glad you're feeling better," said Evanchuk.

"What's going on with Tizzard?" asked Windflower.

"He's still in jail in Las Vegas," said Evanchuk. "But he's got a lawyer now, so we're hoping he'll be out soon. I can't imagine what he's got himself into out there."

"I'm sure it'll be fine," said Windflower. "What's going on at the shop?"

"It's busy," said Jones. "A few break and enters we're looking at from the weekend, and we've got some cannabis awareness training at the high school."

"Plus, the inspector has got us digging into the Spurrell case," said Evanchuk. "We don't have a lot to go on. Paul Spurrell wasn't from around here. He came to visit his girlfriend. They have a baby together, but I don't know what their current relationship is."

"So how did you find him?" asked Windflower.

"He came to us, remember?" said Jones. "We don't often get people turning themselves in."

"Oh yeah," said Windflower, realizing with a little dismay that he might be feeling the impact of his fall a bit more than he thought. "But all he had was a breach of probation, right?"

"That's right," said Evanchuk. "That's why I took him over to Marystown. He'll get processed there and then likely be transferred to St. John's."

"What's next then?" asked Windflower.

"I'm going to speak with his girlfriend," said Evanchuk.

"And I'm going to check in with our usual sources to see if they know any more about what brought Paul Spurrell to Grand Bank," said Jones.

"Maybe just a family visit," offered Windflower.

"Maybe," said Evanchuk. "But from what I heard from Inspector Quigley, HQ thinks it might be something more."

"Okay," said Windflower. "Keep me in the loop."

Both of the constables stood to leave. "Jones, can you stay for a minute?" asked Windflower.

Evanchuk nodded her goodbyes and left.

"Yes, sir?" asked Jones.

"I've been watching your work lately, and I am very impressed," said Windflower. "I think you have consistently shown your leadership capacity. And I want to recognize that. I am going to recommend you for corporal."

"Thank you, sir. Thank you very much." But her face didn't match her words, and Windflower could tell from her expression that she was concerned or maybe confused.

"I will still be here to provide support, and we'll have a transition period to ease you into your new role," said Windflower.

"It's not that, sir," said Jones. "I know that this is a great honour, and I also know that it's very important for the Force to show that women and racialized people are welcome in the leadership ranks. But I'm not sure I can accept, sir."

"I don't understand."

"I was going to talk with you about it, Sergeant. I was thinking about applying for a transfer out west. Since Harry and I have become involved, it has been hard to be so far apart from each other. Can you give me a few days to think about it?"

"Absolutely," said Windflower. He knew that she and Harry Frost, who had been stationed in Grand Bank for a number of years, had been in a relationship but wasn't sure how serious it was. Obviously, it was serious enough for her to consider trying to be closer to Frost, who was now in Portage la Prairie, Manitoba. "Take your time and let me know when you want to talk again," he said.

"Thank you, sir," said Jones. "I'm really sorry that we didn't have a chance to talk before this came up, and I really appreciate you considering me."

"You have earned it."

Jones nodded and left.

Windflower didn't have a lot of time to process that conversation before his cell phone rang.

11

Hello, Betsy," said Windflower, not expecting to hear Betsy Molloy's voice, considering how deathly ill she had appeared the previous morning.

Betsy's voice was faint, but her spirits sounded high as she gave Windflower an update on the office and her health. "I was feeling pretty poorly yesterday. But my Bob made me a beautiful pot of soup, and I had a great sleep. So I'm good to go today," she pronounced.

"Well, just be careful. You don't want to be catching pneumonia or anything. We really need you."

"Thank you, Sergeant. You're very kind. I know that young Smithson is happy I'm back. He near kissed me when he saw me this morning."

Windflower laughed. "I'm sure he is. Is the inspector still around?"

"No, sir," said Betsy. "He's gone back over to Marystown. But I can radio him, if you want me to."

"No thanks, Betsy. I'll call him later."

"Okay, then, you rest up now, and I'll see you in a few days."

"I'll likely be in before that," said Windflower.

He waited, and it seemed like Betsy was pausing, too, before she replied. Finally, she spoke up. "Yes, Sergeant, we'll see you soon."

What did Betsy know that he didn't, he wondered?

He called Ron Quigley and left a message. Then, realizing he was much more tired than he had thought, he fell back to sleep. This time he didn't have any dreams.

Somebody else who didn't have dreams was Eddie Tizzard who had spent the night in the Las Vegas jail, determined not to fall asleep.

He had paced the open space between prisoners in the holding cell for most of the night, afraid of what might happen if he
dozed on one of the cracked vinyl benches along the walls. Already,
more than a couple of fights had broken out, all because of people
too high or drunk to care. Tizzard cared a lot. That's why he was
determined to stay awake.

He succeeded in that feat and was drinking his cup of luke-
warm breakfast coffee when he heard his name being called. When
he went to the door of the holding cell, he saw it was Sanchez.

"It's your lucky day, boy," said Sanchez. "Somebody upstairs has
given you the green light. But first, we got some questions."

Once again Tizzard came to the hallway where the interview
rooms were located and was gently shoved inside by Sanchez.
Sitting there waiting for him was Detective Sergeant Rutherford
and Hillebrand from the FBI.

"We have confirmed who you are," said Rutherford. "Now we
need to figure out why our dead guy had your name in his pocket.
We're releasing you, but we'd like you to stick around to help figure
that out. What do you say, Mr. Tizzard?"

"I'd love a large coffee and a breakfast sandwich," replied the
aspiring private investigator. "Then I'm all yours."

All three other officers laughed.

"You're the cheapest informer we've ever had," said Sanchez.

"And once we get through the basics, I'd love to have a shower,
too," said Tizzard.

"Detective Sanchez, would you get our friend some food and
send somebody back to his hotel to get his luggage?" said Rutherford. "Let's get started while we're waiting, shall we? Agent Hillebrand, why don't you begin?"

"We've had our eye on Martin Spurrell for a while now," said
Hillebrand. "He's not a big fish, but he's connected to one of the
gangs based in Las Vegas, and they in turn have a business relationship with bikers across the States and into Canada. We think he
was laundering money for them using some of the smaller casinos
here and in Reno."

"Our connection is crystal meth," said Rutherford. "It's been
here for years, but because it's cheaper to produce and easier to

distribute, it's taking over, even from opiates and fentanyl."

"So, the FBI's got the national and international angle, and the LVPD is trying to stem the tide locally," said Hillebrand, who then turned to Rutherford so she could describe what was happening in the local jurisdiction.

"We've got seven murders already this year directly related to the fight over meth territory," said Rutherford. "We need to make some inroads into the distribution network and slow this thing down before we have an all-out war. It's not that we care if they kill each other, but we've lost five civilians in crossfire, and everyone is upset with us." After taking a long sigh, she added, "The mayor promised action."

"I'm not sure how I can help you," said Tizzard. "I don't even know my way to the airport."

Hillebrand and Rutherford looked at each other and gave each other a nod.

"There's another brother," said Rutherford.

"I know. Paul Spurrell's in jail in Newfoundland," said Tizzard.

"No," said Hillebrand. "There's another brother." He picked up a file folder on the table. "Walter Alexander Spurrell, known as Willy. He's in Los Angeles right now but on his way to meet his brother Martin here in Las Vegas."

"He doesn't know he's dead?" said Tizzard.

"Not yet," said Hillebrand. "Same with his brother in Canada."

"What do you want me to do?" asked Tizzard.

Rutherford and Hillebrand looked at each other again.

"We want you to meet up with Willy Spurrell and see what you can find out," said Hillebrand.

"He's going to find out his brother is dead," said Tizzard. "And he won't be happy."

"Yes, it's a risk," piped in Rutherford, "but we'd have you under surveillance."

Tizzard didn't know whether he was more scared or excited. He decided he couldn't turn down the adventure or the FBI.

"Do I have to wear a wire?" he asked.

12

Windflower woke from his nap feeling quite a bit better, refreshed even, and a little peckish. The young girl who brought him his soup at lunchtime smiled and wished him a good day. Despite the circumstances, a good day was exactly what he was having when Ron Quigley called.

"Good morning, Inspector. Jones is likely out for corporal," said Windflower when he answered the phone.

"How come?" asked Quigley.

"She's going to ask for a transfer out west. Wants to be closer to Harry Frost. She said she'd think about it, but by the looks of it, I'd say she's gone in the next couple of months. Young love. 'Love looks not with the eyes, but with the mind. And therefore is winged Cupid painted blind.'"

"Nice one. But that's too bad for you. Is there anybody else to consider?"

"Evanchuk is probably ready," said Windflower, "although I've been reluctant to move in that direction until Tizzard gets himself sorted out. But she is a great officer."

"Speaking of Tizzard, he's getting out of jail."

"That's great news. I'm pretty sure Eddie is innocent of everything besides, of course, overeating when given the chance. He'd be a terror on those buffets."

"He's going to be working with the Las Vegas police and the FBI. I just got the notification."

"Wow, that's pretty exciting," said Windflower. "Dangerous?"

"Might be," admitted Quigley. "Las Vegas is not the most dangerous city in the States, but it's up there. They got the major street gangs like the Bloods and the Crips and then some homegrown gangs like the Gersons. There's also a white supremacist group called the Aryan Warriors that heavily recruits inside the prison system."

"You seem to know a lot about gangs. I'm impressed."

"It was part of our study work when I was on the drug task force. Meth is big time, and the gangs were major suppliers all across the United States and even in Canada."

"Here too?"

"You know, the stuff here is mostly run through the local bikers, but their connections go back into those gangs in the States."

"Is that what Tizzard is going to be involved with down there?" Windflower was beginning to feel a bit uneasy. Eddie Tizzard was a capable investigator, but Las Vegas wasn't anything like Grand Bank.

"All I know is that I've been asked to segregate Paul Spurrell and keep him safe and away from everybody else," said Quigley. "Is your holiday over yet?"

"I think I like this," quipped Windflower. "But I'm ready to get out of here as soon as the doctor gives me the okay."

"You'll have to take it slow for a while."

"No worries," said Windflower. "Once I get out of here, I plan to definitely take it easy."

After he got off the phone, the nurse came to help him get to the bathroom. That's when he realized how easy he would have to take it. Part of it was stiffness from lying around, but when he tried to put weight on his injured ankle, the pain was indescribable. He moved very slowly back to his bed and lay down.

Doctor White was his next visitor, and he tried to make his best impression of a person being perfectly fine. The doctor was having none of it.

"A couple of more days here would do you the world of good," she said. When Windflower looked disappointed, she added, "But I have to tell you that you don't really need to be in the hospital; you just need to slow down."

"You're not the only one telling me that," said Windflower. "But I promise to be good if you let me go home."

"Okay, but you have to stay off that ankle. It's the only way it will heal," said the doctor. "I tell you what. I'll release you, but you can't drive for a week."

Windflower thought about saying something like 'you can't do that', but he really wanted to go home. And besides, who would know what he was up to once he left the clinic?

Doctor White apparently would because she gave Windflower a note with NO DRIVING FOR ONE WEEK written on it in large block letters. She also wrote down some Tylenol for pain as required.

"I'll make a copy of this and keep it on file, just in case you lose yours," she said.

Windflower smiled through his teeth and simply thanked her. He called Sheila after the doctor had gone. "I've been given a reprieve," he said. "But you'll have to pick me up. I think I'm grounded."

The nurse helped him pack up his belongings and wheeled him out to the waiting area. She got him a set of crutches that Doctor White had prescribed and rested them next to him while he waited for Sheila. He wanted to walk to the car when Sheila arrived, but the nurse insisted on moving him in the wheelchair.

Sheila was really happy to see him and helped him into her car. Amelia Louise was delirious in the back seat and squealed "dada, dada" all the way home.

When they got home, Levi Parsons was coming back from a walk with Lady, who was even more excited to see Windflower than his daughter.

"Thank you, Levi, we really appreciate your help," said Sheila.

"I'm happy to take Lady for the next few days if it helps," said Levi. "This is study week, and it's a good break to get out with the dog. And it looks like you might need some help," he added, pointing to Windflower's crutches.

"Thanks, Levi. Yeah, that'll be great. I have to try and stay off this ankle. Doctor's orders," said Windflower.

Levi patted both Amelia Louise and Lady on the head as he left.

"Such a nice young man," said Sheila. "We're lucky to have him to help us out, especially with the B & B."

"I know. It's really been a relief not to have to be there every day," said Windflower.

"Are you hungry? I've got some halibut."

"I'm famished."

With that, Sheila left Windflower with his daughter and the pets, warned him to be careful and then set out to make her husband the best fish dinner he had ever had.

13

Windflower tried playing on the floor with Amelia Louise and Lady, but two or three painful bumps on his heavily bandaged ankle moved him to the couch where he directed operations.

Sheila was busy in the kitchen getting dinner ready. She prepped the halibut by sprinkling it with black pepper and sea salt and covering it in a mixture of melted butter, garlic, lemon juice and basil. She put it in a baking pan and tucked it into the fridge.

Next up were the roast potatoes. She peeled her potatoes, cut them in half and tossed them with olive oil, some salt and a heavy hand of black pepper. Both she and Windflower loved the spicy taste of pepper on just about everything. Then she added minced garlic and parsley and tossed everything again to completely coat the potatoes. She arranged the potatoes in a single layer on a large baking sheet and put it in the oven.

She went back to the living room and took Amelia Louise upstairs with her to give Windflower a little break. He was happy for the chance to relax at home for a few minutes and picked up Sheila's book while he waited. He was busily engaged in reading when she came back down with their little girl and a book for him to read to her.

"This is a great book," said Windflower of Sheila's novel.

"Wait your turn," she said as she handed him Giraffes Can't Dance. It was a story that they often read together as a family, and Windflower loved how poor Gerald the giraffe learned that he didn't have to be like everyone else to be great. Amelia Louise loved it, too, and moved closer to her daddy to get a good look.

Sheila smiled at her two favourite people curled up on the couch as she returned to the kitchen. "I've got to put the fish on," she said.

Sheila took the potatoes out of the oven. The aroma filled the kitchen and wafted out to the living room.

"What's that smell?" Windflower yelled.

"Roast potatoes," shouted Sheila as she covered the vegetables with tinfoil and took the halibut out of the fridge. She put the pan in the oven and turned on the broiler. While she waited for the fish to cook, she made a small green salad and set the table for dinner.

Ten minutes later, she called out to Windflower, "Dinner's ready."

"My favourite two words," said Windflower as he put Amelia Louise in her high chair and sat at the table.

"Oh my God, this is so good," said Windflower when he took his first bite of the fish. He was oohing and aahing as he worked his way through one side of potatoes and another piece of fish. "A few more potatoes, too, please," he said. "This is so good."

"I'm glad your appetite still works," said Sheila.

"Appa, appa," said Amelia Louise, throwing another piece of potato over the side for Lady and Molly to scrap over. This time Molly got there first and with a slight snarl sent Lady back to wait for the next missile.

"Room for dessert?" asked Sheila.

"I'd like to, but I'm thinking that I'll be in a lot of trouble if I eat like this and not be able to walk it off," said Windflower.

"Well, I guess Amelia Louise and I will have to eat this chocolate peanut butter cheesecake on our own," said Sheila, taking the famous white cardboard box from the Mug-Up café out of the fridge.

That was enough for Windflower to change his mind. "Well, maybe a little piece."

"I knew you couldn't resist." Sheila cut him and Amelia Louise each a small slice and cleared away the table, putting the dishes in the dishwasher.

"That was a great investment," said Windflower, pointing to the dishwasher as he savoured his dessert.

"Even better since you are going to be relatively useless around here when it comes to cleaning up."

"I can give Amelia Louise her bath."

"Baff, baff," said the little girl.

"Be careful what you say," said Sheila. "She's taken to repeating everything."

"Ting, ting, ting," said Amelia Louise as if to emphasize the point.

"So I hear Eddie Tizzard is in a bit of trouble in Las Vegas," said Sheila.

"Yeah, somehow he came into contact with a fellow Newfoundlander in Las Vegas. Unfortunately, the other man was dead at the time."

"Is Eddie going to be okay? Is he in trouble?"

"Last I heard he got out of jail, and he may even be working with the police out there. That's what Ron Quigley told me."

"Lots of things seem to be changing around here, at least in your world."

"Jones may be leaving, too. She wants to be close to her beau."

"That's a great reason, although I never thought the two of them would hook up."

Windflower nodded in agreement. "Gruff Harry Frost must have some charm hidden inside him that he didn't show us," he said.

"I'm more surprised by Yvette," said Sheila. "I had her pegged as the rising black female in the RCMP."

"'Love looks not with the eyes but with the mind.' Anyway, that will mean another shift at my ever-evolving workplace."

"Does it make you think more about your situation? Our situation?"

"You know I thought about it a bit when I fell in the hole."

"Any conclusions, other than we're not moving to Marystown?"

"Other than I'm sticking with you, no," said Windflower. "How about you? What's your thinking these days? Still ready to give up the political spotlight?"

"Good diversion," said Sheila. "I'm ready to move on from politics. That's the only thing I'm sure about. But one thing I've been thinking about is maybe we should move to St. John's."

"What? A Grand Bank girl turning into a townie?" Windflower

threw up his hands in mock horror. Of course, Amelia Louise held her arms straight up as well, loving this particular game.

"Only temporarily," said Sheila. "But it would be easier if I wanted to take classes full-time. I'd really like to finish up my formal schooling before old age happens."

"You are still young and beautiful."

"Bootifull," piped in Amelia Louise.

"I told you," said Sheila.

"She was just agreeing with me," said Windflower as he picked up his daughter with his one good arm. Amelia Louise rewarded the effort with a squeal of delight.

"Hey, what about you? You hardly said anything," said Sheila.

"It's bath time," said Windflower, and Amelia Louise chorused behind him, "Baff time, baff time."

Sheila laughed at their antics while Windflower mimicked dancing without moving his feet. "I guess I need your help to get her upstairs," he said. "That was another of my inspirations. I'm supposed to ask for help."

Sheila took Amelia Louise from Windflower. "Asking for help isn't a sign of weakness," she said. "It's a sign of strength."

"Oprah Winfrey?" he asked.

"No, Barack Obama. Although smart women like Oprah, or me, for that matter, know when to show our strength."

14

Windflower started to follow slowly up the stairs when his cell phone rang. It was Jones.

"Good evening, sir, calling in to see how you're doing," she said.

"I'm fine," said Windflower. "Is there any more news on Tizzard?"

"Nothing. The inspector called over to tell us to back off on interviewing the girlfriend. Said there had been a development. But I don't have any more news."

"Okay. Anything else for me?"

"Well, sir, we were wondering if you were coming to work tomorrow."

"Of course, I am. I'm not dead."

"How will you be getting here? Do you need a ride?"

"Why would I need a ride?" asked Windflower a little defensively. Then he realized Jones already knew he wasn't supposed to drive. "Betsy," he said.

"Yes, sir. She talked to the doctor. Would you like Smithson to pick you up? He's agreed to be your driver for the next few days, if you want."

"That would be fine," said Windflower, closing his phone and basically crawling up the stairs. Sheila had Amelia Louise's bath running, and Windflower played on the bed with them for a minute until it was bath time. Sheila put the baby in the bath and left her with Windflower to watch over while she tidied up the bedroom.

After her bath Windflower read Amelia Louise one of her favourite stories, If Animals Kissed Goodnight. It was a cozy bedtime chat for a child and her mommy, but Windflower served as a suitable substitute, and it was a great book for cuddling. Sheila came in and kissed her, and Windflower tucked her in with another kiss on her forehead. He turned out the lights and listened in the hallway as Amelia Louise hummed her way to sleep.

Windflower joined Sheila in their bedroom where they watched the news. After Sheila had turned off the lights, Windflower asked her a question.

"If we went to St. John's, what would we do with the B & B?"

"I see you're taking my idea seriously," said Sheila. "I think we could keep it and let Levi run it for us. Beulah can continue with the cooking, and we could come back for most of the summer when it's really busy. I'm not talking about living in St. John's forever. I'd still like to come back to Grand Bank eventually."

Windflower didn't say anything else but allowed the warmth and comfort of the bed and Sheila to lull him to sleep.

Someone who wished he were in Grand Bank was Eddie Tizzard. But rather than being in his beloved town wearing his pajamas, he was sitting in a seedy motel just off the strip in Las Vegas wearing a wire and waiting for Willy Spurrell to appear. His new associates had set it all up, and it was certainly not like anything he'd seen on TV. He was alone and vulnerable, and even though his contacts were sitting outside in a panel truck listening and ready to jump in if needed, they weren't the ones sitting in his seat, sweating as he waited for Spurrell brother number three to arrive.

Tizzard had called Willy Spurrell to tell him that he had showed up in a hotel room in Las Vegas and had found a note from his brother along with the phone number. He didn't know anything more but thought it might be a good idea to get together since they were both from Newfoundland.

Willy Spurrell sounded suspicious, so Tizzard told him to forget about it. Except, he told him, somebody had said his other brother Paul was in trouble in Newfoundland, maybe in jail, and if Willy had any message to give him, he'd be happy to take it back. After much hemming and hawing Willy finally agreed to meet Tizzard. He directed him to the motel where Tizzard was now cooling his heels and having his heart pound out of his chest.

Willy Spurrell was much calmer than Tizzard. He had arrived at the motel early and was parked out back. Tizzard hadn't seen him until he moved in close. Not a good start, thought Tizzard. It didn't get any better when Willy poked a gun in his back and told him to get up and come with him. Tizzard started to speak, but the other man told him to shut up. Tizzard hoped that those watching over him heard all this because the next thing he knew he was pushed in the trunk of a car and the door was slammed on top of him.

Tizzard started speaking, softly at first and then loudly when the noise of the rolling car drowned everything out. By the time he was shouting, he feared that nobody could hear him, and since he didn't have an earpiece—he had thought that would be too risky— he had no idea if anyone knew that he had just been taken prisoner by one of the most sought-after criminals in Nevada, maybe the whole United States.

Eddie Tizzard had a calm and gentle exterior. But that didn't mean he always felt cool inside. Right now, he definitely was not cool. It was dark, it was dirty, and it was hot inside the trunk of a car that was moving very quickly down some highway in the middle of nowhere. He was afraid.

Back in Grand Bank, Windflower woke from a great sleep and was still lying in bed when he heard Sheila rise and pad her way over to get Amelia Louise. He heard Sheila singing softly to their daughter as she changed her and Amelia Louise giggling back. When they were ready, Sheila released her, and Amelia Louise came running into her parents' bedroom. "Dada, dada, dada," she cried. Windflower could have cried, too.

"Who wants pancakes?" asked Sheila

"Me, me, me, me," said Amelia Louise, both arms raised completely straight up in case there was any doubt about her intentions.

"Me too," said Windflower.

"Okay, you look after her and I'll put some coffee on. Levi should be here soon to walk Lady, so I'll pop her in the back for now. Then I'll make our pancakes."

"Yay," said Windflower.

"Yay, yay, yay," shouted Amelia Louise as she did a little impromptu dance routine to show how really excited she was.

Father and daughter went back to her room where she took him by the hand to her toy box. One by one she took her toy animals out and handed them to him. He tried to put them back, but she took them out again and started lining them up one by one. "Oh, we're playing zoo," said Windflower. "Great."

"Zoo, zoo, zoo," murmured Amelia Louise until all the animals were out of the box. Then she clapped her hands and started dancing. Windflower joined in as best he could with his bum ankle, and they were still dancing when Sheila announced that their pancakes were ready.

15

After breakfast Windflower did what he could to help Sheila clean up, and when they were finished, he hobbled to the living room.

"You're supposed to use these," said Sheila, pointing at the crutches in the hallway. "Hey, isn't that Smithson out front in that car?"

Windflower peeked out the window. "Looks like him," he said.

"What's he doing?" asked Sheila.

"Wash she doin?" asked Amelia Louise. "Wash she doin?"

Windflower picked up his cell phone. "Smithson, what are you doing parked outside my house?"

"I'm here to pick you up, whenever you are ready, sir. No rush."

"Oh yeah." Windflower realized he had forgotten about his conversation with Jones the day before.

"Do you need any help?" asked Smithson cautiously.

"No, Constable, I do not. Why don't you come back in half an hour?" he asked and then ended the call.

"The cavalry?" asked Sheila.

"More like the minders," said Windflower. "I'm going to get cleaned up."

He tried to hurry up the stairs, but he only managed to find himself falling and stumbling and almost sliding back down them. "I'm okay, I'm okay," he shouted.

Taking longer than he thought possible, he washed up and got dressed. When he got back downstairs, he kissed Sheila goodbye and gave Amelia Louise a great big bear hug. He grabbed his crutches reluctantly and hopped down the driveway. Smithson had jumped out to open the door for him but retreated quickly when he saw the glare on his sergeant's face. Windflower threw his crutches in the back and half jumped, half fell into the front seat beside Smithson.

Smithson hardly dared look but summoned the courage to ask Windflower where he wanted to go.

"To work, Constable," said Windflower gruffly.

A few minutes later Windflower gingerly got out of the car and started to walk in. Then he remembered his crutches and opened the back door. Smithson had rushed around to help.

"I got this, Smithson," said Windflower, grabbing his crutches under his arm and hopping into the detachment.

Betsy greeted him as warmly as she could without getting too near. "Don't want to get all my germs over you," she said. "You have enough problems."

Windflower smiled grimly and made it into his office. Betsy was behind him soon after with a hot cup of coffee.

"Thank you, Betsy," said Windflower.

"You're welcome, Sergeant. If you need anything else, anything at all, you let me know, okay?"

Windflower forced a smile.

When Smithson came in to ask if he needed anything, Windflower didn't even bother with that, opting instead to give the young constable a scowl while digging into his paperwork. "I'll call you if I need you," he shouted to Smithson's back.

When he was gone, Windflower sat back, sipped his coffee and tried to breathe slowly. That was one of his meditative routines that almost always worked to bring him back to an emotional balance. But not this morning. He thought about the situation and realized that he hated being dependent on other people, even those who loved him, like Sheila, and those who deeply cared about him, like Betsy. Did he have a stubborn streak? Maybe, he thought.

He didn't have much more time to think because Evanchuk arrived at his office door. "Jones called, sir. There's been an accident on the highway, up near L'Anse au Loup."

"How bad is it?" asked Windflower.

"Serious," said Evanchuk. "Paramedics are on their way."

"Okay. You go up and take traffic control. I'll come by with

Smithson," he said just before yelling, "Smithson!" He couldn't have been far away because he was there before Windflower was up and on his crutches.

"Let's go," said Windflower. "What are you waiting for?"

Once they were back in the car, Smithson sped to the accident scene. The paramedics were already there, and Windflower heard the fire department coming, too.

Evanchuk had taken over directing traffic from Jones who was walking to the car to talk to Windflower. He could see the car in the ditch and the paramedics lifting a person onto the stretcher to put them into the ambulance. As Jones got closer to him, he noticed she had something in her arms. It wasn't a something, he realized. It was a little someone.

"She was in the back seat," said Jones, lifting the blanket off the face of a little girl who looked to be about three or four by Windflower's estimation. "Doesn't appear to be hurt, which is kind of a miracle. She was in a car seat. Fell asleep a few minutes ago."

"Thank goodness," said Windflower. "Why don't you put her in the back? Smithson can watch over her while you check out the victim and take a look at the car."

Smithson once again wisely resisted the urge to say anything but got out and opened the door for Jones. She placed her bundle in the back seat, and Smithson slid in. "She'll be fine, likely won't even wake up," said Windflower. Smithson wasn't so confident but kept his own counsel.

Jones came back quickly with one of the paramedics. "They're taking the woman driver, Marla Fitzgerald, to the clinic."

"She's in bad shape, Sergeant," said the paramedic. "We've patched her up, but she's lost a lot of blood, and we can't do much more here."

"Fine," said Windflower. "We'll send someone over right away."

"That's Paul Spurrell's girlfriend," said Jones. "The one we were supposed to stay away from."

"Her daughter is in the back?" asked Windflower.

"I think so. If that's his girlfriend, maybe she's Paul Spurrell's daughter, too," said Jones. "I'll go take a quick look at the vehicle."

As if she knew that people were talking about her, the little girl in the back seat woke up. Smithson tried to soothe her, but she was having none of it. "I wants my mommy," she started screaming over and over and tried to get out of the car. Smithson held her gently but would not let her move. The little girl screamed and tried to get away.

"Bring her up to me," said Windflower. He took the girl in is his arms from Smithson and started talking quietly to her, telling her that everything would be okay. He had no idea if it really would be okay, but that's all he had for now. Somehow it worked, at least to settle her down a bit, and she started to drift off to sleep in Windflower's arms.

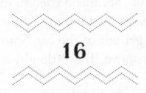

16

Eddie Tizzard was at no risk of falling asleep as the vehicle he was riding in the trunk of swerved off the highway and onto a dirt road. At least he assumed it was unpaved because of the numerous bumps that tossed him around like a marshmallow. He managed to awkwardly wedge himself in next to the wheel well and hung on the best he could until the car screeched to a stop. He heard a car door open, and when the trunk was opened, he squinted as he tried to see what was going on.

"Get out," said Willy Spurrell as he pulled Tizzard out. "Don't make me have to shoot another Newfoundlander."

Tizzard wasn't sure if that meant he'd be the first or another Newfoundlander that got shot by Willy Spurrell. He didn't want to find out so he planned to be as compliant as possible. When his eyes adjusted, he glanced around. He saw a lot of low brush and right in front of him a ranch-style bungalow with several vehicles in the yard. Nothing was remotely familiar to him, and he wondered if anyone, anywhere, knew where he was.

He was pushed ahead of Willy Spurrell into the house and then into a chair in the living room. Tizzard looked anxiously at Spurrell to try and gauge his mood. He actually seemed pretty calm, which Tizzard took as a good sign. Another good sign was when Willy Spurrell pulled a bottle of Jack Daniel's out of a cupboard and poured them each a couple of ounces. You don't usually kill the people you're having a drink with, at least not right away.

Spurrell took a swig and pointed to Tizzard. He took a sip. Jack Daniel's wasn't really his thing, but as it might help, he decided to take a couple more.

"Okay, let's talk," said Spurrell. "Tell me again how you know my brother and what you're doing here."

Tizzard told Spurrell he had got his number from his brother Martin and decided to call him. He told a fib about being in Las Vegas on a business trip and going to an ice-making machine sales convention for the plant in Grand Bank. Willy Spurrell didn't seem to care about that. What he really wanted was info about his brother. He poured himself another drink and offered a second to Tizzard, but he begged off. Tizzard didn't want his senses to be dulled. That was a good thing because he could hear a vehicle pulling up in the yard outside. Both men jumped up.

Willy Spurrell went to the window to take a peek through the curtains. Tizzard saw his chance and darted into the kitchen, hoping there was a back door. Luckily, there was, and by the time he got around to the front of the house, a group of men in FBI jackets had Willy Spurrell on the ground and handcuffed.

"That was pretty smooth," said Hillebrand.

"Not for me," said Tizzard.

The other FBI agents bundled up Spurrell and put him in the back of a black Yukon.

"I didn't know if you were coming at all," said Tizzard.

"We had you all the way," said Hillebrand. "He surprised us a bit when he pulled you out the back, but we had this on you." He reached over to Tizzard's jacket to take out the microphone in the lapel and a small circular object that was in the inside pocket. "GPS," he said.

"Great, except I didn't know anything and was stuck in the trunk of a car with a crazy man," said Tizzard, not too impressed as he realized the personal danger he had agreed to.

"We needed to track him back here. We think there might be a meth lab in here or somewhere on this property."

"What was Spurrell's role?"

"He had worked himself up pretty high. Our sources say that he was overseeing the production and bulk distribution."

"That means he was dealing with some heavy-duty dudes."

"And there's always competition," said Hillebrand. "There's a turf war going on in the Western United States that stretches from California to Colorado. The epicentre is Los Angeles, but Nevada is pretty hot, too."

"Gangs?" asked Tizzard.

"Used to be straight up Bloods and Crips. That's still true in many areas. But they seem to find a way to carve up the pie so that everybody gets a slice. The new kids on the blocks are the white supremacists, neo-Nazi skinheads."

"I think I saw some of them when I was in jail. They scared me more than the others."

"They are the most dangerous because they're the most violent," said Hillebrand. "They're not driven by money. It's straight up hate. They think they're in a race war."

Tizzard shook his head as he watched the Yukon being driven away and several other large trucks being brought up. Teams of what he assumed were FBI people got out and started putting on their hazmat suits.

"I guess you're free to go, with our thanks," said Hillebrand. "I'll take you back to your hotel."

Tizzard got an upgraded suite at the hotel but made sure to check the bathroom and under the bed before he finally relaxed. Then he took a long hot shower, ordered a large steak from room service and called his fiancée, Carrie Evanchuk.

17

Windflower left Jones and Evanchuk at the accident scene. Jones knew enough to get the pictures and do the site investigation while Evanchuk diverted traffic. Since there was no fatality, at least not yet, they could likely wrap up quickly. Cradling the little girl in his arms, both under his seatbelt, Windflower got Smithson to drive to the clinic.

When they arrived, he sent Smithson in to get a nurse, and when she came, he handed over the girl. She woke up and started screaming for her mommy.

"She needs to be checked out. I hope she's okay," said Windflower.

The nurse gripped the girl tightly and was already trying to soothe her. The girl was having none of it, and Windflower could hear her screaming even after the emergency doors closed behind her and the nurse.

"Do you want me to get you a chair, sir?" asked Smithson. The answer he got from Windflower was another icy stare.

Windflower thought about tearing up the young constable but resisted. "No. I do not want a wheelchair," he said. "Hand me my crutches out of the back."

Smithson gave him the crutches and got out of the way as quickly as possible.

Windflower walked into the emergency department and nodded hello to the nurse at reception. He could hear the little girl screaming from somewhere in the examination area but didn't have time to stop and check that out. He was headed for the ICU. He reached the door of the unit but knew he couldn't go in. He tried to peek inside. The frosted glass on the window might as well have been solid steel.

So he sat down and waited. Smithson joined him soon after. They were there for about 15 minutes when a doctor Windflower hadn't met before came out. He clumsily tried to stand to greet her and nearly fell over. Smithson tried to be helpful by approaching him but got another death stare and moved back quickly.

"I'm Sergeant Winston Windflower," he said, holding out his hand.

The doctor took off her gloves and removed her face mask. Windflower noticed her pretty smile first and then that she was wearing a hijab. "Nice to meet you. I'm Fatima Mohamed," she said. "I've heard a lot about you."

"Some of it nice, I hope," said Windflower.

"Most of it," said Doctor Mohamed with a smile. "I'm guessing you would like to know about the accident victim who just arrived."

"Yes, please."

"Miss Fitzgerald has serious injuries and has lost a lot of blood," said the doctor. "The blood we can replace, but we won't even know the extent of her problems until the swelling goes down. We have induced her into a coma, and we'll see what happens in the next few hours. But I would suggest that you call her relatives to come as quickly as possible. Anything can and might happen."

"She has a little girl," said Windflower. "The emergency nurse was taking a look at her. Can you check her out, too?"

"Okay, I'll go there now."

Windflower watched the doctor walk down the hallway. He'd seen lots of women wearing hijabs in his travels around the country but wondered what the reaction from locals had been to the rare sight of a self-identified Muslim woman in their midst. He didn't have much time to ponder that thought as Jones came into the ICU waiting area.

"We need to notify next of kin," said Windflower.

"I'm not sure there are any around here," said Jones. "That's what the paramedics told me. I guess she'd only been living here for a month or so when her brother moved to Fort McMurray. He got hired back on after all the layoffs and was going to stay there for as long as the job lasted. I can see if we can find him, but that will take some time."

"What about Paul Spurrell?" asked Smithson.

"What about him?" asked Windflower.

"If he's the father, then shouldn't we notify him?" asked Smithson.

Windflower wasn't so sure about that. "I'll check with Inspector Quigley," he said.

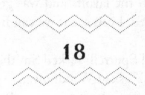

18

Windflower decided to use the area outside of the ICU so he could be updated on the latest developments from the accident at L'Anse au Loup that was now threatening the life of Marla Fitzgerald and may well have injured her young daughter, too.

"Is Evanchuk still at the scene?" Windflower asked Jones.

"Yes. She'll be there until the tow truck arrives. She's pretty happy though. Tizzard called her, and he's out of jail."

"That is good news," said Windflower. He sighed a little, relieved that his friend was safe, but soon turned back to the business at hand. "Anything from the scene?" he asked.

"Skid marks and signs of braking," said Jones. "By the looks of it I'd say she wasn't wearing a seatbelt. She likely bounced around a bit, and even with the airbag blowing up, it wouldn't have been enough to help her. Might have been distracted by something outside the car, an animal or another vehicle maybe. I did find this in the glove compartment."

Jones held up a clear plastic bag with clear glass-like fragments inside.

"Crystal meth," said Smithson. The other two officers looked at him as if to ask why he knew what crystal meth looked like. "I saw a video on YouTube of the bust that happened on the west coast."

"Put it in evidence," said Windflower. "We'll have to get prints from the bag, and make sure we go through the car completely."

"Evanchuk will stay with the car and do the full search at the yard," said Jones. "I had a quick look in the trunk and the back seat but couldn't see anything."

"Okay," said Windflower to Jones. "You go back and see what's going on at the office. Tell Betsy that we won't release any information about the crash until we have more details. The media won't be happy, but we've got too many moving pieces."

Jones left, and Windflower sent Smithson to the machine to get them both a coffee. He phoned Quigley in Marystown and reached his assistant, Sergeant Bill Ford. Ford and Windflower were old fishing buddies. Ford was a real fisherman, and he had introduced Windflower to salmon fishing in Central and Western Newfoundland on the mighty Gander and Exploits rivers. Ford was a nice man and a good cop, but he had run into trouble with the bottle that almost cost him his career in the Mounties. He had pulled himself back from the brink and was now working with the inspector in Marystown.

"Good day, Winston. How are you, man?" said Ford.

"I'm good, Bill, nice to talk to you. How've you been?" replied Windflower.

"Best kind," said Ford. "Although I'm already missing the salmon fishing. I think I'm going to take a trip up to Labrador next year. I've never been, but I hear the fishing is amazing. You should come."

"Man, I'd love to, but it's hard to get away now with the family and trying to keep the B & B going. You know Paul Spurrell, the guy that Evanchuk brought over on a breach?"

"Yeah. All of a sudden, he's somebody important. I don't know much about it except that it's a big deal. The boss is looking after it with HQ. I just know we have to keep him safe and secluded until we get some other direction."

"Well, his girlfriend and her little girl, who we think might be his daughter, were in an accident. The girl looks fine, but the mother is in bad shape. We're trying to notify next of kin."

"Gotcha," said Ford. "Spurrell is in seclusion with no visitors, but let me talk to the inspector, and I'll get back to you."

"From what the doctor said, you better hurry," said Windflower.

After he hung up, Smithson came back with his coffee and a visitor.

"Good day, Sergeant, how's she goin' b'y?" asked Doctor Vijay Sanjay.

"I am well, Doc. How's Repa and the boys?" said Windflower.

"The boys are well, but distant, and Repa is still the light of my life. She was asking about you and that beautiful little girl and when we were going to see her and your lovely wife again."

"Let me talk to Sheila and we'll see if we can work something out very soon. Maybe you come over for dinner? Although it won't be anything like the quiet oasis of your home."

"She is a joy. And you are raising her so well. It's good to expose her to many people and many cultures. 'Do not limit a child to your own learning, for she was born in another time.'"

"That's very wise advice."

"And you have to come to sample my darling Balvenie," said Sanjay. "It's the lesser known of the Speyside distilleries, but it is simply gorgeous. I heard they age it for twelve years in a combination of bourbon barrels and sherry casks and then transfer it into other containers to allow the liquid to mingle."

"That's the same area as Glenfiddich, isn't it?" asked Smithson.

"How'd you know that?" asked Windflower.

"My brother started a small craft distillery a few years ago. He had samples of some of the best Scotch around to try and get his taste right. Best summer of my life," said Smithson.

"I bet," said Windflower, thinking that young Smithson was turning into a much more interesting character than he had ever thought possible.

"In any case, it would be my pleasure to come sample your Scotch," said Windflower to Sanjay. "Although I'm not sure I should be sampling any Scotch in this condition. I can't even drive."

"No problem," said Sanjay. "I will pick you up, and Repa would be happy to drive you back home. So why not talk to your good wife and see if you can't get away for an hour or so this weekend?"

"You are very persuasive, my friend," said Windflower. "I will get back to you on that. I'm kind of struggling to get around right now."

"That is very temporary," said Sanjay. "If nothing is broken and you are careful, you should be back to normal soon. Now to business. I assume you are here about the crash victim, young Miss Fitzgerald."

"Do you know her?"

"I know her daughter, Stella. Her mother brought her in several times for the usual things. Colds, a sprained wrist one time. Nothing too serious. A sweet little girl."

"And the mother?" asked Windflower.

"Not my patient," said Sanjay. "But I could tell she was in distress and using drugs. She tried to hide it, but amphetamine users are pretty easy to spot."

Smithson piped in. "Jittery, picking at their face and hands. Serious tooth decay and non-stop talking."

Both men stared at him. Then Windflower said, "YouTube." Sanjay nodded.

"Talk to Sheila and let me know. My chessboard is as dusty and bored as I am." Doctor Sanjay left and went back to his office at the other end of the building.

"I guess we should go back," said Windflower. "Can you talk to the desk and get them to update us on the woman's condition?"

"What about the little girl?" asked Smithson.

"They'll call social services."

Smithson looked at him as if he had decided to sell his puppy. "What?" asked Windflower.

"They don't need to call social services. Why can't she stay here for now? She's scared and alone, and her mother may be dying in there."

"Okay, you check in on her while I talk to the nurse at the desk."

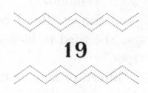

19

Tizzard was on his laptop trying to rebook his flight when his cell phone rang. He thought it might be Evanchuk and tried to sound as cheery as possible for his fiancée. But it was Detective Sergeant Rutherford.

"Hey, Tizzard," said Rutherford.

Tizzard was a little surprised at the sudden informality of the police officer, but what did he care? He was going home. "Hi," he replied.

"I heard you were great with our perp," said Rutherford.

"Thanks. Although I don't know how great one can be when they're locked in the trunk of a car."

Rutherford laughed. "Sorry about that. But the good news is that the FBI got a very bad guy and are getting ready to shut down a major lab that is supplying most of this region."

"That is good news. I'll be sure to tell all my friends about it when I get home."

"That's what I want to talk to you about," said the detective. "The FBI has given us a window of the next twenty-four hours to try and round up some of the people running meth in Las Vegas."

"That's nice of them," said Tizzard, wondering why Rutherford was telling him all of this.

"Not really. They don't want to release any information because they want to completely secure the scene and wait for some of the gang members and meth patrons to show up."

"Well, good luck with that."

"Thanks," said the detective. "I know you haven't exactly been treated well as a guest of the LVPD, but we have a favour to ask."

Tizzard paused for only a moment. "I think I've done enough

for one week, and with all respect to your police department, I'd really like to go home."

"Understood. But here's the deal. We have never been able to get inside the Aryan Warriors."

"The white supremacists?"

"You know about them?"

"Hillebrand was talking about them, and I think some of them were in the holding cell with me. Creeps."

"Dangerous creeps," she said. "They've taken over the coke trade and are trying to muscle in on the meth side."

"Anyway, I wish you well with that. But I'm going home."

"How would a commendation from the Las Vegas Police Department look on the wall of your new office?"

"I don't think I'm going to like what I hear next," said Tizzard. He was right.

Back in Grand Bank Windflower had managed to tug a reluctant Smithson away from the little girl at the clinic with a promise to come back and check in on her again after lunch.

"She'll be fine for an hour or so," said Smithson. "The nurse got her a snack and some crayons and paper to colour on."

"I'm pleased," said Windflower, a little more sarcastically than he intended. "Let's go for lunch."

Smithson drove them to the Mug-Up, which was still quite full. Today, the patrons consisted of some locals and a few tourists who were heading over to the island of St. Pierre, just off the coast. A ferry took them from Fortune to the French territory, whose ownership dates back hundreds of years to some of the last major battles between England and France. England got Newfoundland, and France got the two tiny islands of St. Pierre and Miquelon.

Windflower had been over many times, including one of his first dates with Sheila. He often thought about those early days whenever he heard French being spoken in the café, just like today with the couple in the corner trying to decipher the English-only menu. Windflower didn't need any decoding to decide that he wanted a bowl of pea soup and a grilled cheese sandwich. Smithson happily agreed.

Marie, the long-time waitress, took their orders and came back a few minutes later with their soup, still-warm dinner rolls and two cups of black tea. Herb Stoodley came out of the kitchen with his apron still on to greet them as they were testing the soup.

"Perfect," said Windflower. Smithson agreed by nodding his head vigorously.

"That's good," said Stoodley. "We aim to please. 'Things done well, and with a care, exempt themselves from fear.'"

"How's Moira?" asked Windflower as he sipped on his soup and broke off a large chunk of the roll to dip into the creamy broth flecked with pieces of salt meat.

"She's grand," said Stoodley. "She's gone to do some shopping and left me in charge."

"That's a scary thought," said Windflower. "But you know, 'some are born great and some achieve greatness, and some have greatness thrust upon 'em.'"

"I would be the latter," said Stoodley. "I've got that CD in the back for you. You can pick it up on the way out. I've got to get back to the cash."

"What's the CD?" asked Smithson as Marie delivered their sandwiches.

"It's Debussy," said Windflower. "Herb is my tutor in the classical music world. He wanted me to listen to a flute piece called Syrinx."

"I know that music," said Smithson. "I played the flute in high school. Thought I might go to music school."

"What made you change your mind and become involved in the law?" asked Windflower.

"Music and the law have a lot in common. Just different approaches to life," said Smithson. "'Music is a moral law. It gives a soul to the Universe, wings to the mind, flight to the imagination, a charm to sadness, gaiety and life to everything. It is the essence of order and leads to all that is good and just and beautiful.'"

Windflower's jaw dropped, but he didn't have a chance to respond as Jones walked into the Mug-Up and came to their table.

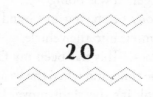

20

"I've got some more information about Marla Fitzgerald," said Jones. "Her neighbours seemed happy to talk about her."

"What did you find out?" asked Windflower, finishing the last of his sandwich and wondering if he had room for some dessert. He surveyed the list of cheesecakes on the board above the cash.

"Sir?" asked Jones, jolting him back to reality from anticipatory cheesecake heaven.

"Go ahead," he said.

"She was just back from rehab when she arrived here," said Jones "Her friendly neighbour told me it was her third time. She said Fitzgerald moved here to get away from that Spurrell fella. Said he was bad news."

"Run her through the system," said Windflower. "Likely she would have had some contact. Where did she come from?"

Jones looked at her notes. "She came from St. John's about six months ago. Before that, she was somewhere on the mainland. Said that Spurrell arrived on the scene about two months ago. For what it's worth, she blames him for getting the woman back on the drugs."

"Okay. We're going back to the shop. Why don't you write up your notes from the accident scene and take a break? You must be exhausted," said Windflower.

"Yeah, we're all a little tired," said Jones. "Everybody except superman here."

"I'm okay," said Smithson. "But what about the girl?"

"You go see how she is. Jones will give me a ride back," said Windflower.

He hobbled out with Jones while Smithson went to the clinic

to see how Stella Fitzgerald was doing.

"I'm sorry you won't be staying in Grand Bank," said Wind-flower once he got himself into the vehicle.

"Me too," said Jones. "This has been my favourite posting. It's super quiet most of the time, and when the weather is good, it really is paradise. But I think it's the right move. I knew that I would eventually have to move on, and this makes sense for me. At least right now."

"I get it," said Windflower. "I just wanted you to know that we'd miss you,"

"Thanks, Sarge. I really appreciate that."

As they pulled up to the Grand Bank RCMP Detachment, Windflower noticed two vehicles out front. One was from VOCM News, and the other was the familiar sight of Inspector Ron Quig-ley's SUV.

Windflower managed to dodge the reporter who was talking to Betsy and make it successfully to his office where Ron Quigley was waiting for him.

"You're pretty quick for a man on one leg," said Quigley.

"'There is more to life than simply increasing its speed,'" said Windflower.

"Nice," said Quigley. "What's the latest on our accident victim?"

"She's in trouble. We found a bag of meth in her car, and her little girl in the backseat. Both are at the clinic."

"Paul Spurrell's girlfriend?"

"That's what we hear, although we don't know how close they are. And he is likely the father of the child. Either way, that would make him the closest relative that she has anywhere around here."

"I've got permission to bring him over. But he will need round-the-clock supervision," said Quigley.

"We don't have the resources for that."

"I know. Ford is bringing him over from Marystown and will babysit him. If you can make sure Ford gets food and bathroom breaks, that would be good."

"We can do that," said Windflower.

"I also wanted to tell you that I am recommending that Ford take over for me, on an interim basis."

"Are you asking for my advice? 'Cause if you are, I think it's a great idea. Bill's a good man, and everybody around here likes him."

"Good, but you may not like my next suggestion as much. I'm also recommending that Smithson come to Marystown to help him. Ford is a great guy, but he is lost technologically, and he needs some young blood around to support him. Smithson is the best choice."

"You're right. I don't like that idea as much. In fact, it sucks. But I get it. We train 'em, you take 'em. That's the way it always works."

Quigley laughed. "'How sharper than a serpent's tooth it is to have a thankless child!' Or a thankless sergeant. I'll start working on getting someone else transferred in as quickly as I can. Thank you again for your support."

"Are you staying around tonight? Why don't you come over for supper? I was thinking about picking up some pizza. Sheila would love to see you."

"Yeah, seems like Grand Bank is where the action is right now. That would be great. I'll even drive you home," said Quigley. "Let me check and see where Ford is. Can you see if you can get rid of the media guy out there before Ford arrives with Spurrell?"

Quigley left, and Windflower called Betsy on the intercom.

"I can see the person from VOCM now," he said.

A relieved looking Betsy arrived moments later with a male reporter in tow.

"Bill Withers," said the reporter. "VOCM radio news. Can you do an interview about the accident?"

"Sure," said Windflower.

"Bill Withers, VOCM News, reporting in Grand Bank about the accident at L'Anse au Loup. I'm with Sergeant Winston Windflower of the Royal Canadian Mounted Police. Sergeant, what can you tell us about the accident this morning?"

"It was a single vehicle accident, and there is one person in serious condition at the Grand Bank Clinic. The driver of the car was a woman in her twenties from Grand Bank. The cause of the accident is still under investigation," said Windflower.

"We understand that there was a child in the car at the time of the accident. Can you give us an update on their condition?" asked Withers.

"There was a minor in a car seat in the back of the car. She is being examined right now, but her injuries, if any, do not appear serious."

"What do you think caused the accident?"

"That is under investigation at this time, and no further information will be released until that is completed."

Withers turned off the tape. "I've talked to some of the neighbours," he said. "They say drugs were involved."

Windflower didn't take the bait. "Have a great day and thank you," he said.

Withers took his pad and equipment and followed Betsy. She'd been standing in the doorway, out in the lobby area. Windflower watched through his office window as the VOCM car pulled away. Soon Spurrell would be led in, and Windflower wasn't sure he'd be able to handle any more in his day. He thought about his accident at the mine. It had taken more out of him than he had thought. He put his head back on his chair's headrest and felt himself falling again...falling, falling and falling.

He 'woke' with the sensation that he was flying, not in an airplane but by his own power. He had had this type of dream many times. Auntie Marie had called them eagle dreams. She said that dreams like this might be asking us to look for perspective or the big picture. "Look carefully, my boy, not just at the rivers or mountains, but see the rocks and the birds and the animals," she often said.

In his dream Windflower swooped down low like a hawk seeking his prey and flew close to the ground. He flew over the forest and saw deer and a fox and several moose tromping through the trees. It appeared that all the animals were going in the same direction, towards what Windflower could see farther ahead was a wide river. He followed their trail and landed near the remnants of a fire.

"We're too late," said one of the moose. "They're gone."

"Who's gone?" asked Windflower, but in his heart he knew. He looked on the other side of the river and could see his Auntie Marie sitting in a circle with a great gathering of animals and people. They were singing and dancing and getting ready for a feast.

He called out to her, but there was no answer. He woke, startled, and grabbed his cell phone to check for messages. None. Hardly any time had passed. That's what it was like in the dream world. Much could happen in a short amount of time because in the dream world time had no limits.

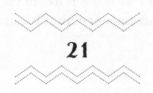

21

Windflower decided there was still time to do a quick check-in with Sheila to make sure it was okay to bring Quigley over for dinner. She said she would be happy to have him join them and offered to make a salad to go along with the pizza.

Windflower was expecting to see Ford first with his prisoner, but Evanchuk popped her head into his office.

"Got a sec?" she asked.

"Sure," said Windflower.

"Not much else in the car, but I've got some prints to run through the system," she said. "Anything else you want me to do?"

"Yeah, can you go over to Fitzgerald's apartment and pick up a change of clothes for her and her daughter. Some pajamas and stuff, too. Take a look around the place while you're there, just whatever is in plain view."

"That way we don't need a search warrant."

"Exactly, or to make our case stronger for one if we need to. By the way, how's Eddie?"

"He's good," Evanchuk told her boss. "He got tied up in some part of an investigation out there. But he was making plans to come home the last time I heard from him."

"Great," said Windflower. "Glad to hear he's okay. Did you ever find out what it was all about?"

"Not really. He told me some story about going into a hotel room and finding a dead man and thousands of dollars on the bed."

"Maybe he got lucky at the casino."

"Eddie is kind and smart and more than a little gullible. He'd be nervous in a Las Vegas jail and quite possibly be targeted by someone in there with him," said Evanchuk.

"He knows how to look after himself."

"I know, but I worry. Anyway, I'll make my stop at the apartment and then head over to the clinic to drop off the stuff."

"Send Smithson back when you see him, will you?"

Evanchuk had barely pulled out of the parking lot when the RCMP prisoner transport van stopped in front of the detachment. Windflower saw Bill Ford open the back and lead a prisoner into the office.

"Sergeant Windflower, meet Paul Spurrell," said Ford.

Paul Spurrell didn't look very happy. "Why are you dragging me around?" he snapped at Ford. "Do you know anything about my brother?" he asked Windflower.

"Nope," said Windflower. "What's your relationship to Marla Fitzgerald?"

"She's my girlfriend," said Spurrell. "What's it to you?"

Windflower looked Spurrell over. He was trying to figure out whether he should tell him what was going on when Smithson came in with Stella Fitzgerald skipping by his side. Before Windflower could ask Smithson what he was doing, the little girl looked up at Spurrell and then shrunk back towards Smithson right away. Windflower observed that the child looked surprised to see Spurrell, but not at all interested in getting close to him.

"Stella, what are you doing here?" asked Spurrell. "That's my daughter. What's she doing here? Where's Marla?"

The little girl stood stiffly against Smithson and didn't move a muscle. "Let's put him in back," said Windflower to Ford, and Ford pushed and pulled Spurrell towards the back and into a jail cell. Spurrell was yelling for his daughter all the way, but she didn't move an inch.

"What's this all about?" asked Windflower, looking at Smithson and the girl.

"I can explain," said Smithson.

"Start talking. Fast."

"They couldn't reach a social worker on short notice, so she would've had to stay there at the clinic on her own. I said I would take her back here for a couple of hours and look after her."

"This is a police station, in case you haven't noticed, and there are jail cells back there. This is no place for a child," said Windflower.

Stella Fitzgerald sat on the floor and started to cry. Smithson looked at Windflower as if to say 'now look what you've done' but didn't speak. Instead he sat on the floor next to the little girl and whispered that it would be okay.

"Two hours max," said Windflower. "It's not safe for her here."

"We'll stay out of the way. Betsy's making a snack right now for her."

As if on cue Betsy appeared with a cut-up apple, two cookies and a juice box. "C'mon with me, my ducky," she said to the girl.

Stella followed Betsy to the lunchroom, and the arrival of Inspector Quigley at Windflower's office let Smithson escape, too.

"What's that about?" asked Quigley, watching the parade go down the hallway.

"It's Marla Fitzgerald's little girl," said Windflower.

"So that's what the yelling was all about," said Quigley. "Let's go talk to Spurrell."

"What are you going to tell him?" asked Windflower.

"As little as possible until we find out what's going on. What's the status of our patient?"

"Let's ask Evanchuk. She's coming back in now." Windflower pointed to the window.

"Not good," said Evanchuk when she came into Windflower's office. "The nurse said there's apparently little brain activity, and they are waiting for her to die. Could be anytime."

"I guess we should tell Spurrell and see if he wants a visit," said Quigley. "We'll have to secure the scene. Can you help with that?"

"Not personally," said Windflower. "But Evanchuk and Smithson can. You go talk to Spurrell, and I'll get that organized. Can you get Smithson?" he asked Evanchuk.

Moments later Evanchuk, Smithson and Stella Fitzgerald were standing in front of him. Windflower gave directions on how both officers would proceed, and they both stayed stuck to the same spot.

Finally, Smithson spoke up. "What about Stella?" he asked.

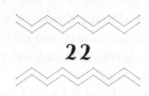

22

At the mention of her name, Stella sat on the floor again. She looked like she was going to cry once more. "I'll look after her while you're gone," said Windflower. The girl still wasn't sure, and this time did start crying. Smithson sat down beside her and began speaking softly to her. "The Sergeant will look after you," he said. "He's got a little girl, too, Amelia Louise. Maybe he can read you a story. Let's pick one."

Smithson and Stella rummaged through the bag that Evanchuk had brought from the apartment and pulled out three books. Stella picked one and held it up. It was called Sparky and had the picture of a sloth sleeping in a tree on the cover.

"This one?" asked Smithson.

Stella nodded yes. He handed the book to Windflower.

"She doesn't talk much. But she likes to have stories read to her and to play cards. There's a deck of Go Fish cards in the bag."

"Thanks," said Windflower as he heard Paul Spurrell being loudly led up the hallway to go to the clinic. He tried to stop at Windflower's office, and when he saw Stella again, he went crazy. The little girl almost jumped into Windflower's arms, and he held her tightly. Evanchuk went first to get the route clear, and Smithson followed soon after.

Now it was only Stella and Windflower, and realizing the danger had passed, she slid out of Windflower's arms and sat on the floor staring up at him. There was nothing for Windflower to do but read the story. To his great surprise he liked it. Sparky was about a girl trying to get her pet sloth to do something, anything. But Sparky was a sloth, and in the end the girl had to accept Sparky as the lazy sloth he really was and stop trying to make him into something else. Stella loved the story, and Windflower suspected she'd read it, or had it read to her, dozens of times before.

When the story was done, she smiled at Windflower. That was a great reward for very little effort. "I think we're going to be friends," he said. "Would you like that?"

Stella smiled again and nodded her head at Windflower. "Do you want to play cards?" he asked.

Another smile and a nod, yes. This is fun, thought Windflower.

Not having as much fun was Eddie Tizzard in his hotel room in Las Vegas. After having received a quick briefing from Rutherford, he had told her he needed time to think. Sure, he wanted to help. He'd do anything to catch bad guys. But he also had responsibilities back home. Pacing from one end of his hotel room to another, he thought about his dad and how he was aging and needed to have someone to help him from time to time. And he thought about Carrie and how he wanted to have a long, happy life with her. Finally, he punched in the numbers for Rutherford's cell phone.

"I want to go home," he said.

"I know, I know," said Rutherford. "But we really need your help. Will you hear me out one more time, and then you can say yes or no?"

Tizzard was beginning to regret he had bothered to stick around. But curiosity was getting the better of him. "I'm pretty sure I'm gonna say no, but go ahead," he said.

Rutherford ran through the reasons why she wanted him to help, starting with the stats on murders in Las Vegas, then describing how much damage the Aryan Warriors were doing and ending with how the police had never been able to infiltrate their core group.

"There must be other young white guys you can get," said Tizzard.

"None with the police training and cool-under-fire that you have," said Rutherford.

"I'll take that as a compliment, although I still want to run away as fast as I can."

"Let me get right to it then. We want you to do a coke buy with them. We have a contact number for you to call. But we only want to do it if you get one of the main guys to be part of it. We've got lots of lower-level gang members, but none of them will talk. They seem to like being in jail."

"Anybody particular in mind?" asked Tizzard a little sourly.

"Robert Wilson, also known as Tiny. He's one of the founders of the Las Vegas chapter and is one of the meanest sadistic creeps we've ever come across. I won't even tell you some of the stuff he's done and what he's got gang members to do over the years. He's running the show."

"Tell me again why I should do it. I understand your problem. It's just that I don't know why I should risk my life again for you guys."

"Fair enough," said the detective. "The reason you work for this job is because you're from Newfoundland, from Canada, same as Martin Spurrell. He was their meth connection, and they don't know he's dead yet. You can say you know him, and that, along with your complexion, might be enough to get you in. It's a long shot and they may not go for it. But it may be the only chance we have to put a real dent into a group of people who are not just spreading dangerous drugs but hate and bigotry and racism."

Rutherford paused. Tizzard was hardly breathing at the other end of the line. "They are tearing our city apart," said Rutherford. "This is a racially mixed community, despite what you see on the strip. Latinos are the fastest growing group, and whites are starting to become a minority. Those white supremacists want to ignite a race war. We really need your help."

"Okay. If I'm going to do this, and I'm really not sure I am, my partner, fiancée, has to sign off. Don't worry, she's a cop, too. But I don't think I can commit until I talk to her. And if she says no, it's a hard no."

"Perfect. I'll wait for your call."

Tizzard hung up the phone and sat on the bed. The food he'd eaten earlier sat in his stomach like a lump. But that wasn't indigestion, he thought. It was fear. Pushing through that emotion he picked up the phone and called Evanchuk.

Evanchuk was at the Grand Bank Clinic when she felt her phone buzzing in her pocket. She waved to Smithson to tell him she'd be waiting outside. She walked out into the emergency parking area and opened her phone.

"Hey, what's up?" she said. "When are you coming home?"

"Soon," said Tizzard. "But something else has come up."

After listening to Tizzard describe what he'd been asked to do, Evanchuk was very quiet. "It sounds dangerous, but I'm not going to say yes or no," she said. "I couldn't forgive myself if I said yes and something happened to you. And I don't want to stop you from doing what's right. I think you should talk to Sergeant Windflower."

"I had a feeling you might say that," said Tizzard. "In fact, I thought about calling him first. Let me call him, and I'll call you back."

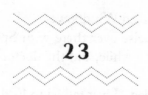

23

Tizzard called Windflower as he was losing his second game of Go Fish to Stella Fitzgerald.

"Eddie, how's it going?" asked Windflower. He gave Stella her crayons and colouring book while he talked to Tizzard.

"I'm okay," said Tizzard. "But I have a bit of a problem." He walked through what had happened since he got to Las Vegas, including his experience in jail and then with Willy Spurrell.

"Willy Spurrell?" asked Windflower.

"The other brother," said Tizzard.

"There's another one?"

"Yeah, and this one is really bad news, a big player in the crystal meth business."

"It sounds crazy out there; you better come home."

"That's my dilemma," said Tizzard, and then he told him about Rutherford and what he was being asked to do.

"Sounds dangerous."

"That's what Carrie said. My head tells me to run away as fast as I can, but somehow my heart is resisting. I feel torn between what is right and what is right for my family and me, assuming I live long enough to have one."

"I think you've done your part," said Windflower. "I know you want to do more, but I think you should walk away. It's too risky. Just my opinion of course, but I do think about Sheila and Amelia Louise now before I make a big decision. And this is a big decision."

"Okay, thanks," said Tizzard. "That's about as direct a 'no' as I could ask for. I think you're right. I should be back home soon."

"Good luck, Eddie. See you soon."

Windflower hung up the phone, and Stella was already rummaging through her bag for another game when Quigley came into the office.

"Back so soon?" asked Windflower.

"I left everybody else over there with Spurrell," said Quigley. "He asked to stay for a while, and the doctor said it may not be a long wait."

Windflower nodded. "I just talked to Eddie Tizzard."

"Is he on his way home yet?" asked Quigley.

"He will be soon. He's been having quite the adventure with the FBI and the LVPD. Did you know that there's another Spurrell? Willy?"

"I did not," said Quigley. "But you know what, there's a lot I don't know about this situation, and I'm beginning to feel a little used. I'm going to see if I can't get full access to all the files on this, including the ones from the FBI."

"Can you do that?"

"I'm going to try. Looks like you've got your hands full here," Quigley said as Stella offered Windflower another book.

While the inspector went to search the database for more information on the Spurrell brothers, Windflower read Stella another story. It was a Berenstain Bears book called The Trouble with Friends. It was a book that helped kids figure out how to solve problems together. Windflower thought that it would be great for many of the adults he knew, too. Lots of people could use help getting along with others and learning to negotiate instead of argue.

After he finished the story, Windflower could hear his tummy grumble, and he asked Stella if she was hungry too. She nodded yes.

"Would you like to come to my house for pizza?" he asked.

That produced another vigorous nod of the head from Stella.

Windflower called the pizza shop and ordered two large pizzas: one meat-lovers and one vegetarian. That should please everybody, he thought. Quigley came back to Windflower's office, and he was quite happy with the selections and to help with pizza delivery.

Quigley took the pizza boxes. Windflower managed to hold Stella's hand and his crutches at the same time and still make it up the driveway at his house. Everyone was glad to see him, the pizza and Quigley. Stella stood very quietly in the doorway and allowed Amelia Louise to inspect her and Lady to sniff her.

"It's okay," said Windflower as he took Stella by the hand and introduced her to everybody.

It didn't take long for Stella to respond to Lady, and soon they were running around the living room with Amelia Louise in hot pursuit. Sheila dished up the pizza and organized the salad while Windflower filled her in on Stella and her mother.

Sheila gathered up Amelia Louise and put her in her high chair with a small piece of pizza and some carrots and cucumber, and then she led Stella to her own chair at the table. The men had already started eating and were almost on their second piece by the time Sheila sat down.

"Have you heard anything from Eddie?" asked Sheila.

Windflower put down his pizza long enough to bring Sheila up to date.

"I hope he doesn't do it," said Sheila. "He and Carrie have their whole lives ahead of them."

Quigley and Windflower wisely went back to their pizza instead of engaging further in a discussion that would inevitably lead to how dangerous police work was and how worried the spouses were about their partners on the Force.

Quigley was helping Sheila clean up when they heard a car outside and a knock on their door. It was Smithson.

"We just brought Paul Spurrell back to his cell. Marla Fitz-gerald passed a little while ago," said Smithson.

All three of the adults in the house instinctively looked at Stella. But she was fully engaged with Lady and Amelia Louise and openly laughing for the first time that day. Even Molly had joined in, as only a cat could do, by observing their antics from a safe distance.

"What happens to her now?" asked Sheila to no one in particular.

Windflower started to speak, but Smithson spoke up first. "There's a social worker on the way," he said. "We suggested that she come here instead of going back to the detachment. I hope that's okay."

"That's fine," said Windflower. "Why don't you go home? You've had a long day."

"Good night," said Smithson. He waved goodbye to Sheila and left.

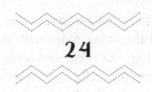

24

Windflower sat silently on the couch and watched the little girls and his dog play while Quigley and Sheila finished putting everything away. Sheila brought a pot of tea and a plate of cookies out and put them on the table. Amelia Louise grabbed one and Stella was right behind her with Lady trying to get a bite out of both of their cookies.

Both girls squealed, and the three adults laughed despite the seriousness of the situation. They sipped their tea quietly for a few minutes, enjoying the scene, until there was another knock on the door.

Sheila answered and led the social worker into the living room. Almost immediately, everything grew deathly still. Even Lady stopped her earnest efforts at getting more dessert as everyone waited for what would come next. Windflower instinctively went to Stella and picked her up with Sheila doing the same for Amelia Louise.

"Hi, Stella," said the social worker. "My name is Anne Dyson, and I've come to take you to a nice safe place for the evening."

Stella Fitzgerald put her arms around Windflower's neck and buried her head in his shoulders. She squeezed so hard it almost hurt, but Windflower didn't mind. He knew this was not going to be easy. He was right.

When the social worker tried to take Stella from his arms, she started to scream. She managed to wiggle her way out of his grasp and slide to the floor where she began to scream even louder. She didn't stop all the way out the door, and Windflower thought he could still hear her as the car pulled out and was driven away.

He looked at Sheila, and all the blood seemed to be drained

from her face. Ron Quigley didn't look much better. "I think I better go," he said. "We'll talk in the morning. Thanks for dinner, Sheila."

Amelia Louise had sensed that something bad was happening, and she was now sobbing in her mother's arms. Sheila soothed her and rubbed her back. Lady retreated to her bed in the kitchen.

Windflower felt a wave of emotions wash over him, from sadness to anger to worry about the little girl who just lost the only real connection she had to the world. He had no words and neither did Sheila. They went through the motions and did everything they had to do to look after Amelia Louise and get her to bed, and then both of them lay on their bed in the dark without saying a word.

When Windflower heard Sheila softly crying, he put his arm around her and together they lay there until they both fell asleep. She woke first and started to stir.

"What will happen to her now?" she asked, knowing the basic answer but hoping for some other, more positive outcome.

"She'll go into care," said Windflower. "She's already been there before, on a temporary basis. Now they'll try and find something more permanent. But it's hard for a four-year old to get adopted. People want newborns and babies."

"But she's so small and vulnerable," said Sheila, holding back a sob before finally releasing it.

"I'll make you a bath," said Windflower. He went into their bathroom and ran a hot bath. As he did so, he thought about telling Sheila about his dream that afternoon and that Auntie Marie had visited him to say goodbye. Not yet, he decided. He didn't know when would be the right time, but he knew it wasn't at that moment.

He found Sheila's favourite bubble bath and poured in a capful. He made sure it wasn't too hot, and when the tub was halfway full, he called her.

She slid into the bath and sighed. "This is so nice," she said.

"Enjoy," said Windflower. "I'll turn everything off downstairs."

He walked slowly downstairs where Lady lay subdued. She knew something wasn't right. Molly kept vigil on top of the couch in the living room window, and Windflower wondered if she was waiting for Stella to come back.

"That's it for tonight," said Windflower, and he turned off the lights and went back upstairs. He looked into Amelia Louise's room as he passed and could see her lying on her side holding her pink pet rabbit by one ear. He went closer and gave her a kiss on the cheek and watched her briefly from the doorway.

Windflower quietly undressed and got into bed. Sheila came in a little later, and without saying another word they held each other until they drifted off.

It didn't take long for Windflower to enter his dreamland again. He arrived inside the familiar clearing of his previous dreams. This time he walked by himself through the forest path and came again to the river. The beaver was sitting by himself in the sunshine by the side of the river. Windflower looked across and saw that there was a great celebration with many animals gathered around a woman wearing a beautiful coloured shawl.

"Is that Auntie Marie?" he asked the beaver.

"It is," said the beaver. "It is the beginning of her welcoming feast to the other side. Soon she will be moving there."

Windflower tried to go into the water to swim across, but the current was too strong. He was pushed back onto the shore.

"You can't go there," said the beaver. "It is not your time. Those are all of your aunt's spirit animals who are getting her ready to join the spirit world."

"Can I talk to her?" asked Windflower.

"Not now, but soon," said the beaver. "You can ask me questions, and I can take them to her though. I am able to move between the worlds underneath the water."

"Can you ask her a question? Should I leave the RCMP?" asked Windflower.

The beaver paused and rubbed the fur on his tail. "She says that you should use all of your allies to help you make a decision. Use your eagle eyes to see the opportunities that are presented and think about all the people in your life and not yourself."

Windflower had many more questions he wanted to ask Auntie Marie, and he called out to her.

But there was no answer. He woke from his dream drenched in sweat and reached for his cell phone. But still there were no messages.

"What's wrong, Winston?" Sheila asked.

"Auntie Marie is passing," he said.

"How do you know? Did you get a message?"

"Kind of. You go back to sleep. I'll get up with Amelia Louise when she wakes up."

Sheila cuddled into her husband, and he held her while he thought about his aunt. She had been such a great person in his life that it was hard to imagine her not being there when he called. She was one of his last connections to his birth family and often told him stories about when he was growing up that he had long forgotten. But she had also taught him a very important lesson about learning to miss people well.

That was a great gift he had received from someone who actively practiced that in her life. Auntie Marie always talked of people who had passed as still being with them and reminding them of their good qualities and the good things that arose in life. Richard Wagamese, Windflower's meditation guru, had the same message. Miss people well by seeing them or their image or memories of them in a beautiful sunrise or a startling sunset. Miss them really well. He would miss his aunt dearly, but he would also try his best to remember her and to miss her well.

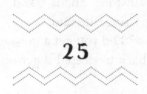

25

He was thinking about his Auntie Marie and trying to miss her well when he heard Amelia Louise stir and start to softly sing in the other room. Windflower had a very pleasant time with his daughter and even managed to make them both a bowl of fruit and let the dog out before Sheila came downstairs. She made some oatmeal for Windflower and herself and boiled an egg for Amelia Louise.

He had got himself cleaned and dressed and was sipping his second cup of coffee when an RCMP cruiser came into their driveway. "That's my ride," he said. He kissed his family and gave each of his pets a rub before grabbing his crutches and slowly ambling down the driveway. He had expected to see Smithson, but Evanchuk was at the wheel.

He was grateful that she didn't try to help or pamper him but let him struggle and stumble his way into the vehicle. "Good morning," he said.

"Morning," said Evanchuk. "We going to the detachment, sir?"

"Yes, please," said Windflower. "Did you talk to Eddie again last night?"

"I did. Thank you for convincing him not to do it. I wanted to but didn't think it was my place."

"We helped him make the right decision. But you do have the right to speak up if you feel he is in danger. We all need someone in our lives to do that for us."

"Yes, sir," said Evanchuk. "It's awful about Marla Fitzgerald and her daughter," she added.

"I know. One life cut too short and the other, I just don't know. It's all very sad."

They drove in silence the rest of the way to the detachment. Ron Quigley's SUV was again parked out front.

"Morning, Betsy," said Windflower.

"I've got a draft statement on the woman's death on your desk," said Betsy. "And a wonderful grand morning to you, too, Sergeant."

"Thank you, Betsy," said Windflower. "I'll take a look at it."

"Good morning, Sergeant," said Ron Quigley when Windflower turned the corner into his office. "Must be nice to be on banker's hours now that you've got an excuse."

"Very funny, Inspector," said Windflower. "So, what did your early-bird searching come up with?"

"Three brothers, all connected in various ways to gangs, bikers and even the Mob."

"Wow, they really did have adventures in the United States."

"Not just there, in Canada, too. Even here on the island," said Quigley, holding up sheets of printed paper. "Willy Spurrell was the kingpin, but Martin and Paul were no slouches either. The FBI has been tracking them for years, and HQ was advised over twenty months ago."

"They've been sitting on this for almost two years?"

"Not really sitting on it. They've been picking apart pieces of the network in Ontario for years. Just last month they managed to get inside the Hells Angels and broke up a major route. When I called back in about it, they said they were trying to get Paul Spurrell to come on board."

"As an informer?" asked Windflower. "Against his brothers? That's not very likely."

"The guy I spoke to said they thought Paul was trying to keep his brothers alive and saw this as the only way to do it. Maybe that's why Martin Spurrell had your number in his pocket when he died."

"What? He had my number?" asked Windflower.

"Martin Spurrell had your name and number and Eddie Tizzard's as well. That's why the Las Vegas police were initially holding him. They thought he was connected, too," said Quigley.

Windflower was still processing this information when Jones came by and stood in the doorway. "Come in," he said.

"I've got the printout on Marla Fitzgerald," said Jones. "Two bits in Ontario, both for being a mule, coming back from the States with crystal meth. Got her medical files, too. Rehab in St. John's last year. Reference to previous stints in treatment centres going back ten years."

"You can't do drugs like meth for very long without serious health effects. Stroke, overdose, brain damage are common," said Quigley.

"I saw somewhere that the life expectancy of a meth user was under forty," said Jones.

"She didn't even make that," said Windflower. "And she may not have been the best mother, but she was the only one her little daughter had. And now she's gone."

"The only good news I have is that we are able to talk to Paul Spurrell now," said Quigley. They gave me the green light to see if he wants to play ball while they work on Willy in Las Vegas."

"You might as well do it here," said Windflower. "I'd like to sit in if you don't mind."

"Fine by me," said Quigley.

"Let me get Betsy to set it up," said Windflower.

Soon afterward, Betsy had the large interview room prepared with microphones and recorder, all ready for the interrogation of Paul Spurrell. She gave Windflower a press release on the sudden death of Marla Fitzgerald to review. It was short and to the point, perfect. He initialled it and handed it back.

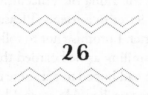

26

Eddie Tizzard was getting ready to head to the airport for his early morning flight. Right after he spoke to Detective Sergeant Rutherford, he booked his trip back to Newfoundland—three hours to Chicago, an hour plus to Toronto and then home via Halifax and St. John's. He tossed and turned all night, afraid that the forced insomnia he had experienced while in Las Vegas might cause him to sleep through the alarm he had set on his cell phone. But he was up even before the alarm sounded. If all his connections were on time, he'd be on his beloved island by midnight, stay overnight in St. John's and then drive back to Grand Bank the next morning. And then he reminded himself he was flying back to Newfoundland. When were connections to Newfoundland ever on time, given how the fog seemed to have a mind of its own?

Rutherford had been understanding, but upset, when he spoke to her about his decision. He could definitely get her frustration, but he wasn't prepared to take a chance. Another chance actually, he thought. He'd been shot by a crazed coke user a few years back and had nearly died. That was one of the reasons he'd got out of the Force. Well, that and the fact that he'd jumped Acting Inspector Raymond.

As he reviewed his decision, he felt more comfortable with it, especially when he thought about how dangerous the situation had been with Willy Spurrell. Now, that was crazy. He also thought his dad would have been proud of him for taking Windflower's advice and coming home instead of taking on another dangerous job in Las Vegas. His dad always said that there was no point asking for help or advice unless you were prepared to take it.

On the other hand, he knew his dad could also offer some oddball advice. Once he'd asked his dad for some advice, even though he'd already made up his mind about what he was going to do. His dad gave him the Edna St. Vincent Millay quote that she apparently wrote in a letter to a friend. 'Please give me some good advice in your next letter. I promise not to follow it.'

Tizzard was still smiling as he boarded the plane and took his seat near the back. He had hoped to get some room to himself back there, but the flight was packed. He stowed his bag and put in his earplugs thinking that at least he could get some sleep on the plane. But that was not to be. He had just settled away in his middle seat when the aisle passenger sat down next to him. The old Chinese lady had a sign around her neck that read: "I do not speak English. I only speak Mandarin." Then she proceeded to talk to Tizzard non-stop for almost the next three hours.

Someone who wasn't as communicative was Paul Spurrell.

"Why should I talk to youse guys?" he asked the Mounties in Grand Bank. "I can get a deal with the big boys."

"Not anymore," said Quigley. "Now you've got to deal with us."

"I don't think so," said Spurrell. "I got info."

"Maybe. But now they're focused on your other brother."

"Martin don't know nothing."

"I regret to inform you that your brother died in Las Vegas," said Quigley.

Paul Spurrell looked stunned. He was not expecting that news. Windflower watched as he processed that information.

"That's not true," said Spurrell. "I wants my lawyer. You're just trying to trick me."

"Sorry, but that is the case," said Quigley. "And the reason those big boys don't need you anymore is that they've got your other brother, Willy."

Spurrell sat back in his chair with his hands behind his head. "I still got nothing."

"Okay, I'm going to send you back to Marystown and then on to St. John's. You won't get much for the breach, maybe another six months in Renous."

"I can't go back there. I'm a dead man," said Spurrell.

"I think we're done here," said Quigley. "Sergeant, would you arrange transport for our friend back to Marystown?"

Windflower stood to leave.

"Wait, wait," said Spurrell. "I'll talk. But I can't go back to that jail. Can you guarantee that?"

"I can make the breach go away. But depending on what else you tell me, I can talk to the powers that be," said Quigley. "But let's have a conversation and see where it goes, shall we?"

"Okay," said Spurrell. "I gave Martin your name," he said, pointing at Windflower, "and Tizzard's. I thought I had a deal cooked here, and he wanted out, too. I told him to contact Tizzard and see if he could swing a deal as well."

"Tizzard found him, but he was already dead," said Quigley.

"Willy tried to protect him, but he didn't have the juice. Those guys out there are mean. They don't screw around."

"Which guys?" asked Quigley.

"The Aryan Warriors," said Spurrell. "I only met up with them a couple of times. White skinheads. They said they were fighting a race war with the blacks and Mexicans. I didn't want no part of that stuff. But Willy saw a way to make money and be protected."

"What were they running?" asked Quigley.

"Coke, weed to start with, and then they switched to meth. Said they could make more money with less expense and overhead. Real businessmen. Willy was the perfect in-between because he already had connections and knew a chemist."

"So he went into business with these guys, the Aryan Warriors?"

"Yeah. Pretty soon they were running the whole show on meth in Vegas, Reno and starting to move into California. Then they decided to go international."

"That's how you got involved?"

"I just made some introductions," said Spurrell. "Some biker friends. They took it from there."

"What about local connections?" asked Quigley.

"Some of my best friends in Newfoundland are bikers," said Spurrell.

"Can you give us some more details about who's running the show down here?"

"Anything's possible if there's a get-out-of-jail card in my future," said Spurrell.

"Let me make some calls," said Quigley.

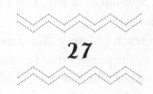

27

Quigley and Windflower left Spurrell in the interview room and walked outside. Betsy interrupted them on the way to Windflower's office.

"There's a call for you," she said. "It's your Uncle Frank. I thought you'd want to take it."

"Thanks, Betsy," said Windflower.

"You take your call," said Quigley. "I've got some of my own to make."

Windflower nodded and followed Betsy down the hall. She closed his office door behind him.

"Uncle Frank, how are you?" asked Windflower.

"I am well," said his uncle. "But it's your Auntie."

"I had dreams," said Windflower.

"She is resting comfortably, but the doctors say it is only a matter of time," said Uncle Frank. "Even though she is nearing the other side, she seems very peaceful."

"That is a blessing. Should I try and come out?"

"No, Nephew, you have already said your goodbyes. She will not likely wake up from this dream."

"I will miss her."

"We all will. But she has lived a long and full life and is ready to live on the other side. She said she would wait for me there."

"Thanks for calling. Give her a kiss for me."

Windflower sat in his office with the door closed and allowed himself to feel the growing sadness inside of him. It welled up into tears, and he allowed them to flow freely. Once they had subsided a little, he called Sheila.

"Oh, Winston, I am so sorry. She is such a beautiful soul," said

Sheila. "Are you going out there? I can go with you."

"No, I think it would be better to wait," said Windflower. "But I would like to go afterward for the ceremony, and I think we should all go."

"Okay," said Sheila. "I love you."

"I love you, too," said Windflower.

He thought for a few more minutes about his Auntie Marie until he heard a knock on his door.

"You okay?" asked Quigley.

"I will be," said Windflower. "My Auntie is really sick."

"Oh, that's too bad," said Quigley.

"Yeah, she's likely going to pass soon. But she's not in pain, and she has my uncle with her."

Windflower thanked the inspector and his friend for his concern. He then asked if he had any more news about the Spurrell case.

"Yeah, I've got a green light," said Quigley. "As long as Paul Spurrell hasn't killed anybody, I think we can get him a deal."

"Excellent," said Windflower. "Be good to clean up some scum from around here."

"I'm still going to have him brought back to Marystown. I think Ford can handle it, though. I'll keep you posted on developments."

"Perfect," said Windflower.

Bill Ford stopped by to bring Windflower a coffee and have a chat while he was waiting for transport back to Marystown.

"I'm going to apply for the job," he told Windflower.

"I think you'll be great."

"Thanks, Winston. Are you sure you don't want it? Because I would gladly step aside if you were interested. I'd be glad to serve under you."

"Thanks, Bill, but it's not for me. I'm not quite sure what my next move is, but it's not likely going to be Marystown. Sheila's talking about moving to St. John's."

"St. John's is nice, although it's a bit big for me. I thought Corner Brook was too big," Ford said with a laugh.

"Well, we'll see what the future has in store for us," said Windflower. "'It's not in the stars to hold our destiny, but in ourselves.'"

"True enough," said Ford. "Although our job has something
to do with that from time to time. Anyway, here's my ride." He
pointed to the RCMP van pulling up in the parking lot.

Windflower watched as Ford loaded Paul Spurrell into the van
and got in front with the driver. After he left, Windflower's office
grew very quiet, as if the universe knew he needed a little peace
and quiet. Windflower took advantage of it to clear up the backlog
of paperwork that had overfilled his basket. He was making great
progress when Ron Quigley came back in.

"Time for lunch," he announced.

"I guess it is," said Windflower, and he followed Quigley into
his SUV for the short trip to the Mug-Up.

The café was warm and bustling, and Quigley and Windflower
sat at an uncleared table while they waited for service. Marie came
along soon afterward and took their orders. Windflower ordered
the cod au gratin, and Quigley decided on the turkey soup. But they
only managed a couple of bites from their meals before Quigley's
phone rang.

"Where did it happen? Is everyone okay?" Quigley asked,
listening intently and then hanging up. Lunch was over.

"Something's happened on the highway. Paul Spurrell's gone.
Let's go," he told Windflower.

As fast as he could, Windflower scrambled behind Quigley and
into his vehicle. As they were pulling out of the parking lot at the
café, they heard the sirens and saw two RCMP cruisers heading
towards the highway in front of them. Quigley turned on his lights
and siren and raced behind them.

"I didn't want to say anything inside, but Bill Ford's been shot,"
said Quigley.

"What?" asked Windflower. "What happened?"

"I don't know yet. Sounds like some kind of ambush. That was
the van driver on the phone. He said they stopped to help a driver
on the side of the road, and three guys jumped them. They got Ford
to open the back. Ford tried to stop them, and then they shot him.
That's all I got so far."

Quigley's radio crackled all the way out. Quigley barked
orders to the command centre about roadblocks and bulletins and

notifications to other jurisdictions. It sounded like every police officer in the area was involved, and that was exactly the way he wanted it.

The first thing they saw when they came over the hill was a wall of blue flashing lights and the two ambulances. One was from Grand Bank and the other from Marystown. Quigley jumped out of his vehicle and ran towards the RCMP van. Bill Ford was lying on the ground by the side of the van, and he was not moving. Windflower followed behind as fast as he could on his crutches, and when he arrived, he could see that Ford was in trouble, big trouble. He was barely conscious, barely alive. The first responders had placed a compress on the wound in his chest area. The bullet must have missed his heart or aorta or he'd be dead, thought Windflower, although he kept that conjecture to himself.

The paramedics gently raised Ford and put him on a stretcher. Then, two of them carefully brought him to the ambulance and put him in. One of them looked at Quigley. "Burin?" he asked.

"What do you think?" he asked back.

"He's bled a lot. But we've got that stemmed. He's in and out of it. We won't know until they see him in emerg," said the paramedic.

Quigley nodded, and the paramedics finished loading and roared off with an RCMP cruiser leading their way. His next stop was to see the driver of the van. He was sitting in the back of an RCMP vehicle with a blanket wrapped around him.

"Mitchell's already given us a statement," said a young Mountie who was standing outside the car. "A woman was standing beside the road with the hood up and waved them down. Ford got out and went over to her. As soon as he did, a guy jumped out of the bushes and pointed a gun at the driver. Then three guys jumped out from behind the car and grabbed Ford. There was another guy with a vehicle up the side road right there, a blue Honda CR-V, and he drove down. They forced Ford to open the back and grabbed the prisoner. They started loading everybody into the vehicle to take off, and Ford tried to stop them. That's when he got shot. Mitchell took off into the woods and kept running. He crept back when he thought it might be safe and called it in."

"Okay," said Quigley. He opened the door to the vehicle and

leaned in. "How are you?" he asked.

"I'm fine," said Mitchell. "How's Bill?"

"He's gone to the hospital in Burin," said Quigley. "Did you recognize any of the people involved? The woman look familiar?"

"No," said the young officer. "I didn't even get the plate number." He looked like he was going to cry. "The girl was pretty young, eighteen or nineteen. The guys were big, and they had bandanas over their faces. The only thing I really noticed was one guy had a tattoo on his neck."

"It's okay," said Quigley. "Try and relax. You might remember more. Someone will drive you back to Marystown and debrief you again later."

Windflower followed Quigley with his eyes as the inspector went over the scene carefully. Windflower had done that sort of thing many times before. Sometimes it helped to look from afar while the rest of the team did a meticulous review close up. But, this time, nothing stood out.

"I'm going to the hospital and then back to Marystown," said Quigley. "My crew will clean up and collect all the evidence. You can get a ride back?"

"I'm good," said Windflower, although no one on the scene was truly good. The shooting of a police officer was almost the worst thing that could happen—almost, because no one could contemplate the worst. It brought back every fear to every officer and every family member waiting at home.

He called Sheila on the way back to Grand Bank with Jones.

"I heard there was a shooting," were Sheila's first words.

"It's Bill Ford," said Windflower, "although that information isn't public yet."

He could almost feel Sheila's anxiety through the phone. "Is he going to be okay?" she asked.

"He's gone to the hospital."

Windflower paused and thought about what and how much he wanted to share with Sheila and if it would help or hurt the situation. He decided to simply tell the truth.

"He was hit in the chest area, but it looks like it might have missed his heart," he said.

"Or else he'd be dead," said Sheila, finishing the sentence. "Okay, call me later."

"I love you, Sheila," said Windflower, but the line had already gone dead.

There were no words between Windflower and Jones for the rest of their journey. When they arrived, Evanchuk pulled in beside them. Smithson met them inside the detachment. Betsy was on the phone but laid down her receiver when Windflower and the other officers came in.

"Everybody, listen up," said Windflower. "I want you to put the word out that we're looking for a woman and three big guys. One with a neck tattoo. Go to all your informants. Everyone you know. Shake them down. Somebody around here knows something. They must have been watching this place and waited for their chance to grab Spurrell. Go."

The three officers scattered and left Windflower standing alone with Betsy. "See what you can find out," he said. Betsy looked terribly concerned but pleased that she was being asked to help in the investigation. "Yes, sir," she said.

It wasn't much of a reach for Windflower to recruit Betsy. She probably had the best informal network in town. Between all of them they just might have a chance at finding out where Paul Spurrell was and who had tried to kill Bill Ford.

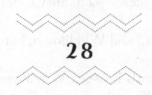

28

Windflower reviewed all the information that had been circulated so far and sat at his desk to wait for news. He didn't have to wait long. Jones was the first one back in.

"My guy says that everybody knew Spurrell was here in Grand Bank," said Jones.

"How'd they know that?"

"They got it from the Marystown jail. That place is like a sieve. My guy also says that it's probably bikers. They're running the dope and girls on the island, but it's not the locals. They've sent in some heavies from the mainland to oversee the operations."

"That makes sense," said Windflower. "Keep digging."

Jones left, and Windflower's phone rang. It was Evanchuk.

"We've found the vehicle," she said. "It was parked on the side of the road near the Fortune Head turnoff." That's about 10 minutes away, thought Windflower.

"Have you called Quigley?" he asked.

"Yes. But I thought you'd want to know. There's a dead man in the car. Paul Spurrell," said Evanchuk.

By the time Jones and Windflower got to that scene, Evanchuk, Smithson and an ambulance were waiting. Soon after they arrived, Windflower saw Doctor Sanjay get out of his car and walk towards the CR-V. He noticed Windflower and waved hello. Windflower waved back and followed him to the vehicle.

"He's dead b'y," said one of the paramedics.

"Yes b'y, looks like it," said Sanjay as he leaned into the back seat of the vehicle. "Shot multiple times at close range, judging by the damage done in his chest area and the splattering of blood. You know him?" he asked Windflower.

"Paul Spurrell," said Windflower. "He was originally in custody."

"How's Bill Ford doing?" asked Sanjay. "Bad news travels fast around here."

"I don't know," said Windflower. "He was in bad shape when I saw him."

"If you're okay, we can take the body out now," said Sanjay. Windflower nodded, and the doctor pointed to the paramedics as Windflower's cell phone rang.

"Spurrell?" asked Quigley.

"Yeah, they're just loading him up. Shot in the chest multiple times," said Windflower. "We can look after the scene here. Any word on Bill?"

"Nothing yet."

"We think it's bikers. That's what our people on the street say."

"Yeah, same here," said Quigley. "We've started picking them up. I've also set up a roadblock past Swift Current. Nobody gets off this peninsula without being checked."

"I have a feeling they might still be around here," said Windflower.

"If they are, let's find them. Fast."

Windflower hung up and noticed Doctor Sanjay getting ready to leave.

"Hey Doc, can I get a ride back with you? I need to leave all the rest of my gang here to clean up."

"Absolutely," said Sanjay. "It would be an honour and a privilege."

"Give me a sec." Windflower spoke quickly to Jones, giving her directions about managing the on-site investigation. They would do all the preliminary work including getting photos and fingerprints. If need be, they could get the forensics people in to do a more thorough search. Jones was gathering Smithson and Evanchuk as Windflower and Sanjay left to go back to the detachment.

Sanjay was surprisingly quiet on the drive. Just before they got to the detachment, Sanjay asked Windflower if he was okay.

"I'm fine," said Windflower, almost automatically. Then he paused as Sanjay remained silent. "Not really. There's a lot going on, and I'm really lost."

Windflower then spent the next 10 minutes talking about his life while Sanjay nodded and listened. He talked about Bill Ford and how what had happened to him brought back memories of

Tizzard almost dying, how Sheila had reacted to the news about Ford and how he didn't know if he could continue as a Mountie.

"I understand," said Sanjay when Windflower finally grew quiet. "Not the police officer stuff. I have no idea how you get up and go to work every day not knowing if you will be attacked or shot. But when it comes to the daily challenge of trying to be a good person in a sometimes very bad world, there are times when we simply must answer the questions that trouble us. Tagore says that every difficulty slurred over will be a ghost that disturbs our sleep later."

"Good advice, and thank you for the company," said Windflower as they arrived at his office.

"Repa and I and that beautiful bottle of Scotch are waiting for your visit. Tomorrow, we hope."

"I'd like to, but things are really crazy. I'll talk to Sheila. My dear Auntie is very sick and will pass soon."

"I am so sorry," said Sanjay. "'Death is not extinguishing the light; it is only putting out the lamp because the dawn has come.'"

Windflower waved goodbye and went into the office. Betsy was waiting for him. "I think I know who the girl is," she said. Of course, she would, thought Windflower. She knew everybody and everything that moved in Grand Bank.

"Patti Lewis," said Betsy. "She's been hanging around those bikers and some other really bad guys. Her mother is worried sick, and she's only barely nineteen."

"Do we know where she is now?" asked Windflower.

"The last time her mother saw her was night before last. She came home to have a shower and change. I have a picture of her."

"Okay, scan it and put it on the wire. Send it directly to Inspector Quigley. Good job, Betsy."

Betsy beamed and walked away to post the picture.

The rest of the afternoon whizzed by with people coming and going and popping in and out of his office. Finally, he had enough. When Smithson came in with one more tidbit of information, Windflower listened and then asked him to drive him home.

Sheila met him at the door and held him tightly for a few minutes. Lady and Amelia Louise fought over his legs, and he nearly tumbled over. Finally, Sheila released her grip, and he slipped to the floor to play with Lady and his daughter.

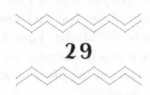

29

Dinner was a simple one that evening: tomato soup, with a spicy shot of cayenne in the adults' bowls, along with a baguette and a tray of cheeses and grapes. Comfort food, thought Windflower as he took a chunk of bread and dipped it in his soup. That was a mistake because Amelia Louise thought this was a great game, and soon there was soup not only all over her but in a wide arc around her chair. Windflower got up to start cleaning, but Sheila was ahead of him. She took away the remaining few drops of soup in Amelia Louise's bowl and gave her some bread and cheese which made the little girl just as happy.

Soon she was feeding herself and Lady and Molly while the two adults got to enjoy the rest of their meal. Levi Parsons came by as they were cleaning up and took Lady out for her big evening stroll. Windflower played with Amelia Louise as Sheila made tea, and while he was sitting on the floor, he found one of Stella Fitzgerald's books. She must have left it behind, he thought. It was the sloth book.

When Amelia Louise saw what he had, she came closer and sat on his lap. She thought it was reading time. So, Windflower read Sparky to her, and then when it was finished, he read it again.

"What are you reading?" asked Sheila.

"Sparky," said Windflower.

"Parky," said Amelia Louise.

"Stella must have left it here," said Windflower as Amelia Louise was pushing the book towards him, hoping for one more reading.

"Winston, I can't get that little girl out of my head," said Sheila. "I know we've got an awful lot going on, but it feels like she is somehow supposed to be part of our lives, more than just coming to us in a crisis."

Windflower hadn't thought about it that way so he took a few seconds to process what Sheila had said while he wrestled with Amelia Louise and the book. "Maybe," he said. "We certainly had a connection. But maybe it was just because we were kind. I bet she hasn't had a lot of kindness in her life. I mean, her mother would have tried, but she was an addict."

"Is there anything we can do?" asked Sheila.

"I don't know. I guess social services will try and place her in a foster home eventually. I could ask around and see what they have planned."

"That would be good. I'd feel better if I knew she was in a safe place, a good home. She deserves to be happy."

Windflower smiled and swung Amelia Louise above his head. "If you get her bath ready, I will dunk her in it," said Windflower.

"Dunk, dunk, dunk," said Amelia Louise.

After bath and story time Amelia Louise was kissed by both parents and tucked safely away in her bed. Windflower called Marystown, but there was no further update on Bill Ford. "Still under observation," he was told. "We'll know tomorrow." He then joined Sheila in the living room and poured himself a cup of tea from the fresh pot that she had made.

"I'm worried all the time now," said Sheila. "It's like cumulative anxiety. Every time I hear about an officer being hurt or shot, I think about you."

"I have to admit that every time there is a serious incident, I worry about you and Amelia Louise," said Windflower. "That sort of thing doesn't happen every day in Grand Bank, but it does sometimes."

"We're not going to fix it tonight. Let's go to bed."

"I've got some good news."

"Please, please, share it."

"I think my ankle is getting better." To prove it Windflower stood and walked around the living room without grimacing in pain. Just as he was about to shout his good news, he stumbled and felt a sharp twinge. "Ow," he said. "Okay, almost better."

"Turn off the lights and come to bed."

Windflower said goodnight to Lady and Molly and made sure

their water bowls were full. Then he followed Sheila's directions and turned off the lights. He crawled into bed.

"Be gentle with me," he said.

"Come closer," was her reply.

When he woke, the rest of the house was quiet. He thought about his Auntie and all the good things he had in his life, and even though it was still early and dark, he left his bed and wandered downstairs to find his medicines and his smudging bowl.

Molly barely blinked at his early morning presence, but Lady was her enthusiastic self. She was quite happy to follow Windflower out into the backyard where he mixed his medicines and sat on the porch to smudge. Lady explored the dark corners of the garden while Windflower allowed the smoke to float all over him. He felt the air grow damp as the fog from the nearby Atlantic Ocean started to creep into Grand Bank, and he sat and thought about his Auntie Marie.

His heart was aching, but he tried to miss her well. He remembered the many walks through the forest in Pink Lake and their talks around the fire. She had told him about his ancestors and how to spot his allies and receive them into his life as partners on the journey. She had taught him about the many moons that ruled their skies at nighttime throughout the year and how to appreciate the dream world and the messages it gave everyone to help them live their lives fully.

He laid down a little tobacco for his Auntie Marie and said a quiet prayer of thanks for the gifts she had given him and the world. Despite all of the things that were happening around him, Windflower was grateful. He was even grateful for his bum ankle and broken arm because they had forced him to slow down and take a good look around him. They also reminded him to not just be more careful, but to recognize that he needed to stay connected and close to the people he cared about at home and work, and to learn from his mistakes, too. One of the Grandfather teachings of his people was wisdom and that we learn from our mistakes and misfortunes.

Windflower thought about his family, about how much joy Sheila and Amelia Louise had brought into his life and how much they gave him every day. Being limited in his ability to help out made him realize how much more he could do, if he weren't selfish or lazy. Even Lady and Molly offered him much more than he could ever give back—unconditional love from Lady and as much care and concern that a cat could give to a helpless human from Molly.

As he petted Lady and thought about his Auntie Marie, a wave of sadness rose in his chest and moved to his throat. The fog moved in, and he could feel her close to him. Windflower let himself drift into the thick fog and be embraced by it. He thanked Auntie Marie for the gifts she'd given him. He also prayed for Uncle Frank. Her passing would not be easy on him.

After he finished, he stood and watched the fog start to lift. By the time he got inside the house, he could see the whole yard again and out past the driveway. He took that as a sign from his Auntie Marie that her path to the other side had been cleared. He felt her spirit rise with the fog. He knew in his heart that she would soon be gone.

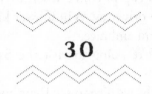

30

As soon as he got into the house, he heard Amelia Louise on the monitor and went to her. He picked her up, and together they looked out the window. The fog was completely gone now, and the sun was shining brilliantly in the east.

"It's a beautiful morning," he said.

"Bootifull," said Amelia Louise.

He managed to get them both safely downstairs, and by the time Sheila woke, he had scrambled eggs in the frying pan and was cutting up a melon while Amelia Louise and Lady were play fighting over a stuffed toy.

Sheila finished off making breakfast so Windflower could shower and change his clothes. When he came downstairs, he noticed the fruit and homemade blueberry jam, fresh from September's pickings, that she had put out on the table. Just seeing the jam reminded Windflower of the many pleasant hours he had passed sitting and picking blueberries, sometimes with Sheila and Amelia Louise, but many times alone. It was reflective, almost meditative, and he recalled picking berries many times in his younger years with Auntie Marie and enjoying cups of wild mint tea with her after their work was done.

"What are you smiling about?" asked Sheila, seeing the happy glow on her husband.

"I was thinking about Auntie Marie and picking blueberries," said Windflower.

"Two of your favourite things."

"Tings, tings, tings," said Amelia Louise.

"Yes, indeed," said Windflower.

The family ate heartily, and Windflower and Sheila were

enjoying their second cup of coffee when they noticed an RCMP cruiser come into the driveway. Windflower kissed Amelia Louise and gave Sheila a warm embrace.

"Don't forget. We're going to visit the Sanjays tonight," said Sheila.

"I can't wait. It's always nice to see Repa and the doc away from work."

"Doc, doc, doc," said Amelia Louise.

Windflower kissed his wife and daughter, grabbed his crutches and walked slowly out to join Smithson.

"Good morning, Constable," said Windflower.

"Good morning, Sergeant," said Smithson, somewhat subdued.

"Anything wrong?" asked Windflower.

"Inspector Quigley called me last night. I'm being transferred to Marystown today."

"That should be good news. The inspector wants you because of your experience and technological expertise. It's a great opportunity."

"I know. But I fit in here. I belong here. I never really had that before. I'm really going to miss being here."

"You're a good officer. You'll not only fit in but be an asset wherever you go. And as I understand it, it's a temporary assignment. If you don't really like it, I think the inspector might let you come back."

"Thanks, Sarge. I really appreciate that," said Smithson as they pulled into the RCMP parking lot.

"Keep an open mind, if you can, Smithson," said Windflower. "'We know what we are, but know not what we may be.' Give it a chance, as you so often have before in your life."

Smithson looked puzzled.

"You are kind of like an iceberg," said Windflower. "I keep finding out things about you that you have kept well hidden. You have a lot of experience for such a young person, and that means you've taken some chances in life."

"I'm not really hiding anything, sir. It seems to me that people aren't all that interested in finding out about each other."

"That may be true. But I'd like to know more. Tell me about

you and your family, where you grew up, what you're interested in today."

Smithson started talking about growing up in Listowel, up towards Kincardine and Lake Huron in Ontario.

"I know that area a little," said Windflower. "I took the ferry from Tobermory over to Manitoulin Island. I love that place."

"It's a great little part of the world," said Smithson. "I miss it and try to get back every so often, but that feels like so long ago."

"Tell me about it. I miss Pink Lake, but I'm happy here, too. I feel like I know you a little better. I wish it had happened earlier and not just as you're about to get transferred out."

"I'm still hoping that will be slowed down until we hear about Bill Ford."

That quickly brought Windflower back to reality, and he hurried, as best he could on his crutches, into the office to get an update on the injured officer.

The news, for a change, was good.

"He's moved out of intensive care," said Ron Quigley. One bullet passed completely through and out the other side. The other bounced around a little bit apparently, but miraculously didn't hit any of his organs."

"That is a miracle, although I don't know if you could call getting shot lucky," said Windflower.

"'Fortune brings in some boats that are not steered,'" said Quigley. "In any case, I'm sure he'll take it. But he's certainly not out of the woods yet."

"Fingers crossed. Are there any developments on your end with the Paul Spurrell case?"

"Slow going. I've got a jail full of bikers and a waiting room full of lawyers trying to get them out."

"'They shall have justice, more than they desire.'"

"The quote may not be precise but the sentiment is exact. We do have a good lead on the girl. Thank Betsy for the photo. We think she's in St. John's, so we're watching at the airport."

"We'll keep beating the bushes over here."

"Great. Talk soon."

Windflower thanked Betsy again when she came into his office with his paperwork. "Inspector Quigley was very happy with the picture you provided. They're looking for her in St. John's," he said.

Betsy beamed and walked away. She returned later with a fresh cup of coffee and a muffin with butter. "I made them this morning before I came in," she said. "My Bob loves them."

"Partridgeberry, my favourite, too," said Windflower as he opened the still-warm muffin and took a bite. "Thank you."

Betsy beamed even more and walked away. Her mission was complete.

As Windflower was finishing off his muffin, Jones came in with an update from overnight. Both she and Evanchuk had been talking to their contacts who knew some of the local bikers. "We knew that the Relics had been partnered with Bacchus for some time, but there are new players in the game now. The Angels and some of their crew were here last summer, and they picked up some prospects. They're the ones who've been running meth on the peninsula."

"I thought they were only in Central," said Windflower.

"That's where they're mostly headquartered," said Jones, "but it's pretty crowded out there with both Bacchus and the Outlaws. Since the Angels established themselves in New Brunswick, they've been looking at setting up here. And it's a little easier in this area than in some others."

"The path of least resistance," said Windflower. "Are there any of these prospects around now?"

"If there are, they're pretty well hidden. But we'll keep looking."

"Okay. Can you also check something else for me? Can you find out where Stella Fitzgerald is and what her status might be?"

"Of course," said Jones. "I'll call over to social services and see what I can find out."

31

After Jones left, Windflower spent half an hour going through his papers. There wasn't really much of anything, just more policy updates and notices for upcoming training. There was also the usual handout on available positions in the RCMP. Windflower almost never took more than a cursory glance at it, but today, for some reason, he took his time and went through the whole listing. Most postings were for vacancies in headquarters, but one in his region stood out. It was a one-year acting assignment as a public outreach coordinator in St. John's. It was within his salary range, and when Windflower checked the qualifications, it looked like he was a fit.

He circled the position and put the notice in his briefcase. Then Evanchuk came in with a guy with a hoodie over his head. She brought him into the back area.

"I've got somebody I think you should meet," said Evanchuk. "He claims to know the girl, Patricia Lewis. Said she was his girlfriend before the bikers came around."

"What's with the hoodie?" asked Windflower.

"Nobody wants to be seen as a snitch with these guys," said Evanchuk. "You want to come back or have him brought up?"

"I'll go back. I need another cup of coffee anyway. What's going on with Eddie?"

"On his way home, last I heard. Connections didn't work out, and he just clawed his way through Pearson this morning. Hopefully he'll be back tonight sometime."

Windflower decided it was time to see their hoodied guest.

"You may have seen him around," said Evanchuk as they walked to the back. "He's been in the drunk tank a few times, mostly just drunk and disorderly. Got an addiction to opiates like many of his friends, but when he's clean he's okay. He's also on probation for trafficking and terrified about going back to jail."

"That's a card we can play," said Windflower.

"Sergeant Windflower, meet Leo Grandy," said Evanchuk. "Why don't you tell my boss what you told me?"

The thin, short young man hesitated and then spoke in a low, gravelly voice that suggested too many cigarettes and too much weed.

"Listen, I've been clean for two months now. I can't go back in. There's no way to stay clean inside," said Grandy.

"Let's see what you have to tell us," said Windflower. "You cooperate and we'll do what we can. Tell me about your relationship with Patricia Lewis."

"Patti and I were together since grade school," he said. "That all changed last year when she hooked up with her other friends."

"The bikers?" asked Windflower.

Grandy looked a little scared at even the mention of the bikers. "They can't know I'm talking to you," he said. "I'd be a dead man."

"Nobody has to know," said Windflower.

"Patti started going to parties with them. Some of her friends were going. I went once or twice, but they really didn't want other guys around, if you know what I mean."

"Where were those parties held?" asked Evanchuk.

"Those guys had houses everywhere," said Grandy. "There was one out in L'Anse au Loup, and I heard there were others in Winterland and Marystown. Money was nothing to them. Cases of liquor and bags of weed everywhere, often lots of coke, too."

"Where's your girlfriend now?" asked Windflower.

"I dunno. I haven't seen her for a few days. I don't want to get her in trouble, but she was bringing in some stuff for them."

"What kind of stuff?" asked Windflower.

"Meth. She said she was only doing it to get enough money to go to Europe. She's got an older sister who moved to Ireland. Loves it over there."

"Okay. I want you to show Constable Evanchuk where the house is out in L'Anse au Loup. And let us know if you hear from your girlfriend."

Grandy nodded, and Evanchuk led him out to her car.

Windflower watched as they drove off. He was about to call Quigley to tell him what he'd learned when his cell phone rang.

He said hello to Sheila.

"Repa Sanjay called and asked us over for dinner tonight. I said yes. Hope that's okay," said Sheila.

"Did you tell her we were bringing a one-child wrecking crew?" asked Windflower.

Sheila laughed. "She's not that bad."

"Okay, when she knocks over one of Sanjay's glass antiques, you're paying. By the way, we're expecting Eddie Tizzard back sometime later today, maybe tomorrow morning if the weather gets bad.

"That's great. It will be good to have him back here. This is his home," said Sheila.

Next came the call to Quigley.

"We've got a lead on a possible biker house," said Windflower. Evanchuk found the girl's old boyfriend. He says the bikers had houses here and in Winterland and Marystown."

"Yeah," said Quigley. "We found the Marystown one already, but it's been cleared out. We're still trying to track down the Winterland one. Did the boyfriend have anything else to say?"

"Not much," said Windflower. "Just that he thinks the girl was bringing in meth for the bikers. And she was planning a trip to Europe."

"Where in Europe?"

"Ireland, I think."

"Might be worth checking out," said Quigley. "Talk soon."

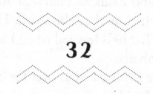

32

The minute Windflower got near Betsy's desk he was handed a fistful of messages. He walked to his office, noticing that his ankle seemed stronger. He was really hoping to be able to get back to normal, including driving by the weekend, and if not then, at least by the start of next week. His arm was starting to itch inside the cast, too, although he knew there was little he could do about the cast or the itching. Maybe he could get to the clinic to see about getting some relief on both ends.

He was still thinking about that and was a bit lost in the messages when Jones came into his office.

"I've got some news on Stella Fitzgerald," she said. "She's in temporary care with a family in Burin. But that's very short term. Social services will try and place her in a foster home, but she's had some behavioural problems according to the case worker I spoke to. That also means that adoption will be trickier as well."

"She's only four years old," said Windflower. "How bad can her behaviour be?"

"Biting, hitting other children," said Jones, looking at her notes. "It just adds another level of concern that many adoptive parents, even foster homes, don't want or have the time or resources to deal with."

Windflower shook his head. "So, because her mother is an addict, now dead, that little girl gets punished again. Doesn't seem right. Is there anybody we can talk to?"

"I've got the name of the regional manager, Noreen Corrigan. She's in Marystown. Here's her number, but I'm not sure what she can do."

"Thanks, I'll give her a call later," said Windflower.

Windflower continued flipping through his messages. Most were from the media, so he ignored them and took another look through his in-basket. He saw a course on marijuana's impact on teenagers that he thought might be interesting for the staff and opened his briefcase to put the information in for a look later. The job vacancy in St. John's was sitting right on top. He was going through it again when Betsy came on the intercom.

"Constable Evanchuk on line one."

"Thanks, Betsy," he said.

"Windflower."

"Sarge, I think we're going to need that warrant," said Evanchuk. "You should come take a look. I'll get Smithson to drive you over."

Windflower stuffed the job handout in his pocket and got ready for Smithson. It didn't take him long to grab his crutches and hop out to the car. Smithson could tell when his boss meant business, and so he made sure to get to the L'Anse au Loup house in record time.

"Whaddya find?" asked Windflower as soon as they got to the bikers' house.

"More like what we didn't find," said Evanchuk. "Certainly a party house, so lots of garbage—roaches, pipes, cases of empty beer bottles, scales. Some ammo, too. Looks like powder residue in a few places."

L'Anse au Loup had once been the summer house location for many families in Grand Bank. They would move everything they needed from their 'downtown' house up to L'Anse au Loup and live there almost like campers for the summer months. It was easier to cook and less to clean for the women in the family while the men sometimes went off to fish for July and August. The children and their mothers looked after whatever animals they had and grew great amounts of root vegetables to last them through the long winter months.

Over the years the area became mostly designated for cabins, as the locals called their cottages. Then it was used for year-round homes as some people wanted to be away from the busyness of the community. The Mounties were now in front of a house that most likely had been abandoned by its owners and then bought up or rented by one of the bikers or their associates.

"I want you to check the registry and see who owns this property," said Windflower to Smithson.

"Already looked online."

"Of course you did. And?"

"It was bought by one Melissa Fraser from Port Coquitlam, British Columbia. I talked to the real estate agent. He said nobody even came to look at the place. There was an email from this Fraser woman, and then all the monies were wired electronically. A lawyer in Marystown handled the paperwork."

"Okay, Smithson," said Windflower. "I want you to start gathering up that paperwork. We might need to show ownership of whatever we find. What did we find, Evanchuk?"

"Let's walk through," she said, handing him and Smithson a pair of gloves.

"Pee-yew, that's awful," said Windflower.

"It's pretty stinky. Guess they weren't big on cleaning up," said Evanchuk as she led Windflower back through with Smithson, his handkerchief over his mouth, a few steps behind.

Evanchuk was right about the mess. In the main area that passed for a living room, there were two low couches stained and starting to break open. The kitchen wasn't much better with empty pizza boxes and two nearly full green garbage bags in one corner. The ashtrays were filled with butts, tobacco and weed, and Evanchuk pointed out the powder on the countertops in a couple of places. There was also a set of scales and boxes of empty gelatin capsules.

The bedrooms were a little cleaner in that there was no stacked garbage, but Windflower sure wouldn't sleep in any of the beds. One bedroom looked like it was just being used to store sleeping bags and some camping equipment. There were also more boxes of gelatin capsules and plastic straws and a small collection of glass pipes.

They tried not to disturb too much, but Windflower saw something sticking out from underneath one of the beds. It was a shotgun. He gingerly pulled it out.

"That's what we call a duck gun," said Smithson looking over his shoulder at the slender rifle. "Although, it's a pretty expensive one."

"Semi-automatic," said Windflower. He pulled it up and looked through the sights. "Pretty special piece, probably over a grand."

"Easily," said Evanchuk. "But the ammo I found is for a handgun. I wonder if that's still around here?"

"I guess we'll have to do the search to find out," said Windflower. "Get the warrant and call forensics. They're probably still around the area after the shooting. Let them go through, and make sure we don't miss anything. Smithson, you drive me back, and then you can organize the warrant and forensics."

Evanchuk got her camera out of her car and waved to Windflower and Smithson as they headed back to the office.

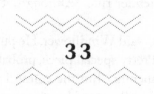

33

Windflower called Ron Quigley to give him an update on what was found at the bikers' house in L'Anse au Loup.

"That's great," said Quigley. "And I've got news of my own. We've got the girl. She was stopped by airport security last night, trying to leave the country with a false id. A pretty good fake passport, too, I hear. She's on her way here now. I was going to call you. Do you want to sit in? You're a great investigator."

"I could do that. I guess I could get a ride with Smithson if you could arrange a ride back. Be interested to see what she's got to say. You should know that Smithson's pretty upset about leaving. I'm not that thrilled about it either."

"He'll get over it. And we'll get you a fresh body. It'll be good for him. Ah, the course of true love, or policing, never did run smooth."

"When do you think Patti Lewis will be there?" asked Windflower, ignoring Quigley's attempt to mollify him with a quoting duel.

"Just before noon," said Quigley.

"Okay. I'll get Smithson to drive me over."

"Perfect. Thanks, Winston."

"Ron, while I have you, do you know what a public outreach coordinator does?" asked Windflower.

"Outreach with the public?" said Quigley. "There's a unit in Ottawa that was started a few years ago to work with at-risk youth. They expanded it to the regions last year. Why are you asking about that?"

"I saw a job posting in St. John's, a one-year assignment."

"You going to St. John's? I thought you were a bayman. Do you even know how to drive in the big city?"

"St. John's is not a big city, by any stretch. I've seen the drivers in town. Most are too slow and the others are crazy. Anyway, I'm just exploring my options."

"That's partially why I called. I'm not going to Ottawa, at least not yet. They've pulled my assignment for six months because of what happened to Ford and everything else going on."

"Well, that's too bad for you, but good news for us," said Windflower.

"Well, not all good news. I still need Smithson to come over and help me. Bill Ford is going to be okay, but he's out of commission for a while. Between you and me, he may not come back at all."

"I'm glad he's okay. And not surprised. Getting shot would shake anybody up. Plus, Bill must be close to retirement, if he wants."

"I think he might explore that route. He was looking at doing this gig for a couple of years and then packing it in."

After the call ended with Quigley, Betsy popped into his office to see if he needed anything.

"We've got forensics coming this morning to go through the house at L'Anse au Loup, and I'm going over to Marystown with Constable Smithson."

"I heard he was leaving," said Betsy. "He was pretty sad about it last night."

"It's only temporary," said Windflower. "After I leave, would you mark me out on the board and note that I'm gone to Marystown?"

"Very good, Sergeant," said Betsy, pleased that he was following the internal office procedures. "Anything else?"

"Yes, Betsy," said Windflower. "Could you do a little research for me. Find out everything you can about the Public Outreach Unit in St. John's. When it was formed, what its priorities are. Successes. Anything you can find."

"Yes, sir," said Betsy, happy again to be of service to her boss.

Smithson was the next to report. "Jones called to say that Corporal Brown and forensics are here," he said. Windflower followed Smithson out, and a few minutes later they were at the biker place in L'Anse au Loup. The familiar white forensics van was parked in the driveway, and Jones was standing outside talking to a man in overalls.

"Good morning, Ted," said Windflower.

"Good morning, Sergeant," said Corporal Ted Brown, head of the local forensics unit. "Jones was telling me you think this was one of the bikers' hangouts. We finished up another one in Marystown yesterday. It was crazy what we found there. Right in the middle of town, too."

"You won't likely be surprised with what's here then," said Windflower. "We tried not to disturb things too much, but just in our visual search we found evidence of weapons and heavy-duty drugs."

"Man, it's really changed. Used to be a lot of weed, contraband booze and tobacco, maybe a little coke. Now it's opiates and speed and fentanyl. Killer drugs."

"Good luck and be careful," said Windflower.

Windflower and Smithson drove back to the RCMP offices. Windflower called Sheila to tell her that he was going to Marystown.

"Can you pick up a nice flower arrangement to give to the Sanjays?" asked Sheila.

"You're asking me to pick flowers?"

"You can do it. Man up, Sergeant. Just go to Sobeys and see what they have. Pick a nice bouquet or plant. It's not that hard."

"Okay. I'll see what I can do."

When he hung up, Smithson was looking at him with concern. "Everything okay, sir?" he asked.

"Responsibilities of married life," said Windflower. "They never end." Now Smithson looked confused.

"I'll explain in the car," said Windflower. "We're going to have a nice drive to Marystown."

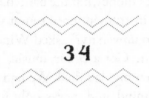

34

Windflower always enjoyed going to Marystown, but this time he got to experience it as a passenger. It was a beautifully gorgeous fall day with lots of sunshine and only a slight breeze shaking the trees as they left Grand Bank and passed by the smaller settlements of Grand Beach and Molliers. They really weren't communities anymore, but there were still houses and cabins all the way down to the lakes and ponds that marked their boundaries.

Then they came to the beginning of the wide, open stretches that would seemingly last forever. They only ended with a turnoff or a side road like the ones to Fisherman's Cove or Garnish, small towns that hugged the coastlines of this part of the world. After that, there was more emptiness. These stretches turned into vast swaths of uninhabitable and inhospitable territory that featured little but rocks and small trees to break the horizon.

Windflower loved the quiet simplicity of this drive and often used it to think about his life or problems that had arisen. He was a careful driver, seldom going much beyond the speed limit and usually settling into a form of driving meditation. Today, he was free to explore that a little further, except that he had a driver who he'd promised to talk to along the way.

"So, tell me more about your life growing up," said Windflower. "Did you go to high school in Listowel?"

"No," said Smithson. "There's a high school there now, but I went to Kincardine. That was a big shift, six hundred kids. But it had sports and a band program. I wasn't very good at sports, but I loved the band."

"Yeah, you said. You played the flute, right?"

"Flute, clarinet, French horn. I played everything I could. My folks didn't have a lot of money, but the band had a lending program. I didn't have my own instrument until senior year."

"Then you went to university?" asked Windflower.

"I went to Western. Got a BA in music," said Smithson. "But I had to drop out when my dad died. We had a farm, and I had to go help out. I didn't mind, and it was only for two terms, but by then I had moved on from music. I knew I was never going to be good enough to play professionally, and I didn't want to teach. So I signed up for the RCMP."

"You were posted out west to start, weren't you?"

"I was in Edmonton, at the airport. The job was good, but I hated Edmonton. The winter started early and went on forever."

"Kind of like here."

"No. This was brutally cold, starting in October and never warming up. I liked the people in Edmonton. But it was a rough town. Downtown they had a lot of gangs. Shootings, stabbings every night. I wasn't afraid. I just didn't like it."

"But you like it more here, in Grand Bank?"

"It's been so nice here. Somehow it feels like home even though it's completely different from where I'm from."

"You know I feel the same way. I have always been fascinated by the wildness of this area—the barrens, the sea, even the way the fog rolls in and takes us all prisoner for a day or a week."

"I know," said Smithson. "Can I play you a piece of music? It's something I always play when I come on this drive. It's Mendelssohn's Hebrides."

"Sure," said Windflower.

Smithson reached into the compartment in the middle console and pulled out his player. He plugged it in and grabbed a CD from the case.

"Mendelssohn was on a tour of Europe in his early twenties when he came to the Hebrides area of Scotland," explained Smithson. "He was captivated by sounds of the ocean and the isolation of the coast. We're on a different coast on the other side of the Atlantic, but it sounds and feels like he wrote it for us, too."

The constable turned on the music, and Windflower got lost in the sounds. He was soon taken away by the waves and the ocean and the intense, rolling melodies of the piece. It started with violas, cellos and bassoons, which reminded Windflower of the solitude that he often felt on this journey. Then it moved to more dramatic sounds that made Windflower feel like he was on the ocean, rolling along forever.

"That was amazing," said Windflower. "Thank you."

"You're welcome," said Smithson as he put away the CD and his player.

The two men sat in silence for the next half hour. Windflower thought about the music and felt a peace and comfort come over him. He even forgot about everything that was troubling him, and it only came back when they passed the turnoff to Winterland.

"They say that's where the other biker clubhouse is, although it must be well hidden," said Smithson. "There's not much in Winterland."

"They seem to be able to hide in plain sight," said Windflower. "But you know 'you can keep as quiet as you like, but one of these days somebody is going to find you.'"

"That's good."

"Haruki Murakami, a Japanese writer somebody turned me on to years ago. I read a couple of his books, translated from the Japanese. He also said, 'If you only read the books that everyone else is reading, you can only think what everyone else is thinking.' I'm glad I read some of his books."

There was little more said between the men as they continued on their journey. Soon they were coming into Marystown. Smithson was heading for the RCMP building, but Windflower directed him into the supermarket parking lot.

"Do you know anything about flowers?" he asked Smithson.

"Not really," the younger man said.

"Here's twenty bucks. Go in and ask the girl on the counter to help you pick out a bouquet. Tell her it's for a friend," said Windflower. Smithson hesitated. "Go on," said Windflower.

Five minutes later Smithson came out with a smile, a potted plant and a couple of wrapped sandwiches.

"What is that?" asked Windflower.

"A quick lunch," said Smithson.

"No, no. But thanks. I mean what kind of flower is it?"

"It's a begonia," said Smithson. "Heather told me."

"Why are you so happy?"

"I think I got a date for the weekend. Thanks, Boss."

Windflower shook his head and laughed. They quickly ate their sandwiches before leaving the parking lot. Smithson dropped Windflower and his plant off at the front door of the Marystown RCMP. I'm going to miss that kid, thought Windflower.

35

Windflower found his way to Ron Quigley's office and shared pleasantries with his admin assistant until Quigley emerged.

"Gotta brief the big boys twice a day now," Quigley said. "It's exhausting. Lewis is downstairs. I've sent word to bring her up."

Patti Lewis was led into the interview room where Windflower and Quigley were waiting. She was not as young-looking as Windflower had expected. She looked far beyond her 19 years but was certainly attractive and knew how to push her breasts forward to make them a focal point. That was a handy skill to have to attract men, thought Windflower despite the fact that she was not even close to his type of woman and not nearly lady-like enough for him.

The female guard nodded to Quigley, and he indicated she should take off the cuffs.

"Might as well get comfortable," said Quigley.

"In that case, I'd like a cigarette and a Pepsi," said Lewis. Quigley ignored that remark.

"I am Inspector Ron Quigley, and this is Sergeant Winston Windflower. We want to ask you a few questions."

"I got nuttin to say," said Lewis.

Windflower wasn't surprised. This was how almost every interview started. He looked for signs of weakness in this young woman, but she looked strong and determined. But then again, so did 95 percent of the witnesses and accused he had interviewed over the years.

"You might want to think about that," said Quigley. "We have you at the scene of the attempted murder of a police officer, to say nothing of helping a prisoner escape custody. A prisoner that has since been executed."

"You must be mistaken," said Lewis. "I don't know what you're talking about."

"If you have information to provide that helps us, we might be able to plead you down to accessory," said Quigley. Right now we're going to charge you with everything. When you add it all up, how much do you think she might get, Sergeant?"

"I'd say twenty to thirty years minimum," said Windflower.

"The people you think you are protecting don't care about you," Quigley told Patti Lewis. "In fact, once I release you into general population in the jail downstairs, how long do you think it will take for them to find you?"

That got her attention, thought Windflower. He decided to jump in.

"You are a beautiful young woman. By the time you get out of jail, even if you don't get beat up or scarred up, you won't be either. They are not your friends. They will turn on you in an instant if that serves their purpose," he said.

Lewis now looked like a deer in the headlights. Quigley went in for the kill. "We need to know where their clubhouse is in Winterland, and we need you to make a statement identifying the men who were involved."

"I need a lawyer," was all Patti Lewis said.

Quigley and Windflower tried other lines with her, but it was clear that she was done talking until she had legal counsel.

"I can get duty counsel," said Quigley finally.

Windflower and Quigley left the interview room and went outside. "We've had all available duty counsel here all week," said the inspector. "You can wait in my office if you'd like."

Windflower went back to Quigley's office and was sitting in his chair when he looked out the window. He could see the Walmart on one side, not his favourite place in the world for a dozen reasons he could easily recite. On the other was an industrial park and an office building. He looked a little closer and saw a sign that said Service Newfoundland: Child Protection and In-Care Division.

Child protection, he thought, wondering if the people there could talk about Stella Fitzgerald. Then he remembered that Jones had given him a name and a number. He couldn't remember either.

Using his phone, he checked for the number and called. Of course, he got the answering machine. But there was an option to scroll through the employee directory. Third on the list was Noreen Corrigan. That was the manager's name.

He punched in her extension, expecting to leave a message. Instead, she answered the phone.

"Noreen Corrigan."

It took a flustered Windflower a moment to respond.

"Hello, hello?" asked Corrigan.

"Sorry, Ms. Corrigan. It's Sergeant Winston Windflower from the Grand Bank RCMP. I'm calling about Stella Fitzgerald."

"Hello, Sergeant. All I can tell you about Stella is that she is in a temporary home, and we're looking to place her," said the manager. "I certainly can't discuss her case over the phone."

"I'm in Marystown at the RCMP building across the way. Can I come see you for a few minutes? It won't take long."

"If you can get here right away. I'm on a break between meetings. It's your lucky day, Sergeant."

"Thank you. I'll be right over," said Windflower, thinking that she just might be right. He got Quigley's assistant to page Smithson.

Windflower noticed Smithson looked surprised when they met up. "Thought you got rid of me? Not so fast," said Windflower. "I'm going right over there." Windflower pointed to the building across the way.

"Stella Fitzgerald," said Smithson after he saw the sign across the road.

"Exactly," said Windflower. He asked Quigley's assistant to let the inspector know that he was going out for a few minutes but would be back soon. Then he got Smithson to drive him to the door of the child protection building. He walked in and asked for Noreen Corrigan.

She came out to greet him and ushered him into her office. She was in her early forties by Windflower's guess and wore a skirt and a smart-looking blouse. Her jacket was on the chair behind her neat and well-organized desk. She pulled Stella Fitzgerald's file out of a drawer and laid it in front of them.

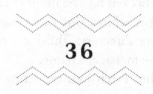

36

What did you want to know about Stella?" asked Corrigan. "As I said on the phone, she is in a safe place right now, and we're looking for a placement."

"Will she be available for adoption? How likely is it that she will be adopted?" asked Windflower.

"Once the situation stabilizes, she will certainly be available for the right family to adopt," said Corrigan. "But I have to tell you that the older the child, the harder the adoption becomes. There are thirty thousand children waiting for adoption in Canada right now, hundreds in Newfoundland alone. And less than fifty get adopted every year, most of them newborns."

"Does she need special attention?" asked Windflower. "Is that a barrier to adoption?"

"Many children who have experienced abuse or neglect have difficulty trusting any adults, even adoptive parents. Stella has certainly had her struggles, and that has meant some aggressive behaviour towards other children as well. But all that can be ameliorated in the right environment and with the right family. Medically, she appears healthy, if a little undernourished. She doesn't talk much, but then again maybe she wasn't encouraged to."

"I noticed that. She was in the office for a short period while her mom was in hospital. She didn't talk very much."

"Not unusual," said Corrigan. "But she can talk. Because I have heard her, not talking to her little friends or to adults, but to herself as she was playing."

"Interesting. Now she has to deal with the loss of her mother, the one person she could rely on, at least some of the time. And she doesn't know it, but she's lost her father, too."

"It's sad and unfortunate, but she and we have to find a way to move on."

"What's going to happen to her?"

"We will try to place her in foster care while she's awaiting adoption. But if that's not possible or doesn't work out, she could be in a group home setting."

"She's pretty small for a group home."

"Those are the options, the best ones we have to offer."

Windflower thanked Corrigan for her time and went out to meet Smithson who was parked nearby.

"How'd it go?" asked Smithson.

"It doesn't look good," said Windflower, and he explained what he'd heard.

"That's awful," said Smithson. "How could a little girl like that live in a group home? She needs a family."

Windflower nodded his agreement but stayed silent while Smithson drove him back to the RCMP building.

"I know it's not my place, but I have to say something, Sergeant," said Smithson. "You and your wife should consider adopting Stella. You are already great parents, and your daughter gets along with her."

"The thought did cross my mind," said Windflower. "But my life, our lives, are already chaotic. How would we manage another child? How would Sheila manage it?"

"You should at least talk to her about it."

Windflower nodded again and walked slowly into the building. He went to Quigley's office and waited outside his door. He didn't have to wait long.

"They're ready for us," said Quigley. "It's Freddy Hawkins."

Windflower knew Hawkins from many appearances in Grand Bank and Marystown on behalf of people who couldn't afford the best legal representation but had to have someone represent their interests while they tried to cut a deal. And everyone wanted a deal. Like it or not, Frederick Hawkins was the man to get the job done. Windflower didn't think he'd ever seen him in court, probably because the lawyer did everything he could to avoid going there. But Hawkins helped make an unworkable system of revolving jail doors work for the many and sundry minor criminals, usually addicts and alcoholics, who got caught in the legal web. He called himself 'indispensable' one time, and Windflower could not disagree.

"Let's see what Freddy's got cooked up for us today," said Windflower.

They opened the door and took their seats across from Freddy Hawkins and Patti Lewis. The young woman still looked a little shell-shocked, but Hawkins, the very wide and not-very-tall lawyer, looked completely at ease in his loose, stained suit and half-knotted tie.

"Let's talk about what evidence you might have against my client, first of all, shall we?" said Hawkins with a smile.

Quigley smiled back. "We have a witness that places your client at the scene of a prisoner escape, a hostage taking and the attempted murder of a police officer," he said.

"My client was an innocent bystander who was also taken hostage," said Hawkins.

"Your client was a known associate of the men who were involved in this situation," countered Quigley.

"Can you prove that?" asked Hawkins.

Windflower got in on the action. "We are currently searching a property in L'Anse au Loup," he said. "I'm pretty certain her prints will show up there, along with evidence of drug use and almost certainly drug trafficking."

"Circumstantial evidence," said Hawkins.

"Enough for us to charge her and hold her," said Quigley. "And given her recent attempts to leave the country, bail would not be an option. That means she will spend at least six months in custody, and we all know how dangerous a place jail can be."

Hawkins looked at his client and she nodded. "Given the fact that you have nothing on her directly, she would like complete immunity and witness protection should she decide to be more cooperative than she has already been," said Hawkins.

"I don't know about witness protection, but I can guarantee her safety while she's with us here in Marystown," said Quigley. "I can make charges disappear, but that will depend on what she has to tell. And that deal only lasts right now. We need all the info about the men she was with and where they might be now."

Hawkins looked at Patti Lewis and got another nod.

"Go ahead," he told her. "Tell them what you know."

37

Patti Lewis cleared her throat and started speaking. She talked non-stop for 15 minutes about how the gang recruited her by offering her weed and alcohol and in turn how she got them more girls for their parties. She wasn't a big druggie or a groupie. According to her version of events, she was more like the social convenor of their world, and there was always a party. She said she was having fun until they sent a biker named Billy Fraser down from the mainland, along with one of his pals. Then things turned more dangerous with harder drugs and a new code that only allowed certain people access to the inner circle. She was not one of them.

As Lewis spoke, Windflower tried to remember where he had heard the name Billy Fraser before. Then it came to him. Smithson had found out that a woman by the name of Fraser had bought the biker house at L'Anse au Loup without even looking at it first. The dots were beginning to connect.

"Did you ever meet Paul Spurrell?" asked Quigley when Lewis stopped for a breath.

"Sure," said Lewis. "He was around for the past few months. He was one of the Ontario connections and brought drugs back and forth. That's when the crystal meth started to become everything and all the boys were expected to push a certain limit. Like quotas."

"What happened to that relationship, with Paul Spurrell?" asked Quigley.

"Fraser said that Spurrell was ripping them off. Cutting the meth with something. Milk powder or sugar. Then selling the product himself. Him and his girlfriend."

"Marla Fitzgerald?" asked Windflower.

"Yeah, although I think she was dipping into the product," said Lewis. "Anyway, it was a real circus. That's why they grabbed

Spurrell. But they told me they were only going to teach him a lesson. I didn't know it, but one of them told me that Fraser thought Spurrell was going to rat them out, if he hadn't already."

"So, you helped set up the ambush by pretending your car was broken down," said Quigley. "Who was with you?"

"Fraser was in the bush, and the other guys, Ronnie Winstone and Fox Raymond, were in the back seat of my car. They were supposed to grab Spurrell out of the back of the van and take off. Then the cop got in the way and Fraser started shooting. I saw the cop fall and everybody was screaming. We jumped in the car and took off."

"Where did you go from there?"

"First, we went to the house in Marystown, but everybody was creeped out there. As soon as I could, I got out. I called a friend and got a ride to St. John's."

"Fraser and the other guys?" asked Quigley.

"I dunno. But I don't think they were planning on leaving. Fraser seemed to think that it would be better to lay low around here, that they, you, would be looking for them."

"Where is their house in Winterland?" asked Windflower.

"I don't know the address or anything. I'm not sure it even has one. It's a cabin in the woods. But I can show you."

"Okay," said Quigley. "That's enough for now. Once she shows us the location, I'll have your client transferred to protective custody," he said to Hawkins. "Then, other people will want to talk to her. I'll give you a few minutes with her."

Quigley and Windflower left the room. "I'll get you a ride back," said Quigley. "Thanks for your help. I'm sure she's not as clean as she pretends, but I think she'll be a credible witness."

"No problem," said Windflower. "Let me know how it goes."

Minutes later Windflower and the begonia were in the back of a cruiser on the way to Grand Bank. "Can we make a pitstop?" he asked Watson, the young constable who was driving him. I want to see Bill Ford."

"No worries," said Watson, and he turned off the highway towards the Burin Peninsula Health Care Centre. He parked in the emergency lot, and Windflower went to the reception area to ask for directions to Bill Ford's room.

Ford was dozing when Windflower came into his room. He almost left but then heard Ford stir.

"Hey, Bill, how's it going?" he asked.

Ford spoke in a very low voice, almost a croak, and Windflower couldn't pick out much, but he did see a slight smile come across Ford's face.

"It looks like you're going make it," said Windflower, prompting another smile. "Only the good die young, I guess."

Ford struggled to speak, but Windflower stopped him. "No need for talk now. I just wanted to come by and say hi. I'll be back later. Maybe we can go trouting together." That brought a broad smile to Ford's face, and he whispered to Windflower, "That's a plan."

Windflower smiled back and squeezed Ford's hand. "We'll see ya later, buddy."

He walked slowly to the car, thinking about Ford and how lucky he was despite his situation. It made him very grateful for his own. For the rest of the journey, there was little chatter and a whole lot of snoring as Windflower took advantage of the ride for a bit of shut eye. He woke as Watson turned off the highway into Grand Bank.

"Thanks a lot," he said to Watson. The other officer waved and turned around for his return trip to Marystown.

It was a little after four o'clock, and Betsy came into Windflower's office just before leaving for the day and dropped off a file with the information he had requested on the public outreach program. She lingered a moment in the doorway.

"Is there anything else, Betsy?" asked Windflower.

"Did you know there was an opening in the unit?" she asked.

"I did, thank you, Betsy," said Windflower. "I'm taking a look at it. Sheila has talked about going to school in St. John's, and the job might be more convenient for us. But I haven't made any decisions. I would ask you to keep this confidential."

"Absolutely, sir," said Betsy. "You can count on me. My lips are sealed. But it wouldn't be the same without you."

"It would only be a short-term assignment, if anything ever happened. And sooner or later, all things come to an end."

"I know, sir, but it would still be sad without you here."

"Thanks, Betsy. But nothing is happening quickly, if at all. Okay?"

"Okay, Sergeant. Have a nice evening. I'm assuming with everything going on, you'll need me in tomorrow morning."

Windflower could always count on Betsy. She never hesitated to work on a weekend when the officers' caseloads piled up.

"Yes, thank you, Betsy, if you could. We'd appreciate it. And have a nice evening, too."

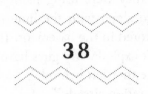

38

Jones came in as Betsy was leaving. "She looks a little sad," said Jones. "Everything okay with her?" she asked.

"It will be," said Windflower.

"Smithson is gone," said Jones. "We're going to miss him."

"I know," said Windflower. "I was starting to really like him."

"I'm not missing him like that," said Jones. "He was like an irritating little brother who knew everything and nothing at the same time. I meant we'll miss him and have to cover his shift."

"I'm happy to do an extra shift to give you and Evanchuk a break, but I can't do any solo patrols. Hopefully, next week."

"Yeah, it's too bad we can't just pull someone in off the street."

"Maybe we can. I've been wondering if we can get Tizzard back as a special constable."

"That would be great. We could really use the break."

"Okay," said Windflower. "I'll call the inspector and see what he thinks before I talk to Tizzard about it, just in case Quigley thinks it's a bad idea. How did forensics make out?"

"They're staying overnight," said Jones. "Corporal Brown is just behind me. Here he is now."

"So, what did you find, Brownie?" asked Windflower.

"More like what we didn't find," said Brown. "A ton of weed, although I guess that's hardly a problem now with legalization."

"We're just tax collectors now," said Windflower. "What else?"

"It looks like they were getting organized to set up a meth lab. Right in the middle of other houses," said Brown. "At least they were smart or crazy enough to keep it outside the house. It was in the shed outside. That's probably why you didn't smell it."

"What does it smell like?" asked Windflower. "All we smelled was garbage."

"Like ammonia. They were using paint thinners, iodine and lye as chemicals to go along with the industrial supplies of cold medicines they had stored in the basement. They're still lucky that the whole thing didn't explode. My guys have to stay overnight to remove the toxic waste they left behind."

"Were they in operation already?"

"They had started but were just getting set up for some mass production. They had the capacity to make a lot of meth and a lot of money with that set-up. Maybe that's why they had all the weaponry, too. Needed protection."

"Guns and ammo? We found some ammunition right out in the open along with a long-range rifle."

"Pistols, long guns and a couple of modified automatic rifles that were pretty close to machine guns. Along with several vests and even a few stun grenades. They were getting themselves ready for an attack by the looks of it."

"A drug war? In Grand Bank? That's crazy," said Windflower.

"It's been moving here for a while," said Brown. "There's already been shoot-ups in Grand Falls and an incident in Clarenville where two people were shot in a drive-by."

"I guess so. Just feels weird, out of place to be happening here."

"Drugs, gangs, guns, bikers and money—a pretty potent mix. Anyway, we're done for the night. We're going to the pub for a drink. Interested?"

"I'd like to, but we're going out for dinner. Over to Doc Sanjay's."

"Say hello to him for me," said Brown. "You around all weekend?"

"I'll be here, or at least close to my phone at home if I'm needed," said Windflower. "We're short-staffed."

"Like everybody," said Brown. "I'll pop by tomorrow before I leave."

Windflower checked his watch. Still time for one more quick call before leaving for the day. He punched in the speed dial for Inspector Quigley.

"We're getting ready to head over to the location in Winterland that Patti Lewis gave us. What's up over there?" asked Quigley.

"Forensics found what they think was the makings of a meth

lab in L'Anse au Loup and a weapons stash. Tell your guys to be careful," said Windflower.

"We're going in full SWAT," said Quigley. "It sounds like the bikers are not just armed but desperate."

"I have a suggestion about dealing with our staff shortage." Windflower paused to make sure he was being heard. "Tizzard."

"Tizzard? How's that going to help you?" asked Quigley. "There's a process for reinstatement. That's going to take some time."

"While we're waiting, we could make him a special constable, if he's interested. It might help him, and it would certainly help us."

"I guess so. He qualifies and has a gun licence already. Go ahead and talk to him and see what he says. I have authority to appoint for 30 days. That should give us time to find a longer-term replacement."

"Thanks," said Windflower. "I'll get back to you and good luck."

He started packing up his stuff and was ready to go. Then he realized that he had lost his driver. Smithson was in Marystown, and he had no ride home. He could call Sheila, but that would involve getting her and Amelia Louise out and dressed only to have to do it all over again in half an hour. Jones had gone with the forensics team for drinks.

He had no choice but to call Evanchuk in from patrol.

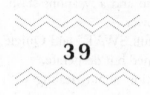

39

Sheila was happy to see Windflower coming up the driveway. When she opened the door, Amelia Louise, Lady, and even Molly rushed over to him, and Evanchuk waved them all a goodbye as she reversed out of the driveway.

"Someone's in a good mood," said Sheila. "And you brought a plant. Good job, Sergeant."

"Moo, moo," said Amelia Louise who was barely being kept in the house by Sheila.

"It's a good day," said Windflower. "It's a good day to be alive."

"You're home early, that's great," said Sheila.

"Gwate, gwate," said Amelia Louise as Lady did her usual happy dance. Molly, on the other hand, as the cat of the house, had to pretend not to care and to be miffed all at the same time. She retreated to her perch on top of the sofa and sent out disdain as far as she could. She did her cat job well.

"I didn't know if I'd get away on time. It's crazy right now," said Windflower.

"It must be," said Sheila.

"Carrie popped in for a few minutes today. Did you know Eddie is thinking he might want to work with the Force again?" Sheila said.

"No, I didn't, but I'm really glad to hear it," said Windflower

"Why the change of heart, I wonder. I thought he was set on being a private eye or something."

"I think his experiences in Vegas shifted him somehow. He seems to be moving in another direction. I personally think he'll be better off in the Mounties."

"But maybe not if he's planning a family."

"Oh that's a ways off," said Windflower. "They're not even married yet."

"She also told me something else," said Sheila, and then she fell silent. Windflower looked at her with raised eyebrows that said, "Well?"

"I'm not sure I can say. It's a secret," said Sheila.

"I'm a police officer, an expert interrogator. You can say I tortured you."

"You have to swear to secrecy and act surprised when you find out."

"Tell me."

"Carrie is pregnant," said Sheila. "A little over three months."

"It won't be hard to act surprised," said Windflower. "I'm a little shocked, actually. I bet Eddie will be surprised, too."

"Surprised, yes, but happy I'm sure," said Sheila. "He seems happy with everything, and he loves children. Doesn't he, Amelia Louise? Uncle Eddie loves you, doesn't he?"

"Unca, unca, unca," said Amelia Louise, looking around for Tizzard.

"He's not here right now," said Windflower. "You'll have to get by with me, your dear old dad."

That was fine with Amelia Louise who started her "dada, dada, dada" chant and didn't stop until Windflower had her on the ground tickling her. After they were both left gasping for breath, Windflower managed to get himself up and went to the closet. He pulled the job notice out of his jacket and handed it to Sheila.

"This is in St. John's," said Sheila.

"It is indeed," said Windflower. "A one-year assignment by the looks of it. But with these things it could turn into something longer."

"What does a public outreach coordinator do?"

"I'm not sure. But I certainly seem qualified for it, and the change might be good for me and us," said Windflower.

Sheila said she agreed and went upstairs to get ready for dinner. When she was ready, she put Amelia Louise in her car seat, and Windflower strapped her in. Then she drove them across the brook to the Sanjay residence.

Doctor Sanjay greeted them at the door, paying particular attention to Amelia Louise. He was soon joined by his wife, Repa.

"This is for you," said Sheila, handing over the plant.

"I love begonias," said Repa as she took the gift and guided the little girl and Sheila into the kitchen.

"Whatever you're cooking, it smells delicious," said Windflower.

"That is all Repa's doing," said Sanjay. "She shoos me out of the kitchen like a house fly. Would you like a small dram of Scotch before dinner?"

"That would be excellent," said Windflower as he followed the doctor into his den. This is where he stored his fine collection of single malt whiskies. On the table along with a pitcher of water and glasses was his latest prize.

"I have been waiting for your visit to try this beauty," said Sanjay, holding up a bottle of Balvenie. He poured them both about an ounce of whisky and a glass of water. He sniffed the Scotch and tasted it on the tip of his tongue. Then he washed it down with a few sips of water. Windflower followed suit.

"What do you think?" asked Sanjay.

"It's marvellous," said Windflower. "Sweet with a taste of honey. I thought it would taste more like Glenfiddich since they're from the same area."

"Different processes," said Sanjay as he took another sip. "It's got vanilla and some spice, too. Beautiful."

The two men sat in perfect silence and enjoyed the rest of their drink until they heard a voice calling to them.

"Dinner is ready," announced Repa. "Come while it's hot."

Windflower followed Sanjay into the dining room where Amelia Louise was sitting on a large pillow on a chair next to her mom, looking very pleased with herself.

Windflower didn't realize how hungry he was until he had sampled several plates of the cucumber salad with beetroot, radishes and lots of black pepper. He also had two portions of aloo posto, a potato dish that Amelia Louise liked so much she hardly threw any on the floor. That pleased her mother, too, who particularly enjoyed the dal that Repa had made.

"What's in this dal?" she asked as she poured another spoonful over her rice.

"It is a very simple dish," said Repa. "You can use any kind of lentils and add turmeric powder, dried red chillies, cloves, cinnamon and green cardamom if you can get it. I like to add some golden raisins and a little grated coconut."

"Simple, but delicious," pronounced Sanjay. "Try the fish," he urged Windflower.

Windflower didn't really need any encouragement. It was a fish curry with sliced mackerel in a ginger-red chilli sauce that was a little oily but soft and very pleasant on the palate. "Mmmmm," he said. "It's delicious. Does it have a special name?"

"The recipe calls for hilsa, or ilish, fish," said Repa. "But we have to make do with its poor cousin, mackerel."

"This might be the national dish of Bengal," said Sanjay. "But only with ilish fish, of course."

"I hope you have room for dessert," said Repa as she and Sheila cleared away the dishes from the table.

Windflower almost said no as he watched Sanjay play pat-a-cake with Amelia Louise but changed his mind when he saw what Repa brought out from the kitchen.

"What is that?" he asked.

"It's called mishti doi," said Repa as she handed everyone their own bowl of dessert. "It is really just sweetened yogurt prepared with caramelized sugar, warm milk and some plain yogurt. You mix it, bake it and chill it."

"Oh my God, this is so great," said Windflower as he tasted the milky goodness in his bowl.

"Ish grate," said Amelia Louise.

"The experts have spoken," said Sanjay as all the adults laughed.

Sheila helped Repa clean up while Windflower tried to prevent Amelia Louise from destroying the Sanjay house. Then they shared a cup of strong black tea with the Sanjays before Amelia Louise's restlessness moved them to take their leave. After many thank yous and grateful hugs, Windflower, Sheila and Amelia Louise were finally in the car for the short trip home.

"What a lovely evening," said Sheila. "Looks like our little rascal has completely tuckered herself out." She pointed to the back where Amelia Louise had slumped in her car seat and was solid as a log.

"Let's take a drive around town before we head back," said Windflower. "She's only going to wake up when we get home anyway."

"Excellent. Let's go to the wharf first."

Sheila loved going down by the wharf in Grand Bank. It had always been where the action was, from years ago when schooners carried goods from all over the world, to generation after generation unloading cod fish that was spread out in the summer sunshine to dry and then salted to feed the world. It was the place where locals gathered to talk about the weather, politics, sports and then the weather all over again.

Tonight, even as the day came to a close, a few men and boys lingered near the side of the harbour down by the bait shed and hung their fishing lines in hopes of catching whatever came closest. It was most likely to be conner or sculpin, but they all lived in hope that a random salmon would swim right onto their hook or spinner, and they could secrete it away and pray the fisheries officer wouldn't come around.

Some of the older buildings had sunk and collapsed in the face of salt, water, wind and neglect. But many of the others had been repaired and restored, giving people like Sheila and long-time residents hope that the memories they held could be maintained.

"I like that no matter what we do, the waterfront almost stays the same here," said Sheila. "Yes, we can and should do more to keep our properties up, but it is a sense of place rather than structures that we all relate to."

"I know what you mean," said Windflower. "When I come down with Lady in the mornings, it feels eternal, like it's always been here. And always will be."

"Let's hope so."

"You will miss it if we go to St. John's."

"I will, terribly. But it isn't going anywhere. I can always conjure it up in my mind, too."

"As I do with Pink Lake," said Windflower. "I close my eyes and feel myself walking in the bush. I can even smell the trees."

Sheila smiled and drove back through town, down to the beach and all the way to Fortune where they sat in the car and looked out over the Atlantic Ocean. Amelia Louise stirred but stayed asleep in her car seat.

"We may never get her down tonight," said Windflower.

"That's okay. Tomorrow's Saturday," said Sheila. "I'll have to go into the office for a bit, but not 'til later."

"I have to go in for the day tomorrow, too," said Windflower. "Smithson's gone, and there's just too much happening. And I'm hoping to see Tizzard. I'd like to ask him to come on as a special constable, and then we could see where it goes from there."

"That would change a lot for him and Carrie," said Sheila. She paused and looked intently at her husband. He knew she wasn't finished talking but needed time to gather her thoughts.

"Winston, maybe we should consider…"

Windflower's cell phone rang. "It's Uncle Frank," he said.

"Uncle Frank, how are you?"

"I'm calling to tell you that she has passed," said his uncle. "She is sleeping with her friends on the other side now."

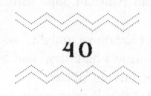

40

I'm so sorry for your loss, Uncle," said Windflower.

"I'm sorry for yours, too," said Uncle Frank. "You were her special nephew. Like the son we never had, she would say."

"I am putting you on speaker so that Sheila can hear as well."

"When will the ceremony be held?" asked Sheila.

"We will let her lay among us for four days as is our custom and her wish," said Uncle Frank. "If it is okay with you, we will have it on Wednesday afternoon."

"Should we come now to be with you?" asked Windflower.

"No, no," said Uncle Frank. "This part is for the community to visit with her. Come when you can to say your personal goodbyes, and then we will have the ceremony."

"Okay," said Windflower. "Call me if there's anything you need."

"I will be fine. Sad, but fine," said Uncle Frank. "People are already starting to bring food and gifts. She will be missed by many."

"I am sure," said Windflower. "I will miss her greatly."

"She may come to visit you before she leaves," said Uncle Frank. "And she will always be with us in spirit."

Windflower hung up. He and Sheila gazed out over the ocean again. The dark cloud cover gave way to light as the moon appeared, and the stars twinkled and shimmered on the water.

"Grandmother Moon is watching over us," said Windflower.

"I heard that she watches over the waters and the tides, and that she calls women to be the water keepers on the earth," said Sheila.

"You've been doing your research," said Windflower. "We are getting close to the full power of the Freezing Moon when the lakes and rivers start to freeze and close in for the winter. But not yet. This is still the Migrating Moon when the geese and other birds are flying south for the winter."

"Maybe Auntie Marie is watching over us, too."

"I think so. Let's go home."

The drive home was quiet, each lost in thought, until they reached their driveway. Then, Amelia Louise woke up, and all their attention turned to her and her needs until a couple of hours later when they finally got her to sleep.

"I'll make the travel plans tomorrow," said Sheila. "We'll travel on Tuesday probably. When do you want to come back?"

"Let's come back on Friday if we can, then we'll have the weekend to recover. You were going to tell me something before Uncle Frank's call. What was it?"

"Oh, we can talk about it later," said Sheila. "I'm bushed. Let's go to bed."

Windflower did not disagree. Not long after, both were snuggled tightly and fell asleep. His sleep was fitful, and he woke several times. He thought it might have been all the food he had eaten. He finally fell into a deep sleep, and though he 'woke' again, he was not disappointed. He was on the same side of the river as Auntie Marie, sitting next to her friends and allies.

"Welcome, Nephew," she said.

"I didn't think I was allowed over here," said Windflower.

"It's only while my time with my community lasts," said Auntie Marie. "I can go back and forth, and I'm allowed to invite guests."

"It's the spirit world protocol," said the beaver who was sitting next to Auntie Marie by the fire, sipping on a bowl of stew. "Ask me anything you want."

"He's a bit of a know-it-all," said his aunt. "But he is right. You can ask him or me any questions you might have while you're visiting."

"What's it like on the other side?" asked Windflower.

"Everything, except that," said the beaver, sounding exasperated. "Why do they always ask the same question? Instead of asking for something that might help them, the humans always ask for something that is beyond their capacity to understand." With that, the beaver threw down his bowl and slid into the water, his tail slapping as he swam out into the river and then disappeared from sight.

"He's right, you know," said Windflower's aunt. "You only

realize that when you get over here and start thinking you'd rather be back over there. It's too late, and we have to make the best of what we have. We can't just survive but must thrive and grow."

"How do I do that?" asked Windflower.

"Now you're getting wiser," said Auntie Marie. "First of all be grateful for what you have. Then, you might even get to keep it. That's particularly true of relationships. Pay attention to them, nurture them. Be grateful for them, and they will grow."

"Be grateful," said Windflower. "I will work on that."

"Next, be gentle."

"Do you mean be kind?"

"Yes but so much more than that. Be gentle and humble. Be like a blade of grass. It is strong because it can get stepped on, but as soon as the pressure is released, it pops back up. Nothing can keep it down."

"What else?" asked Windflower.

"Remember that all good things come from inside of you first. That's why you have to keep the channel to the earth, Creator and Grandmother Moon always open. That way the goodness of the universe can flow through you and out into the world. You can bring many blessings to your family and community just by looking after yourself."

Windflower had many more questions, but he could feel the dream world fading and Auntie Marie disappearing in the mist that arose from the river. He searched everywhere for her, but she was gone. When he finally stopped searching, he woke in his bed at home with Sheila.

He quietly got out of bed to look out the window. The fog had returned, hiding the moon he and Sheila and gazed up at earlier. Windflower felt sad but pleased that he'd had one more visit with Auntie Marie. Maybe he could ask Grandmother Moon for another visit on some other day, though he doubted that would be granted.

Windflower crawled back into bed, not thinking he would ever fall asleep, yet before he knew it, he was drifting off. And then, as if no time had passed at all, he felt Sheila stir to go get Amelia Louise. She was back soon after and dumped a laughing baby on top of his head. He laughed too and rolled over.

Several hours before Windflower and his family woke up, Eddie Tizzard had turned down Route 210, on his way to Grand Bank. He kept the windows rolled down, encouraging the cold air onto his face to help him stay alert while driving. It had been a long and tiring journey from Las Vegas. He had stopped in Goobies to fill up and get a snack and was now enjoying the open road along with his coffee and apple flip. They would help him stay alert, too.

Fifteen minutes later, on the far edge of Swift Current, he was surprised to see flashing lights and the southern side of the highway blocked with a lineup of cars proceeding through one at a time. Tizzard parked his vehicle on the far shoulder away from the road-block and walked up to the nearest Mountie. The officer started to yell at him to get off the road but then recognized him.

"Tizzard? What are you doing here?"

"Just on my way back home. What's all this about?"

"You don't know?" asked the Mountie incredulously.

Tizzard shook his head. The Mountie gave him a quick over-view of recent events, including the fact that Bill Ford had been shot.

"Bill Ford? Oh my God," said Tizzard. "How is he?"

"Looks like he's okay. But we're trying to find the guy who shot him and took Paul Spurrell."

"How did they take him?"

"Just grabbed him and put him in a vehicle. Ford tried to stop it all, and that's what got him shot. We're just finishing up with the scene now," said the cop.

"Wow," said Tizzard. "You go away for a few days and all this happens."

"I know it's crazy. We're looking for three bikers, one with a tattoo on his neck," said the cop.

"What kind of tattoo?" asked Tizzard.

"Some kind of snake. Why, you know him?"

"I just might. I just might. I'll touch base with Windflower or Quigley on that tomorrow or is that today. What time is it anyway?"

"It's late," said the Mountie.

Tizzard waved, and just before he headed on the last leg of his journey home, he sent a text to Windflower. "Will be home soon."

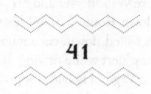

41

Windflower grabbed his cell from the night table, and instinctively looked to see if he had any messages. There was one from Eddie Tizzard. He had got in last night, late and tired, but glad to be home, finally.

"How about pancakes for breakfast this morning?" asked Sheila.

"I love pancakes," said Windflower.

"Pankies, pankies, pankies," said Amelia Louise.

"Why don't we invite Eddie for breakfast, too?" asked Windflower. "He's back home, and I'm sure he wouldn't mind something to eat, and then I can get him to drive me to work. Amelia Louise, do you want to see your Uncle Eddie?"

"Unca, unca, unca," said Amelia Louise.

"Sounds like we're having a guest for breakfast," said Sheila. "You get her cleaned up and call Eddie. I'll get breakfast going."

Windflower called Tizzard. He sounded a little sleepy but was surprisingly alert given his recent adventures.

"Good to hear you're back," said Windflower. "Sheila is doing up some pancakes. Want some?"

"You have to ask? I'll be over in a jiffy. But there's something I want to talk to you about. May be best to do it before I get there. It's kind of personal."

"Now's a good time," said Windflower, having a pretty good idea what was coming next and reminding himself he needed to sound surprised.

"Carrie is pregnant,"

"That's great," said Windflower, trying to sound as surprised as he possibly could. "Congratulations. When is she due?"

"It's early, so we're not telling a lot of people. But we agreed that you should know."

"I'm honoured. You must be excited."

"I can't even imagine it. Am I ready to be a father?"

"You're ready. You'll be a great dad."

"That's what my dad said when I called him this morning," said Tizzard. "He has other grandchildren from my sisters, but he said he couldn't wait to see me with a child of my own. He said something crazy, too, like, 'It is very simple to be happy, but it is very difficult to be simple.' What does that even mean?"

"That's Tagore. Something for you to meditate on as you await fatherhood, I guess."

"But now I have another person to think about besides me and Carrie. How do you manage that?"

"I'm probably not the best example to follow," said Windflower with a laugh. "Just ask Sheila."

"Sheila would say you're the best father she knows," said Tizzard. "That's what she told Carrie."

"It's hard, especially in this business. The job always demands that it come first. But sometimes you have to put them, your family, ahead of that."

"Thanks, Sarge. Now me and Carrie have to talk about my career, together."

"That's the only way," said Windflower. "You'll make the right decision for you and for them. And I may have something that might help with that decision."

Tizzard asked what that was about, but Windflower told him they could talk about it over breakfast. After he hung up, Amelia Louise started again with her 'unca, unca, unca' chant and continued while Windflower got her changed and brought her downstairs to see Sheila. The smell of the cooking pancakes was nearly driving him crazy when he saw Tizzard pulling up the driveway.

Amelia Louise ran to meet her 'unca' Tizzard as he came in the door, and he swung her over his head. She squealed with delight, and he then brought her to the table and put her in her high chair as Sheila served up blueberry pancakes and fruit. It didn't take long for everyone to dig in.

"These are sooooo good," said Tizzard.

"Soooooo good," repeated Amelia Louise.

"Be careful what you say," said Windflower. "She repeats every-thing."

"Ever ting," said Amelia Louise as she stuffed pancake in her mouth and scattered more on the floor for Lady and Molly to scrap over.

"Soon this will be your life," said Sheila.

"I'm looking forward to it but terrified at the same time," said Tizzard. "It feels like a great responsibility."

"It is, but there is so much joy to go along with that," said Windflower.

"Joy, joy, joy," sang Amelia Louise.

"You and Carrie should come over for dinner soon," said Sheila as she served up another plate of pancakes to Tizzard.

"Thank you, ma'am. That would be great. We could also babysit some night. Get some practice in," said Tizzard.

"Hey, we could have a date night," said Windflower. "Maybe go over to St. Pierre for dinner again."

"That would be nice," said Sheila. "Any more for you?" she asked Windflower.

"I'm stuffed," he said. "I've got to clean up, and I'll be ready to go. Eddie, can you drive me to the office?"

"Happy to be of service, sir," said Tizzard. "A few more days?" he asked, pointing at Windflower's ankle.

"I'm determined I'll be driving next week," said Windflower defiantly. "It'll be fine. Doctor said to stay off it for a week. So next week I'll be fine."

"Anyway, if you need a ride call anytime," said Tizzard. "I got nothing but time."

"I might be able to take care of that for you. We're really short-staffed right now and have a lot going on. How'd you like to come back as a special constable?"

"Really? I would absolutely like to. You can do that? When can I start?"

"Today, if you are up to it. Quigley has signed off for 30 days."

"Sweet," said Tizzard. "I get to wear my gun and everything. Right?"

"Everything but the uniform."

Tizzard stayed at the table while Windflower went upstairs to change. He helped Sheila clean up as Amelia Louise fed more of her pancakes to the cat and dog.

"I've been thinking about trying to get back on the Force," said Tizzard as he handed a dirty plate to Sheila. "This might be a way to do it."

"It might be, Eddie. It might be exactly what you and Carrie need right now."

When Windflower came down, he hugged Amelia Louise, kissed Sheila and followed Tizzard out to his car.

"Ready for work?" asked Windflower.

"More than ready," said Tizzard.

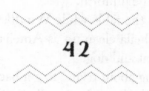

42

At the office, Betsy had already got the paperwork together so Tizzard could sign the release and confidentiality forms needed to start his job as a special constable. Once all the signatures were in place, Windflower called Ron Quigley, and Tizzard went out for his patrol on the highway.

"Morning, Sergeant," said Quigley. "I'm glad you called. We had a very successful raid in Winterland. We got two of the guys, Winstone and Raymond. But Fraser wasn't there. We think he's still around here, but now we have to try and shake loose information about where he is. Sooner or later he'll make a run for it."

"I'll get our people to go back to their contacts and see what we can find out. But good work on getting the other two. Any chance they'll talk?" asked Windflower.

"Probably not, although we'll squeeze them. They look like biker wannabes, and those guys see going to jail as a badge of honour. Forensics will have to go over the Winterland house. There's tons of stuff and a bit of an arsenal, too. I'd say we got in just ahead of a gang war."

"I know. That's crazy, isn't it? I'll let Brownie know you need him back there when I see him. He said he would drop by. Talk later."

Windflower made a note about the still missing biker and made a fresh pot of coffee. It looked like they would need lots of it today. He checked the board. Evanchuk was off, but Jones was due in soon. He would brief Jones and get her to start interviewing their informers and connections. She could also bring Evanchuk up to speed. It might be her day off, but she would want to be part of this.

When the coffee was ready, he poured a cup and went back to

his office. He took out the job notice for the public outreach coordinator and reviewed the information that Betsy had provided. He thought about it for a few minutes and then started drafting up a cover letter to apply for the position. He was nearing the end and hit save when he saw the white forensics van pull into the parking lot.

"Morning Ted," said Windflower.

"Hey, Sarge, how are you?" asked Brown.

"Couldn't be better," said Windflower. "You heading out?"

"Our work here is done."

"That's good because they need you in Winterland. Find anything more exciting?"

"I heard that they had another site on their radar. But they might be interested in this, too." He held up a green garbage bag and opened it for Windflower to look inside.

"Holy moly," said Windflower. The bag was full of money, almost all of it American in twenties, fifties and hundreds. "Must be thousands of dollars here."

"There's ten more bags like this," said Brown. "Drug money, I'd say."

"So, someone down here was laundering this money for them?" asked Windflower.

"Looks like it. But not my area of expertise."

"You know Paul Spurrell and his brothers were heavy in the meth operations. Maybe this was part of the services they provided."

"Isn't that the guy who got shot?"

Windflower nodded. "And maybe this is part of the reason why," he said.

"Always follow the money," said Brown. "Anyway, I got to drop off all of this to Marystown where commercial crime will be picking it up. And then we'll head out to Winterland."

"Safe journeys."

"Thanks. See ya."

Windflower watched the forensics van leave the parking lot and went back to his computer. He noticed the saved document on the screen, looked up the address for applications, entered it and paused for just one second. Then he hit send.

Probably just a waste of time, he thought. Might not even hear back. He closed his computer and was walking back for another cup of coffee when Jones arrived.

He briefed Jones, and she promised to let Evanchuk know what was up with the last missing biker. He could hear her on the phone making contact with some of the locals when Tizzard arrived.

"We've got the other two bikers but not the snake man," said Windflower. He filled him in on what Quigley had told him.

"A snake tattoo?" said Tizzard. "I know a guy with a snake tattoo. I pulled him over one night this spring. He was part of the crew that came down for the tour. I think he was an Angel, a real one. His name was Fraser, Billy Fraser. I think his nickname was Wild Bill. Didn't charge him with anything. He hadn't done much wrong. I just wanted to check him out. But I remember the snake tattoo. Pretty hard to forget."

"Billy Fraser, that's our man. That's the name of the guy we're looking for," said Windflower.

"It's good to get Winstone and Raymond, but Fraser is the big boy around here. I think he's one of the few full-patch Angels in the area," said Tizzard. "He'd be the one calling the shots."

Tizzard got himself a cup of coffee and was scouring the fridge for a snack.

"Good to see you're doing an honest day's work for a change," said Jones as she came into the lunchroom. "You won't find anything in there. We're all fruits and veggies since you left."

"You know 'an onion can make people cry, but I've never heard of a vegetable that can make people laugh,'" said Tizzard.

"Is that one of your dad's sayings?" asked Windflower.

"Will Rogers," said Tizzard. "Anyway, it'll soon be time for pea soup and por' cakes, unless they're outlawed, too."

"They couldn't do that. It's a Grand Bank tradition," said Windflower. "What would Saturday morning be without pea soup and por' cakes?"

"You know what, I've never had por' cakes," said Jones.

Both men looked shocked. Tizzard was speechless. "How could you never have tried por' cakes?" asked Windflower.

"I guess they never really appealed to me, all that fat and pork," said Jones.

"Well, I'm sure they're not the healthiest thing in the world, but they really are sum good b'y," said Windflower.

"You have to try them at least once," said Tizzard.

"What's in them?" asked Jones cautiously.

"They're really just a fat little potato pancake baked in the oven," said Windflower. "There's minced pork, pork back fat and potatoes along with some baking powder and flour to bind everything together. You eat one or two, dipping them in molasses."

"That sounds pretty good, and I like pea soup," said Jones.

On the way to the Mug-Up with Jones, Windflower called Quigley to let him know about the money that forensics had found at the L'Anse au Loup house.

"Interesting," said Quigley. "We found a bit of cash at the Marystown location but nothing like that. We did find money-sorting machines and counters, though. Commercial is already on the case. A meth lab, a biker war and now a money-laundering ring. All right under our nose."

"We don't have the kind of resources to detect that, let alone prevent it," said Windflower.

"I think that's exactly the point. A low police presence, people who don't ask questions or snoop around and a handful of local collaborators—it's a perfect storm," said Quigley. "Did you get Eddie Tizzard settled in?"

"I sure did. We're off for pea soup and por' cakes."

"That makes sense. Enjoy and we'll talk later."

Tizzard was waiting for them outside the Mug-Up. "Ready?" he asked.

"Ready," said Windflower. He got out of the car and noticed that the wind had picked up. Not a little, quite a lot. He pulled his collar up and walked into the café. It was full and warm and lively, and the three officers found one of the few remaining tables.

"Did you hear about the hurricane?" asked Jones.

"What hurricane?" asked Windflower.

"There's a big one coming up the coast," said Tizzard. "It's all over the news. Got all the reports as I was driving to Grand Bank. Just so glad I got here before it hits."

"I guess I've been busy," said Windflower. "Order me a coffee and the usual. I should phone Sheila."

"Did you hear about the hurricane?" he asked Sheila.

"Yes, that's why I'm going in today. We're finalizing our emergency plan. Several of the projections have the storm coming right by the east coast, although it could still blow out to sea," said Sheila.

"When is it supposed to come?"

"As early as tomorrow night. How is your ankle doing today?"

"Almost as good as new."

"Good. You can barbeque tonight. I'll pop by Warrens and see what they have."

"Great," said Windflower. "Whatever you get, put that new Cajun rub on it."

"Planning dinner already? That's the right idea," said Tizzard as Windflower hung up. "But first we have the traditional Grand Bank lunch."

All three Mounties dug into their pea soup and nicely browned por' cakes. Jones dipped hers in the molasses and called it delicious. The men nodded and kept eating. When they were nearly done, Herb Stoodley came by to say hello.

"Hello Eddie," said Stoodley. "Good to have you back."

"It's really good to be back," said Tizzard.

"Did you learn about being a private investigator while you were in Las Vegas?" asked Herb.

"Lots and more than I cared to. I also learned a lot about myself."

"What do you mean?" asked Stoodley.

"I don't think being a private investigator is right for me. It feels like being in between the crooks and the law. I'd rather be on the right side of that equation."

Tizzard had his first por' cake eaten and was well on his way into the second before he continued.

"I'm a special constable right now. Just got brought on for 30 days, and I'm going to ask about being reinstated."

"Great," Stoodley said. "It's what you know and what you're good at. 'To thine own self be true.'"

"Hey, even I know that's Hamlet," said Tizzard. "'This above all: to thine own self be true. And it must follow, as the night the day.' That's what my dad says all the time."

"I guess you heard about the storm," said Stoodley to no one in particular.

Windflower nodded. "Sheila said they're getting ready at the town office. We better get moving on our own plan when we get back," he said to Jones and Tizzard.

"Well, it might just be a big blow," said Stoodley. "We seldom get hurricanes around here, although everybody is talking about Igor again."

"I remember Igor," said Tizzard. "We were still over on Ramea, and everything that wasn't tied down or anchored up got blown away."

"That must have been crazy on that little island. It was bad enough here for people to be really scared," said Stoodley. "They said that Igor was the worst tropical storm to hit Newfoundland in 75 years. We had winds near 130 kilometres an hour here, and there were reports of up to 150 kilometres down in St. Lawrence."

"I remember seeing it on the news," said Windflower. "The road was washed out, wasn't it?"

"We were cut off down here," said Stoodley. "Nobody could get in or out, and our power was gone for days. There are reminders of the damage everywhere on the peninsula. We can only hope that this one gives us a pass."

"Agreed," said Windflower. "We have enough on our hands."

"We sure do. And we need more fortification," said Tizzard as he got up to check out the cheesecake offerings for the day.

"He moves fast," quipped Windflower. "Always has."

Tizzard came back with the cheesecake list for the day—twelve items today plus two specialty cupcakes, caramel and apple-spiced.

"I'm having the coconut cream cheesecake," Tizzard announced. Windflower could not resist and ordered the same, while Jones decided on the chocolate peanut butter. They sat in silence, savouring every moment in cheesecake heaven as though it were the calm before a vicious storm.

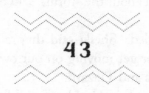

43

The police officers paid their bills and went back to the RCMP office. They were joined by Evanchuk, who had come in after hearing from Jones. She, Jones and Tizzard fanned out across the community to see if they could get any news about the biker with the snake on his neck.

While they were gone, Windflower pulled out the manual and reviewed the procedures for dealing with a storm. He asked Betsy to get the people and paperwork organized, and he contacted the person coordinating the storm watch in Marystown. Then, like the rest of the people in Grand Bank and the whole province, he watched the Canadian Hurricane Centre reports and waited.

Betsy was busy putting together new shift schedules and printing off copies of procedures for everybody when Evanchuk called Windflower.

"I think I might have something," she said. "I'm bringing Leo Grandy in again. He heard something about a helicopter."

"Okay. See you soon," said Windflower.

Ten minutes later, Leo Grandy was led in by Evanchuk, once again with a hoodie over his head.

"I hear you've got something to tell us," said Windflower.

"I don't know much, but people are talking about Fraser," said Grandy. "They said he was looking for a helicopter to get him out of here. I think it's baloney, just another story because people likes to talk."

"Who's saying all this?" asked Windflower.

"Dunno," said Grandy. "Just people. Like I told her, it might be nuttin'. But it'd be better for me and a whole lotta people if he wasn't around here anymore, one way or another."

"Thank you," said Windflower. "Give him a ride wherever he

wants to go," he said to Evanchuk.

She took him back out to her cruiser while Windflower sat in his chair, pondering what he had just heard. Better safe than sorry, he thought as he picked up the phone and called Quigley.

"A helicopter. How would he get one?" asked Quigley.

"Same as you or me. Rent one."

"I guess so. I'll get someone to start checking helicopter rentals in St. John's and Gander. It should be easy enough to find out whether someone has booked one to come here."

"They'll have to come before the storm, too," said Windflower. "No helicopters in a hurricane."

"So that would make their window from now until late tomorrow," said Quigley. "Narrows down the search even further. I'll let you know if we find anything."

The next couple of hours passed quickly, and Windflower got Tizzard to drive him home around five o'clock. Evanchuk would be staying on the overnight shift, and Jones would come in on relief in the morning. They all knew the storm protocols and would monitor the hurricane reports. If anything developed, they would call Windflower.

"How was your first day back?" asked Windflower as Tizzard pulled into his driveway.

"I kinda feel like I haven't been gone at all, yet in other ways it seems forever," said Tizzard.

"Forever is a long time. Enjoy today, or at least what's left of it tonight."

"I will. I'm going over to my dad's for fish stew, and I'll bring a bowl over to Carrie for her dinner. Got to make sure she gets good food for the baby."

"Good work today. Thanks, Eddie."

Sheila was out when Windflower arrived, along with Amelia Louise and Lady. But she had left two beautiful T-bone steaks on the counter covered in a dusting of the Cajun spice that Windflower had got from Herb Stoodley. He loved that spice combination of black and cayenne peppers along with garlic, oregano, thyme and red pepper flakes. It really brought out the flavour of red meat.

Sheila had also chopped up a bowl of vegetables, and they were sitting in a bowl alongside the meat. There were onions, tomatoes, cucumber, zucchini and mushrooms. He would add a little olive oil and seasonings and mix them all together before grilling them with the steak on the barbeque. Perfect, he thought. He also remembered to grab three potatoes out of the cupboard. He scrubbed and cleaned them and went outside to start the barbeque. When it was going, he put the potatoes inside and closed the cover.

He played for a minute with Molly, who was clearly feeling left out, before going upstairs to change. He heard Amelia Louise first. She was singing some nonsense song that made perfectly good sense to her, and Sheila was simply trying to get everybody in and their feet cleaned before they tracked their accumulated dirt all over the house. She had succeeded, mostly, Windflower observed when he came downstairs.

"The steaks look great," he said as Amelia Louise came over to be picked up, a feat he managed with his good arm.

"You can't beat Warrens for meat," said Sheila.

"Let me get set up, and I'll bring her outside with me," said Windflower. Windflower brought the steaks out to the barbeque and came back seconds later to put the vegetables in a grilling pan. Taking one more trip outside, he put the veggies and the steak on the grill and closed the cover.

"Won't be long," he said as he came back in. Then, looking at his little girl, he said, "Okay", and Amelia Louise gleefully grabbed onto her daddy's pant leg as they hobbled together to go outside, followed closely by Lady and Molly. Amelia Louise was soon running around the back chased by Lady, while Molly set up shop near Windflower to observe. After a few minutes Windflower stirred the vegetables, which were starting to cook, and turned the steak, which was nicely grilled on one side. He was aiming for medium rare and so needed to barbeque each side for three to four minutes. He had learned not to turn the meat too often, so he spun the vegetables around again and joined in Amelia Louise's backyard game.

He went back to stir the vegetables one more time and tested the steak. Perfect, he said to himself and turned off the grill. He transferred the steak to a plate and covered it with foil to allow the juices to settle and the meat to tenderize itself while he brought Amelia Louise and the charred veggies inside.

A few minutes later he joined Sheila at the table and oohed

and aahed about the steak. Amelia Louise was doing the same, but Windflower was lost in the flavour of the meat for a few minutes after he took his first couple of bites from his perfect steak. Sheila had cut open the potatoes and smeared them with butter and sour cream, and Windflower mixed some of his with another bite of steak.

"This is sum good b'y," he said.

"Sum good," repeated Amelia Louise.

Windflower's ankle felt strong enough for him to help Sheila clean up. While Sheila extracted Amelia Louise from her potato and veggie-stained high chair, a few pieces fell to the floor for Lady and Molly to scramble after. Windflower even put a bit of meat in Lady's bowl, which Molly fought over as well, even though she didn't even like it. But if the dog had it, she wanted it, too.

Sheila made them strawberries and ice cream for dessert.

"Bath time," she said shortly afterward.

Amelia Louise's eyes lit up. "Baff time, baff time," she said and started dancing around the room. Soon everyone else, including Lady, was dancing beside her. Windflower was more hopping than dancing but surprised himself and Sheila with how well he did. Molly was definitely not dancing. Her look said it all: How incredibly stupid these humans are! She sighed and slunk back to the peace of her bed in the kitchen.

The humans and collie continued their dancing for as long as Amelia Louise would lead them. When she finally sank to the ground, Sheila picked her up and carried her upstairs. Sheila looked after the bath and handed a clean little girl over to her daddy for her bedtime story.

Tonight it was Use Your Words, Sophie, a story about a two-year-old mouse who knows lots of words but doesn't always use them. She thinks it's much more fun to speak like a jellyfish or a hyena, but nobody can understand her. Then, she has a baby sister who her mommy and daddy can't get to stop crying. But Sophie can. Amelia Louise loved the book, and Windflower had to read it three times before she would finally let him go. He kissed her goodnight and went back downstairs.

"She loves that book," said Windflower. "Maybe it's because Sophie has a baby sister."

"Maybe our daughter wants a sister," said Sheila.

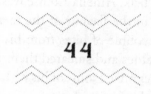

44

"Wow, a few minutes to ourselves," said Sheila, and she brought a pot of tea into the living room.

"Did you get a chance to make our travel arrangements?" asked Windflower.

"All booked for Tuesday afternoon, coming back to St. John's on Friday," said Sheila. "As long as the weather cooperates, we should be back to Grand Bank by lunchtime."

"Great," said Windflower. "You know my ankle is getting better."

"I can see," said Sheila as she poured them both a cup of tea.

"I think I'll try a short walk with Lady in the morning. See how it goes."

"That sounds like a plan. It will be good to have you back in full operation, although I'm kinda getting the hang of this mother thing. Finally," Sheila said with a laugh.

"You are very good," said Windflower. "You were great from the start."

"Thank you, Winston. I've been thinking a lot about what a gift it is to be a mother. Children bring so much joy into your life. Then I think about little Stella Fitzgerald and how little love she has had."

"It is sad. She never had much and now she has nothing."

Sheila paused and Windflower looked over at her. "What are you thinking?" he asked. "I know that look."

Sheila laughed again. "You know me too well, Sergeant. I have been thinking that we should take Stella as foster parents."

She looked at Windflower and could see that it was his turn to pause. "I can tell when you are working things out in your head," she said. "Weighing the pros and cons. Very male and RCMP of you."

"Fair enough," said Windflower. "But I actually like the idea. We can try it out and see how it goes. But really I was thinking about how it would work if we moved to St. John's."

"You applied for the job?" asked Sheila. Windflower nodded. "That doesn't change anything," said Sheila. "I'll be in university, and we can get childcare for Amelia Louise. Stella will be in kindergarten. So it will all work out."

"Let's wait until we get back from Alberta, and then we can talk to the woman in Marystown, Noreen Corrigan. There's probably an application process to go through, but we can start and see where it goes."

"This feels so right. I'm glad you like the idea."

"I think I had it first."

"Did not," said Sheila with fake outrage as she threw a pillow at Windflower's head. He was about to throw it back when his cell phone rang. "It's Quigley," he said to Sheila.

"We've got a lead on a helicopter booked in St. John's," said Quigley. "Booked for a geologist under the name Winstone."

"That's one of the local bikers," said Windflower.

"Yeah," said Quigley. "Your boy Smithson found it and has confirmed a 2 p.m. pickup tomorrow at the wharf in Fortune. We're just setting it up now, but it looks like we'll replace the helicopter pilot with an RCMP guy."

"Good plan," said Windflower. "What do you want from us?"

"We'll surround the dock area in Fortune and protect the highway towards St. Lawrence if you look after the road from Grand Bank to Marystown. Fraser is very likely armed, so get ready."

"Got it. Oh, anything else on the storm?"

"Still blowing our way. Will likely start tomorrow night. Some projections have it moving further out. Let's hope so."

"Indeed."

"What's up?" asked Sheila as Windflower hung up. "Did I hear you talking about the storm?"

"May still hit us is the latest word," said Windflower, a little preoccupied with the other news that Quigley had provided. "I have to make a couple of calls. Why don't you find us something good on Netflix, and I'll make some popcorn?"

Windflower went to the kitchen and called Tizzard and asked him to spread the word that everyone needed to be at the RCMP detachment by 10:30 a.m. for a special assignment. He didn't tell him exactly what. There was no need to burden them, or Sheila, with that news.

He made the popcorn in the microwave and melted butter to go over it. Sheila had found them a movie and it was just starting. It was the Mister Rogers movie, A Beautiful Day in the Neighbourhood. It told the story of a magazine writer who had turned bitter and cynical. He interviewed Fred Rogers as part of an assignment and somehow is transformed by the kindness and empathy shown by Mister Rogers. It starred Tom Hanks who turned in a marvellous and moving performance as Fred Rogers.

"That was much better than I thought it would be," said Windflower as the movie ended. "I never realized that Mister Rogers was so wise."

"I know," said Sheila. "I love the line about 'anyone who does anything to help a child in his life is a hero.'"

"I guess that's why he was so good with kids," said Windflower. "I'll turn everything off. I'll be up in a minute." Sheila came and gave him a kiss before she went upstairs.

Windflower turned off all the lights and sat in the dark for a few minutes before heading up to bed. He liked sitting in his house in the dark sometimes. It was a good place to think, and he had a lot to think about.

He went upstairs and checked on Amelia Louise who was sleeping like an angel and then went into bed with Sheila. They were both tired and happy and fell quickly to sleep in each other's arms.

Windflower woke in the dream world not long after. It was a familiar setting, but this time it was dusk, and the sun was starting to fall into a brilliant red sky.

"Welcome," said a familiar voice.

"Hello, Beaver," said Windflower, perfectly comfortable talking to this creature who had become a regular in his dreams. He looked across the river where there was a fire and several figures sitting around it. "What's going on?"

"It's the welcoming feast for your aunt," said the beaver. "All her ancestors are there or coming soon. Do you want to see?"

"Yes," said Windflower.

The beaver slapped his tail and did a kind of yelp. Windflower waited to see what would happen. Then, with a flash and a whoosh, an eagle landed on the ground in front of him and hopped towards him.

"Look," said the eagle, and he spread his wings as widely as he could. Windflower was surprised when the whole landscape shifted. Suddenly he could see the world around him like a wide-screen TV that he could manipulate somehow just by willing it. He tried to see across the river again, and now the people came into focus. There was his Auntie Marie with a buffalo robe around her shoulders. She was in animated discussions with several others, and as he focused in, he could see that it was his mother and father. He also recognized a man in an eagle headdress. It was his grandfather. All of them were listening to Auntie Marie as she talked to them, as if she hadn't seen them in a long time. Her relatives paid rapt attention, and their faces glowed in the firelight as the sun started to fade even more. Windflower would have loved to have joined that circle, but as he drew closer, the images faded to black. He woke again, this time back in bed with Sheila. He snuggled in closer and fell back to sleep.

Windflower woke early, just as the sun was peeking into the windows of his bedroom. He slipped downstairs, took Lady and her leash and his smudging materials and went to Sheila's car, leaving his crutches behind. He wasn't sure if he should be driving quite yet, but he was going to test things out. Lady had no qualms about joining him in this adventure and happily jumped into the back seat.

He drove down by the wharf and took a look at the harbour. It was quiet, eerily so. There were no creatures moving, not even the gulls. Even the ocean was quiet. As flat as a pancake, thought Windflower. No waves, not even a ripple. He had seen this once before, just before the last big storm that had hit Grand Bank. It was like the ocean was saving up its energy so that it could throw everything it had at the earth once the wind gave its direction.

"Not a good sign," he said to no one but himself, and he checked the latest news on his phone. The hurricane was scheduled to hit the Florida Keys soon and then move up the coast. There was no word about whether it would make it to Newfoundland intact, but all agencies were reportedly on high alert.

Windflower drove through town and down to the beach where he let Lady out of the car. She ran to check out the sights and smells near the water while Windflower walked slowly and carefully behind her. He stopped and sat on a large boulder just out of sight of the road and unfurled his smudging kit. There was no problem lighting his medicines this morning. There was not a breath of wind, and the water below was like a tranquil lake in summer, not the Atlantic Ocean.

He raised the smoke over his head and body and under the soles of his feet. He prayed as he smudged for his heart to be cleansed and his path to be pure. He gave thanks for all his friends, family, allies and fellow travellers. Then, he prayed again for his Auntie Marie and Uncle Frank, that each be given what they needed on the next part of their journeys in this world and the next. By the time he had finished his prayers, Lady was back, and he spent a few more minutes on the beach walking alongside her before heading back to the car and home.

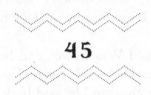

45

When he got home, Sheila had made coffee and was upstairs with Amelia Louise. He called out his hellos and offered to make breakfast.

"That would be great," he called back to Sheila.

"Gwate, gwate," yelled Amelia Louise as loudly as she could.

Windflower laughed as he got eggs and milk from the fridge along with a stick of bologna and a large melon. He cracked the eggs, added a little milk and whipped them for a minute to fluff them up. Then, he sliced off a few chunks of bologna and put them in a frying pan. When the bologna was done, he stirred the eggs into the pan. He sliced up the melon and put on toast while the eggs were cooking. One more stir of the eggs and two more slices of toast, and he was done.

"Breakfast is ready," he called.

"Coming," said Sheila.

"Cumming, cumming," echoed Amelia Louise as she tried to race her mother down the stairs, tumbling over at the bottom. Instead of getting up crying she was laughing as Windflower went to grab her and put her in her high chair.

Sheila set the table and cut up some fruit on a plate with some eggs for Amelia Louise. Windflower served the adults their eggs and bologna and handed around toast to everybody. He cut a small piece of bologna and mixed it into Lady's bowl and gave Molly a similar size piece of toast. Both animals were very happy with their selections as were all the humans. It was an almost perfect family moment for the Windflower household. The only downside was that it wouldn't last. As he was finishing off his eggs, Windflower could see Eddie Tizzard's car pull up outside.

"Good luck today," said Sheila. "I don't know exactly what's going on, but I know it's serious by the look on your face. Promise me you'll be careful."

"I'll be careful," said Windflower, and he held her especially tight as he hugged her. He kissed Amelia Louise who was already waving him bye-bye. "Bye-bye," he said back, and he quickly left the house.

In the car Tizzard was his usual bubbly self, but Windflower knew that Sheila was right to be worried. This would be a serious day. He took a deep breath and said a silent prayer that all of them would be okay. He wasn't afraid, but there were many things that could go wrong when you were dealing with dangerous or desperate people. And Wild Bill Fraser was both.

When they got to the office, everyone else was already there. Betsy was working on the emergency plan for the storm and had her work station all set up as a communications centre in preparation for the worst. Jones and Evanchuk were sitting in the back having coffee, and Tizzard and Windflower went to join them.

"Morning, everybody," said Windflower. "Let's get Inspector Quigley on the phone so we can get our detail for today." He punched in Quigley's number, and when the inspector came on, Windflower put him on speaker.

"We're setting up in Fortune right now," said Quigley. "We've taken over the Border Agency's Customs shed and are running our HQ out of there. All of our team except Smithson will be in place by noon, and no one should come near the wharf area after that time. No marked vehicles and no uniforms. Reid will be flying the helicopter in at about 13:00 hours. Smithson will track him on GPS and keep us posted. Grand Bank is responsible for monitoring the highway in case Fraser slips through, but we fully expect to be able to contain him in Fortune. Once everyone is in position, we will switch all communication to our secure line number one. Don't use any other lines because they could be monitored. Everything okay over there, Sergeant?"

"We're on it, Inspector," said Windflower. "Evanchuk will take the route out of Fortune towards St. Lawrence. Jones and I will be between Fortune and Frenchman's Cove. And Tizzard will take the highway past there. That should give us full coverage."

"Okay. Get in position for 13:30. We don't want to show up too early in case they have someone watching the highway," said Quigley. "This is a fully armed operation. Check your personal weapons before we start out, and Sergeant Windflower will distribute the long guns. Nobody leaves the station without a vest. This is an armed and dangerous criminal. Use caution and be careful. The plan is to take him down in Fortune and have none of you get to see him or anybody that might be with him. But you need to be ready and alert in case it doesn't go down that way."

After Quigley was gone, the mood in the lunchroom darkened considerably. It lightened a little when Betsy came in to tell them that the hurricane had been downgraded to a category two. But all of the officers knew their very own storm was like the one brewing in the Atlantic. Both were a challenge and posed great risks to everyone in their paths.

The rest of the morning passed quietly and quickly, and just before noon Windflower handed out the long guns and checked that all officers were wearing their protective vests. He had been monitoring the secure line and knew that Quigley and the Marystown crew were in position and waiting in Fortune. He also heard that the helicopter was en route from St. John's with touchdown estimated at 13:00 in Fortune. When he got confirmation of the landing, he called everyone together in the lunchroom.

"You know your job. Stay with it, and try to be as casual looking as you can. You never know who's watching you," he said. "Most of all, be careful. Don't take any chances. If there's a problem or anything unusual, call in to the secure line. Otherwise we'll see you back here later this afternoon. Good luck."

Windflower watched Tizzard and Evanchuk walk out together, and just before Evanchuk got into her car, Tizzard grabbed her and hugged her. They held each other for a moment, and then they were gone. Windflower took one more look out the window and then up into the sky when he got outside to get into Jones's vehicle. It was growing darker, and the wind was picking up just a little. It was a soft, mild wind blowing from the south. But Windflower knew that didn't mean it wasn't dangerous.

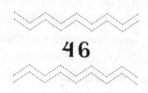

46

The Grand Bank crew were all in position by 13:20 and were waiting for direction from Quigley. There was little chatter on the secure communications line until just before 14:00 hours. Then it seemed like all hell broke loose.

"We've got word that there's been a change in plans," said Quigley. "The pickup location has been changed. It's no longer at the Fortune wharf. Maybe it was never intended to be. Too open and easy for us to control. All we have right now are coordinates. Smithson is mapping them out."

After a few moments Quigley continued, "It's for somewhere out on the highway near Garnish. Anybody know what's out there?"

"It's an abandoned garage," said Tizzard over the radio. "I know where it is. I'm the closest."

Windflower almost said something to Tizzard about not going when he heard Quigley respond.

"Okay, we're going to send the helicopter over there. Tizzard, you are the nearest one to the site. Go there and wait for us. Do not engage," said Quigley. "Everybody else follow Sergeant Wind-flower's lead behind Tizzard and let's go."

Tizzard was at the site first, and he parked his car well back from the crumbling parking lot that looked like it might be the landing spot for the copter. He could hear it in the air as he moved his car as close to the bush as possible. Luckily, he was driving his personal car today. He still didn't have approval for an RCMP vehicle. That meant he could blend in a little more with the surroundings. He took his rifle out from the trunk and crouched in the ditch, waiting.

The helicopter was getting closer, and he could almost feel it as it started to come down near him. He was trying to stay as quiet as he could when another vehicle, a large pickup truck came roaring out of the Garnish side road and stopped just in front of him. A large bearded man ran out and started to run towards the landing helicopter. On instinct Tizzard rose, pointed his gun and yelled at the man to stop.

The man turned, and Tizzard could see his snake tattoo visible above his tee shirt. It was Fraser. Fraser glanced his way and started to reach inside his jacket. Tizzard dropped to his knees in an instant, aimed and fired three shots in succession. The first hit Fraser in the chest and he stumbled. The second missed, but the third caught him in the shoulder, and he slumped to the ground. Tizzard stayed where he was, frozen to the spot as the pickup sped away.

Fraser lay moaning on the ground and was still there when the helicopter landed. Tizzard gave the pilot a wave to stay back and continued to stay trained on Fraser as the line of cars led by Windflower came over the hill and into sight. Soon, the whole area was surrounded by RCMP officers, and two of them secured Fraser while another called for an ambulance.

"Good work," said Quigley as he arrived and surveyed the situation. "We've got the pickup truck already. Two more local bikers to add to our collection." Then looking straight at Tizzard he said, "But I did tell you not to engage."

"It was almost like I didn't have a choice," said Tizzard. "I saw him running and the helicopter coming. I just couldn't let him get away."

"Take him home," Quigley said to Windflower. "We'll look after all this."

"Come on," said Windflower. He wrapped his arm around Tizzard and led him back to his car. "I'm driving," he said as he took the keys from the younger officer. Before they could leave, Evanchuk came running up to their car. She grabbed Tizzard and hugged him and started crying. Windflower almost did, too.

"Let's go back to Grand Bank," he said as soon as Evanchuk released her grip.

Windflower could feel the wind whipping up a bit more now as he walked back into the RCMP office. The sky had gone a couple of shades darker with gloomy clouds filling the horizon. It felt like the storm had been brewing for quite a while and sooner, rather than later, it was going to blow.

Inside the detachment was a completely different story. It was calm and eerily serene. Windflower sent Evanchuk home and got Jones to check on her. He stayed with Tizzard while they awaited the investigators who would be coming from Marystown to talk to him about the shooting. Every time an officer discharged their weapon, there were reports to be filed, and when they shot someone, there was an internal investigation as soon as possible.

Windflower wasn't worried about the investigation, and he tried to reassure Tizzard that things would be okay.

"I've never shot anybody before," said Tizzard. "Even when that guy shot me out on the west coast, it was my partner who hit him. I've drawn my weapon many times, but this is the first time I shot anybody."

"You did what you had to do," said Windflower.

"I thought he was reaching for his gun," said Tizzard. "I only had my rifle out to scare him. It always worked before."

"Not this time, not with this guy. They have a different code, a different set of rules than we do, Eddie."

"But I could have killed him. I was aiming for his chest. And I know he's a scumbag outlaw biker, but I wouldn't want somebody else's life on my hands."

Windflower could see his friend was really upset. But who could blame him? Even though they carried around a gun every day, none of them really expected to have to use it. It was a deterrent. Just not in this case.

"It's part of the job, Eddie," said Windflower. "I've never shot anybody before either. And I hope I never have to. But I also hope that if that day comes, I can be as calm and as brave as you were. I'm proud of you."

"Thanks, Sarge, that means a lot," said Tizzard. "Do you think it'd be okay if I go get us a snack while we're waiting for the investigators? I'm starved."

"Absolutely," said Windflower, relieved that his young friend was going to be okay. "Why don't you make us a plate of cheese and crackers. I have to make a few phone calls."

"Coming right up, sir."

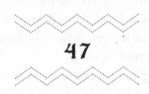

47

Windflower's first call was to Sheila.

"I heard you got the guy," said Sheila. "What was all the commotion about down at the wharf in Fortune?"

Windflower ran through the recent events, leaving out the part about Tizzard shooting the biker. No point in getting her too upset, and besides there was an investigation underway. He promised to come home as soon as he could. Sheila was going over to the women's committee event at the church and would pick up cold plates for their Sunday dinner.

His next call was to Inspector Ron Quigley.

"Everything okay over there?" asked Windflower.

"Good," said Quigley. "Fraser is likely going to live. Looks like most of the damage is in his shoulders. Very painful but not life-threatening. How is Tizzard?"

"He's shook up, but he'll be fine. He's young and pretty resilient. Have you ever shot anybody, Ron?"

"I have. Once I shot someone who was trying to shoot his way out of a bank robbery in Vancouver. There were three of us, and we all shot, but I think I got him in the leg. We kept yelling at him to stop, but he pulled out his gun. Sometimes I wonder if he wanted us to shoot him."

"How'd you feel about it after?"

"You know, it was a clean shoot, and we did what we had to do, but I didn't sleep for weeks. I think every police officer who shoots somebody has that reaction. And if they don't, they should. Or they shouldn't be police officers. Anyway, the special investigations crew are on their way over to interview Tizzard. And did you hear? The storm's been downgraded. It's still big, but now it's a tropical storm and not a hurricane. Might even slip past us."

"That is good to hear," said Windflower. "I don't think we could handle a full-on hurricane right now." He meant the region, but he knew it applied to his staff as well.

Betsy came in to give him the same storm report shortly afterward, and he pretended he hadn't heard so that she could feel like she was giving him some real news.

"That's great, Betsy. I think we can stand down from the storm watch now, and you can go home and have a nice Sunday dinner."

"You, too, Sergeant," said Betsy, looking like she felt pretty pleased about her role in averting disaster from the now weakening storm. The rain started hitting his office window shortly after she left for the night, and by the time the SI guys arrived, it was a deluge. Tizzard came out to give Windflower his snack and went to the back to talk to the investigators.

Windflower stayed in his office for the 45 minutes they spent interviewing Tizzard, and as they left, he called Tizzard to drive him home. Neither was in a very talkative mood on the drive.

"Have a good night, Eddie," said Windflower as they arrived at his home.

"Good night, Sarge."

As best he could, Windflower dodged the torrential rains and pushed his way through the pulsating wind until he reached the door. He waved goodnight to Tizzard and was very happy to enter his safe and happy home.

That evening and night were quiet with dinner consisting of the traditional cold plate of sliced meats and three scoops of various salads. The best part for Windflower was always the homemade Parker House rolls that came with it. There was usually some kind of trifle or custard for dessert, but Sheila had decided to get them a small cake instead.

"Is it somebody's birthday and I forgot?" asked Windflower.

"No, it's just that I thought we needed a little lift," said Sheila. "We have a lot to celebrate."

"We do indeed," said Windflower. "Let's have some cake."

Amelia Louise heartily agreed, and soon there was cake all over her hands, face and high chair and scattered crumbs and bits of icing beneath her. Lady and Molly helped lick the floor clean as best they could, but Windflower got the mop out and gave the floor a wipe as Sheila extracted their daughter from the mess.

After Sheila gave her a bath, it was Windflower's turn to read the bedtime story. Tonight, he chose Just for Me. It was about Ruby, a little girl who has to learn to share. It had lots of illustrations that Amelia Louise liked to point to, and near the end it had one of Ruby's mommy, who was obviously pregnant. Windflower had never really noticed that before, but as Amelia Louise pointed to that picture, he realized that she and all of them would have to learn to share if Stella came to live with them.

Of course, he had to read it twice, and even though Amelia Louise could barely keep her eyes open, she started to whine for one more time. Windflower resisted her pleadings and laid her down in her crib. She cuddled into her pet rabbit, and by the time he got downstairs, there was little sound coming from her room.

Windflower and Sheila had planned to watch another movie since last night's was such a success, but that went out the window when the power started to flicker and went out. It came back about 15 minutes later, but this was something they'd seen before. Sheila called into the town office to get an update, but they had little more information than she had. The latest forecast was that Tropical Storm Pedro would skirt the eastern parts of the island but spare them any direct hit.

"That's good news," said Windflower after Sheila got off the phone and told him.

"It could be worse," she said. "But we are going to get gusts up to 120 klicks in some areas and a boatload of rain. We will almost certainly lose power, but let's hope that's temporary and not a drawn-out event."

"I guess we'll just have to amuse ourselves," he said.

"Oh, you mean play a game of cards." Sheila enthusiastically got up to grab the cards and a cribbage board.

"I did not mean cards," said Windflower. He adored Sheila, but playing cards with her could be like Game of Thrones. She loved to win and hated to lose. And if she won, she gloated. If she lost, she pouted. Either way, Windflower lost.

But the cards were out of the bag now, and soon they were embroiled in a best-of-three games tournament. That got changed to a best-of-five when Windflower won the first two games, and after he was up three to two, Sheila was trying to negotiate a best-of-seven deal.

Fortunately for Windflower, if not the Town of Grand Bank, the house lights flicked one more time, and then there was total darkness. Sheila took up her flashlight and tried to continue the game, but Windflower resisted.

"No más," he said. "You win."

"I win, I win, I win!" said Sheila triumphantly.

"I'll take Lady out in the back before I go around and turn off the lights, at least the ones I can remember we had on," said Windflower.

Sheila was now singing We Are the Champions as she went upstairs. Windflower laughed to himself as he opened the back door to let Lady out. The dog jumped back as the door almost blew off its hinges.

48

Windflower pulled the door closed and went to get his RCMP hoodie and a large flashlight. He pulled the hood tight around his head and led Lady out into the dark backyard. The wind was blowing mercilessly and was starting to pick up anything that wasn't completely secure. He could see that some smaller items like Amelia Louise's plastic gardening tools and a few of her toys were wedged against the back fence. Even the lawn chairs were starting to shift in the wind.

Windflower went to gather them up and was hit in the face by a driving rain that felt like he was being attacked by an army of tiny spikes. He pushed his way through and brought what he could see inside. When he came back out, a drenched Lady pushed her way past him to get inside the house again. It was going to be a hard night, thought Windflower as he filled Lady and Molly's bowls and walked upstairs.

Sheila was waiting for him inside their dark bedroom. She had lit a candle and was sitting up in bed. He went and sat beside her. They could hear the rain being pelted on the roof of the house and crashing against the windows.

"I know we're supposed to be afraid, but I've always loved storms," said Sheila. "Not the hurricanes and really dangerous ones. And I don't want to be out in any of them. But when I'm home and it feels and sounds so stormy outside, I feel safe and warm inside."

"I know what you mean," said Windflower. "Whenever we had a big snowstorm back home, all of the elders would gather in someone's house, later at the community hall, and they would tell stories. That was how our history, our language and our culture got passed from generation to generation. It was a very special time."

"My parents used to let me sneak into their bed when the wind got really bad," said Sheila. "I would pretend to be scared so that they would let me in. Those are some of my happiest memories."

Windflower undressed and slid in beside her. They listened to the wind together and held each other tightly. Sheila was right, thought Windflower, this does feel safe and warm. That was his last thought until he woke in the morning to Amelia Louise crying in the other room.

He went in, picked her up and changed her. Then he took her downstairs where both Lady and Molly were waiting. He went to the kitchen and noticed the microwave clock blinking. Good, he thought. Power's back on. He fixed the clock and put on the coffee. Amelia Louise had already started to take Sheila's knitting out of her basket when Windflower turned around. He grabbed her under his arm and let Lady out in the back to do her morning business.

The wind seemed to be down a little bit because he was able to hold both Amelia Louise and the door without either blowing away. But the rain seemed heavier, if that were possible. It was so far exactly as they had forecast, and a very wet, stormy, blustery day lay ahead. But just like last night, this morning he felt safe, especially knowing Amelia Louise was also safe in his arm. And he welcomed the new day.

Then he remembered Lady, who was so happy to be welcomed back in that she shook her body vigorously and sprayed everything around her, including Windflower and Amelia Louise. The toddler was surprised at first but then realized that this was great fun and screamed for Lady to do it again. Windflower had to chase both of them around the kitchen with a towel to try to dry them off.

"What the heck is going on down here?" asked a groggy Sheila soon after she'd walked in on the chaotic scene.

"Have a cup of coffee," said Windflower, "and join the party."

"Pawty, pawty," said Amelia Louise, and she started dancing around the kitchen.

"I'll leave you to it," said Windflower. "I'm going to have my shower."

"Oh, yeah," said Sheila. "Create havoc and leave me to deal with it."

"True," said Windflower. "But I did make coffee." He kissed Sheila and grabbed a cup for himself. He was about to jump into the shower when he noticed his Richard Wagamese book on his nightstand. He picked it up where he had left off the last time.

When was the last time? he asked himself. He couldn't remember. That wasn't good. Maybe that's why he'd been feeling a little out of sorts and confused sometimes. Grandfather had told him once to keep doing the things that worked for him and not to wait until things got bad in order to start them up again. That worked only if he remembered to do it.

This morning he remembered. He opened the book of daily meditations and started reading. The passage he read this morning had Wagamese talking about how he saw himself. He described looking at a crack in the mirror and not being able to see himself, only the crack. And that meant he felt like there was something wrong with him. But then he realized that once he saw beyond the crack, he could see the whole perfect imperfect being he was.

Windflower thought about the reading the whole time he took his shower and got dressed. Part of what he had read was about forgiving yourself and acceptance. That was important. But the other lesson he took away from the reading was not to expect that others would or could be perfect but to accept them anyway, with all their cracks and flaws. Now, all he had to do was remember all of that.

Sheila had made oatmeal, and Windflower had a bowl with another cup of coffee.

"What's your day like?" he asked Sheila, who was busily scraping oatmeal off Amelia Louise's high chair as the little girl chased Lady and Molly all over the house. "I'm going into the office to check on damages from the storm. There will be lots, I expect. He paused for a moment. "I have to tell you about something before I go."

Sheila stopped cleaning and looked at him.

"Tizzard shot Fraser, the biker guy, yesterday," said Windflower. "Fraser will be okay, but Eddie was pretty shaken."

"Why didn't you tell me last night?" asked Sheila.

"I didn't want to upset you," said Windflower.

"You can't protect me from the fact that you are a police officer and that every time you walk out that door you might get shot," said Sheila. "I knew something bad happened. I'd rather you tell me than I find out somewhere else."

"Sheila, I'm sorry," said Windflower. But Sheila had already got Amelia Louise and was halfway up the stairs. "Bye," he shouted. There was no reply.

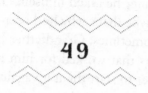

49

That went well," said Windflower to himself as he picked the keys to his RCMP Jeep off the hook on the wall. "What are you looking at?" he snapped at Lady. "I'm allowed to take my vehicle. It's been a week."

He walked to the car, looking up and hoping to catch a glimpse of Sheila in the window for a goodbye wave, but no such luck. "Guess she's not in the waving mood," he said to himself. He got into his Jeep and drove to the RCMP office. Evanchuk was talking to Betsy when he came in, and he wished them both good morning.

"Good morning, Sergeant," said Betsy. "Quite a blow last night."

"Yes, indeed. It's much better today. What's the forecast?" he asked.

"Rain is supposed to continue like this 'til noon and taper off to a few showers. Same with the wind. Should be all over by tomorrow morning," said Betsy.

"Let's hope the wind does die down before we have to travel," said Windflower. "Damage reports?" he asked Evanchuk.

"Jones was here 'til midnight, and she left an incident report on your desk," reported Evanchuk. "I didn't see very much overnight, but there's more than a few rough spots on the highway between here and Marystown. I called them in to the highways department."

"Great," said Windflower. "I'll have a look at the reports and then take a run the other way past Fortune. Are you going home soon?"

"Yes," said Evanchuk. "I was just waiting for you to come in."

"Come and talk to me for a minute before you go," he said. Evanchuk followed him into his office and closed the door behind her.

"How are you and how is Eddie?" he asked.

"I'm okay and Eddie was shaken up, but he's moving through it. He went to see his dad last night, and that calmed him down a bit."

"It's good that his dad is around to help support him, and you, of course."

"I can help, but I'm right in the middle of it, too," said Evanchuk. "His dad said something about getting kicked off a horse and having to get right back on. Anyway, he'll be here later today."

"Okay. I just want you to know that you can talk to me anytime you want about this or anything else."

"Thanks, Sarge. I appreciate that."

After Evanchuk left, Windflower ran through the report that Jones had prepared. There was a flurry of calls every time the power went out, but luckily those outages were short-lived. There was an alarm at the supermarket that turned out to have been triggered when the power went out. Jones investigated and helped them reset the alarm. She also responded to two calls for medical assistance. One was from an elderly woman who needed some company, and another was from a man who thought he might be having a heart attack. Jones got to that call just as the paramedics were leaving. A bad case of indigestion was their diagnosis.

Other than that, there was debris on the highway at various points, but between Jones and the highways crew who were out all night, they managed to keep the roads open. But Windflower suspected that there would be many new potholes and soft shoulders that would need to be patched up and repaired. He was about to go take a look at the other section of the highway beyond Fortune when he heard Betsy's voice on the intercom.

"Inspector Quigley on line one."

"Morning, Inspector," said Windflower. "It feels like 'hell is empty and all the devils are here.'"

"'That, sir, which serves and seeks for gain, and follows but for form, will pack when it begins to rain and leave thee in a storm,'" replied Quigley.

"King Lear, on a Monday morning, no less. I'm impressed," said Windflower. "You were probably up all night trying to find that one."

"I've been up for three days and nights now. What's it look like over there?"

"Power was out for a while, but there appears to be limited damage to people or property. Some issues on the highway, but we've phoned them in. I'm heading out to take a look at the road on the other side soon."

"Same over here," said Quigley. "The same places that always flood are flooded again. There's a washout just outside of town near Jean de Baie."

"Is the road closed?" asked Windflower.

"Should be fixed up after lunch."

"That's good. I'm heading to Alberta tomorrow."

"Oh, yeah, the funeral. Give my condolences to your uncle. How's he doing?"

"I haven't had a chance to really talk to him. We'll visit with him after the funeral. I'll be back sometime on Friday. Anything else on Fraser or the investigation?"

"Fraser is well in hand," the inspector said. "He's in secure lockdown at the hospital in Burin, and once he's able to travel, we're to ship him directly to Halifax. They will interview and process him from there. We don't have the capacity and don't want the trouble. Speaking of trouble, there's been a sighting of what some people are calling skinheads in Marystown. And I guess Patti Lewis has been singing her heart out in St. John's."

"Both interesting developments," said Windflower. "We'll keep an eye out for the skinheads. What's Lewis been talking about?"

"Here's the real interesting part. She says that Leo Grandy was a big player in the area, particularly on the meth side."

"Grandy didn't look like much when we had him in here. Are you sure we're talking about the same guy? He was talking about how scared he was of Fraser and the bikers."

"Maybe he just wanted them out of the way so he could take over."

"We'll pick him up. I'm off to 'unpathed waters, undreamed shores'. Or at least to find the biggest pothole on the southeast coast," said Windflower.

"'One foot in sea and one on shore, to one thing constant

never,'" countered Quigley. And to make sure Windflower couldn't get another quote in, Quigley ended the call.

Windflower called Sheila but got her voice mail. He hung up and thought carefully about what he wanted to say in a message. Then, he called back.

"I'm really sorry that I didn't tell you about Eddie earlier. That was disrespectful, and I did it because, you are right, I did not want an argument or confrontation. In future, I promise to be completely open and forthcoming about what happens with me and around me in my job. And as we move forward, I want you to know that you will be an equal partner in any decision I make to remain with or leave the RCMP. I love you."

He hung up and went to see Betsy.

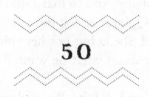

50

"D o you have an address on file for Leo Grandy?" asked Wind-flower.

Betsy rummaged around and found it. "He's living in a base-ment apartment on Evans Street. I know where his mother lives, too, if you need that," she said.

"Not right now," said Windflower. "If Tizzard comes in while I'm gone, tell him I've gone to see Grandy. I'm going to check out the highway down the road towards St. Lawrence, too."

"Okay, Sergeant," said Betsy. "Drive safely."

Windflower was in his Jeep thinking about what Betsy had just said. He couldn't remember her ever telling him to drive safely before. Did she think he was a careless driver or that he shouldn't be driving because of his ankle? Or was she just concerned because of the weather? Windflower couldn't figure that out, so he decided to just drive and go see Leo Grandy.

He pulled up in front of the address on Evans Street. It was a former garage that had been turned into a few apartments—Grand Bank's version of a condo building. There were a number of vehicles parked out front and four mailboxes along the side of the building. One said T. Grandy, 4B. He entered the building, walked down-stairs and knocked on the door marked 4B. No answer. He knocked again and called out Leo Grandy's name.

"Geez b'y, keep it down, willya?" came a voice from upstairs. Windflower followed the voice and knocked on the door he thought it came from.

"Whaddya want?" asked a voice from the other side of the door.

Windflower knocked again.

The door flew open, and the man coming out was loud and angry and looked like he wanted a fight. Until he saw Windflower and his uniform. Then he simply stopped and stared. "Uh, I didn't know it was ye," he said.

"I'm looking for Leo Grandy. Do you know where he is?" asked Windflower.

"No b'y," said the man.

"What's your name?" asked Windflower, taking out his pad.

"Now, dere's no need to involve me in dis, is dere? I'm Gerald Matthews. I'm kinda the super in dis building," said the man as gently as he could.

"When was the last time you saw Leo Grandy?" asked Windflower.

"I don't really keep track b'y. But it was probably last night before it got too stormy. He wasn't here when the power went out or he woulda been complainin' like the rest of dem."

"You said you were the super. Could you open it up to make sure he's not down there sleeping or anything?"

"Well, technickly I probly shouldn't. But he might be in danger, right?"

"Yes, he could very well be in danger," said Windflower.

"Okay b'y." The super walked downstairs with Windflower, unlocked 4B and waited.

"That's good, thank you," said Windflower. "I'll let myself out."

Windflower pushed open the door and went inside, closing it behind him. He looked around. Not the cleanest apartment ever, he thought. But not the dirtiest either. A few dishes in the sink, take-out containers piled up on top of the garbage can. Counters and floors relatively clean. Same with the living room. Rolling papers and a full ashtray, including marijuana roaches, but that wasn't illegal anymore. A battered leather couch, ubiquitous large-screen TV. Normal, so far.

The bedroom was another matter. It wasn't that it was particularly messy. It's just that one Leo Grandy was lying pretty still on the bed, and judging by the blood on the back of his head, he wasn't sleeping. Windflower did a quick pulse check and confirmed the worst.

He called back to the office and asked Betsy to alert the

paramedics and to find Doc Sanjay. "I'll stay here," he said. "Can you call Tizzard and ask him to come in early? Thanks."

After speaking with Betsy, he phoned Ron Quigley. "I've found Leo Grandy," he said.

"What did he have to say for himself?" asked Quigley.

"He's not talking. He's dead. I guess we'll need forensics again."

"Okay, I'll set that up. You need anything else?"

"Can we have Smithson back for a few days while I'm gone? Everybody here is fried, and I'm away 'til Friday night."

"Sure. I'll send him over today."

"And I want to put Jones formally in charge until I get back. We'll need someone to oversee this investigation."

"Fine by me. Get Betsy to send over the paperwork."

"Thanks, Ron." Windflower hung up his phone and walked out of 4B. He went back upstairs and knocked on the super's door. "Mr. Matthews. I'm going to need your assistance," he said.

"Did you find anyting down dere?" asked Matthews.

"We did," said Windflower. "Leo Grandy is dead. Now, we have a few more questions for you." As Windflower took out his notebook, all the blood drained from Matthew's face.

"I didn't have nuttin to do with dat," he stammered.

"Then you have nothing to worry about, do you? Cooperate and don't hold anything back and things will work out," said Windflower. "Screw me around and you're in big trouble. Do you understand?"

Matthews shook his head yes.

Tizzard arrived before Windflower got to ask any more questions.

"What's up?" asked Tizzard.

"Take a look downstairs in 4B, but don't touch anything," said Windflower. "After you're finished, I'll get you to interview our friend here. He has promised to cooperate. Let me know if he does."

Matthews now looked stunned but stayed fixed in place in front of Windflower.

Windflower heard the sirens of the paramedics come closer and then stop in front of the house. "Stay right here."

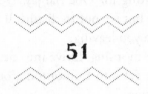
"D ownstairs," Windflower said to the paramedics when they came to the door. Tizzard came up as the others were going down.

"Don't move," Windflower said to Matthews. "We'll be right back." He walked outside with Tizzard.

"Isn't that Patti Lewis's boyfriend?" asked Tizzard. "I thought he was on our side."

"Looks like he was playing all sides," said Windflower. "Talk to Matthews. He knows something. I'm positive of that. Squeeze him hard."

"Got it," said Tizzard.

Tizzard went back in to interview Matthews, and one of the paramedics came to advise Windflower of the obvious.

"He's dead, Sergeant," said the paramedic. "Doctor Sanjay phoned to say he was on his way."

"Thank you," said Windflower. "You can take the body after his examination. Constable Jones will be in charge once she gets here."

He walked to his car and phoned Jones at home. She was surprised to hear from him but agreed to come as quickly as she could.

"I want you to lead the investigation," he said. "I'm making you a temporary corporal until we work our way through the mess here. Tizzard is here now interviewing the super or landlord, whatever he is. I'm sure he knows something. And I've talked to Quigley about forensics. Oh, and Smithson is coming back for a few days, too."

"You've been busy," said Jones. "I'd be happy to lead the investigation. Paramedics?"

"They're here, waiting for Doc Sanjay. Do your best to review and capture the scene but try not to disturb it too much."

"Got it. When are you leaving?"

"First thing in the morning. Drive into St. John's, fly to Halifax and then Toronto. We get into Edmonton around supper time, and we'll stay near the airport."

"That's a long day. I've done it a few times now to get to Manitoba."

"It is what it is. Let's hope our little princess cooperates. I've got to finish my drive around the loop. I'll pop in on the way back."

"Okay. I'm on my way over there. We'll secure the scene and go from there."

Windflower hung up and said goodbye to Tizzard who had a very worried-looking Gerald Matthews sitting on the couch in front of him. He gave Matthews another stern look and resumed his visit to the highway past Fortune.

He really loved this drive, which some from the area called the loop, despite the fact that the last time he took the trip, he fell down a mine shaft. He shuddered a little at the thought of that misadventure and again when he passed by the access road to the old mine site. He thoroughly enjoyed the rest of the journey, however, with its vast wilderness and winding road around the coastline. The ocean was so close he could almost taste it.

He didn't like the condition of the highway though. In more than a few locations the shoulders had been washed away in the rain, leaving only a narrow strip on both sides. Lots of potholes, which were more like moon craters, slowed him down until he finally came to a complete stop somewhere between Lawn and St. Lawrence. He pulled over and called the washout into the highways crew. Then, he turned around and made his way back towards Grand Bank.

Before he could get there, his cell phone rang.

"Hi Sheila," he said as he pulled over.

"Hi Winston. Thank you for your message. That helps and I will hold you to it," she said. "But I'm still pretty upset that you tried to hide it from me. It's too hard to do this all by myself."

"I get it," said Windflower. "You have my promise. It won't happen again."

"And I get a veto on the next move," said Sheila.

"I think I said you get a voice."

"A matter of interpretation. And I am the interpreter. Bye."

With that, Sheila was gone, leaving Windflower feeling pleased that he was back in her good books and terrified of what he'd just got himself into. It was still all good, he reminded himself, as he started back towards town and the murder scene on Evans Street.

There were three new vehicles parked outside the house, and the ambulance was pulling away when he arrived. Smithson was standing in the driveway next to a construction barrier. He waved excitedly when he saw Windflower, who acknowledged him with a smile. He also recognized Jones's RCMP cruiser, and the other black vehicle he knew belonged to Doctor Sanjay. He met the doctor as he was coming out.

"Good morning, Doc," said Windflower.

"How's she goin b'y?" said the doctor. "The deceased is now on his way to the clinic. I will need to do a full exam and workup, but it seems pretty clear that he likely died from a blow to the back of his head. I believe your young constable may have even found a candidate for the murder weapon."

"Is that right, Jones?" Windflower asked as she, too, came out from the house.

"Looks like it might be," she said, holding up a large plastic evidence bag with a round iron fence post inside it. "It's got what looks like blood on the end. I found it in the backyard."

"Good," said Windflower. "Is Tizzard still here?"

"No, he's gone back," said Jones. "But he gave me some info from his interview with Matthews."

"I'll call you if I find anything," said Sanjay, wishing the two officers a good day as he left.

"Bye," said Windflower to Sanjay. "So, what did Matthews tell Tizzard?" he asked Jones.

"I guess there's been a lot of activity around here," she said. "The big thing is that he kept talking about a new guy, a tall bald guy."

"A skinhead?" asked Windflower. "Quigley told me there was one of them spotted in Marystown."

"Could be. Tizzard said that Matthews was more afraid of him than even the bikers."

"Did we get a name?"

Jones checked her notes. "Nobody really knows his name. Matthews called him Big Con."

"When was he last here?"

"He was here last night. Matthews said he was in the building before the power went out. He claims he didn't hear anything, but I think he's just scared."

"Well, he's not going anywhere. Now that you're here, maybe you can ask him if we can let you look around his unit. He doesn't have to let you, but you can get a warrant," said Windflower. "You might find something we can use against him to make him more cooperative."

"Good point," said Jones. "I'll do that. Doc Sanjay took a sample off this pole, and I'll try and get some prints. Be interesting to see if we have any matches."

"I'm going back to the shop. Can you call Inspector Quigley with an update when you get a chance?"

Jones nodded and went back into the house.

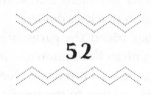

52

Smithson was waiting for Windflower at the end of the driveway. "Hey, Sergeant. I'm back," said Smithson.

"I can see that," said Windflower.

"It's only for a few days," said Smithson, a little sadly.

"Enjoy it while you can. Who knows what the future holds? 'It is not in the stars to hold our destiny, but in ourselves.'"

"That's very good. I like that. Does that mean I can stay in Grand Bank?"

Windflower laughed and walked away.

The rest of the day flew by for Windflower. Jones came in to give him mini-updates, and Tizzard and Evanchuk both stopped by to chat. Jones looked like she had everything under control, so he just tried to stay out of the way. He was happy to leave for home at five o'clock and took one more tour around town to see Smithson before he left.

Smithson waved him down. "Hey, Boss. I got one for you. 'Our wills and fates do so contrary run that our devices still are overthrown.'"

"Very good, Smithson," said Windflower. "'Our thoughts are ours, their ends none of our own.'" He rolled up his window and drove home.

Sheila had heated up a lasagna from the freezer, and when Windflower opened the door, the smell of garlic bread almost knocked him down.

"Oh my God, I love you," he said.

"Me or the garlic bread?" asked Sheila as their pets and daughter fought over who could grab Windflower's ankles first.

"You, of course. But I have to admit that garlic bread is a close second," said Windflower as Amelia Louise won the battle and he fell to the kitchen floor in mock surrender.

"Well, let's see your friend the garlic bread get you business class tickets from Toronto to Edmonton and back," said Sheila.

"What? That's great news. How'd you score that?"

"Connections. I was talking to the tourist board this morning about the summer season for the B & B, and she said she had some passes. They'll be at the airport in St. John's for us."

"That is absolutely wonderful. I was thinking about how we were going to survive. That certainly helps." Windflower put Amelia Louise into her high chair and sat at the table. Sheila served him a large helping of lasagna, and he added some green salad and a piece of garlic bread to his plate.

He took another piece of garlic bread and tore it into pieces for Amelia Louise. She loved garlic bread almost as much as her dad. That meant there were two disappointed pets sitting beneath her chair as she stuffed as much as she could into her mouth and gurgled her approval.

Sheila laughed at her daughter. She gave her a small bowl of cut-up and cooled lasagna and sat down at the table with Windflower.

"I don't really want to talk about work, but I hear there was another dead body found," said Sheila.

"Leo Grandy," said Windflower. "It looks like he might be involved with all the other activity going on around here."

"You know, lots of people must have seen things happening, and nobody reported it. I don't understand. It used to be that everyone was in each other's business around here." When Windflower raised an eyebrow, she added, "I mean in a good way. We looked after each other."

"I think people still care," said Windflower. "But there's been so much change that people can't keep up."

He passed his plate over to Sheila and grabbed another piece of garlic bread. Amelia Louise demanded seconds as well. He passed her another piece of bread as Sheila gave him his lasagna.

"I get that," said Sheila. "But I think I'm going to have a community town hall when we get back. We need to start taking ownership of our town again."

"I agree," said Windflower. "Hooray for our mayor."

"Hooray, hooray," said Amelia Louise.

"Don't get her too wound up," said Sheila. "We have a long day tomorrow, and she needs a good night's sleep."

"Bit too late for that," said Windflower as Amelia Louise dumped the remainder of her bowl of lasagna on the floor. Molly and Lady were there immediately to aid in the cleanup. Amelia Louise thought this was the funniest thing ever and was still laughing when Windflower cleaned her up and put her down on the floor in the living room.

"I can take care of the kitchen if you'd like," said Windflower.

"I would like that," said Sheila. "I'm going to give her a bath early and finish the packing. It's only a couple of days, but we have to take so many clothes and toys, and her diaper bag."

"Takes a village," said Windflower, filling the dishwasher. "You go give her a bath. I'll look after down here."

"Thank you, Winston. I'm glad you feel well enough to help out."

"I thought about faking for a few more days off, but I'm happy to be able to move again. I'm still not running at full speed, but I'll get there."

Sheila took the baby upstairs, and Windflower took the remainder of the lasagna out of the casserole dish and put it back in the freezer, wrapped in tinfoil. It was too good to throw out, he decided, and he wrote 'lasagna' and the date on a label and stuck it to the tinfoil.

He scrubbed the dish and turned on the dishwasher. After he wiped the table and the counter and quickly washed the kitchen floor, he went outside. Lady followed him out and went off exploring. The wind had subsided considerably, and the sky was twinkling now with a million stars. He thought about another star that would soon be shining up there, his Auntie Marie. He opened his phone and called Uncle Frank.

"Uncle Frank, how are you?" asked Windflower.

"I am well, Winston," said Uncle Frank. "Although I won't want to see another casserole for a while. I think I have half a dozen left in the freezer."

"It must be hard," said Windflower. "How long were you together?"

"Almost fifty years. It is hard to miss someone so much. But I have a feeling this is the easy part. There are lots of people around, and I feel Marie is still with us."

"We are getting ready to come up tomorrow. It will be good to see you."

"And you. You were always her favourite. I think she liked you more than me. I know she liked you more when I was drinking." Uncle Frank laughed.

Windflower laughed too. "We'll be there first thing Wednesday morning. Good night, Uncle."

"Good night, Winston."

Windflower called out to Lady, and they went back inside. He could hear Amelia Louise and Sheila laughing. He went upstairs to join them.

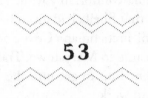

53

I spoke to Uncle Frank," said Windflower as he came into the bathroom and watched Sheila wrestle Amelia Louise in order to wash her hair.

Sheila rinsed her screaming daughter's hair and handed her to Windflower who wrapped her in a towel.

"Oh yeah, now she's all smiles," said Sheila. "How's Uncle Frank?"

"He sounded sad," said Windflower. "I'm glad we're going. He will need our support."

He brought Amelia Louise into her bedroom and put on her pajamas. After reading one of her favourite stories, he put her into bed and went to help Sheila finish the packing. With his help she was done quickly, and they were both in bed early. Not long after they were asleep.

It was good they got to bed early because they were up and out the door before it was light. Sheila made a pot of coffee to put into their Thermos and had a cut-up apple for Amelia Louise. That would get all of them to Goobies where they would stop for breakfast.

"This might be the most pleasant part of the day," said Windflower as he poured them both a cup of coffee.

"She's pretty happy right now," said Sheila, looking in the mirror behind her.

"I'm pretty happy, too," said Windflower. "I'm with my two favourite girls, and I'm not working. Plus, you're driving the first leg so I can enjoy this beautiful scenery."

"Don't forget. You're my moose spotter."

"Relax and enjoy the ride, ma'am."

So they did, chatting comfortably while Amelia Louise played with some of her toys that Sheila had given her. They passed by the well-known turnoffs of Frenchman's Cove and Garnish and made good time until they came to Marystown. Traffic slowed considerably there as people lined up to get into the Tim Hortons drive-through before going to work.

After Marystown the space between wilderness and civilization grew, and Sheila and Windflower drove through the barrens in a pleasant silence until they started to hit the curves before Swift Current. That woke everybody up a little, and Windflower got Sheila to pull over so he could sit in the back to keep Amelia Louise company. Forty minutes later they were pulling up to the gas pumps in Goobies. Sheila took Amelia Louise into the restaurant while Windflower filled up.

Inside, the restaurant was starting to get busy, but they managed to get their orders in and didn't have to wait too long for their breakfast—scrambled eggs and toast for everybody with a side order of bologna for Windflower. He knew he shouldn't eat that stuff, and that it was not at all healthy, but some part of him could not resist. He shared a little piece with Amelia Louise, and she seemed to agree.

"It's sum good, isn't it?" asked Windflower.

"Sum good," replied Amelia Louise.

"You are definitely a bad influence," said Sheila. "But she'll probably hate you when she grows up and turns vegan. So it will all work out."

Windflower smiled, and if he wasn't mistaken, he was pretty sure Amelia Louise smiled back. They finished their breakfast and were soon on the road to St. John's with Windflower at the wheel. This was a less pleasant portion of the trip, at least for Windflower. Yes, there occasionally was some nice scenery, but mostly it was just a two-lane highway, and it was particularly busy the closer they got to St. John's. People commuted from all over the Avalon Peninsula to work in the capital city. Windflower did his best to avoid all that and was able to take the arterial road to the airport.

He dropped Sheila and Amelia Louise at the terminal, unloaded their luggage and went to park the car. When he came back, he went inside to find Amelia Louise already in the play area, trying to convince another little girl to join her in the playhouse. He stayed with her while Sheila went to get them checked in. The timing was great because soon after Sheila returned, they were called to go through security, and even better, Amelia Louise was rubbing her eyes, a telltale sign that a nap was imminent.

They boarded the plane early and got all organized. Amelia Louise was starting to fuss a little, but there were a lot of people and things to keep her occupied, including a kid's package that the helpful flight attendant had handed to Sheila when they got on the plane. Windflower was glad they had purchased a full ticket for Amelia Louise because they could put her in between them, and before they took off, she could and did climb all over them.

Sheila had read that takeoff was the most difficult part of flying with a child or baby because they seemed to be very sensitive to changes in air pressure. But Sheila had a plan for that. Just as the plane started to taxi down the runway, she put her daughter under a blanket and gave her a suckle. There was no sound but gurgling from underneath the blanket, and by the time the plane had reached cruising altitude, she was fast asleep.

She stayed that way until they announced the descent into Halifax, but Sheila had a bottle to calm her on the way down. It was a short stop in Halifax, and Sheila repeated the suckling exercise on the way up. They survived the ascent without incident, and while Amelia Louise didn't fall asleep this time, most of the trip to Toronto was pleasant as she played with and crawled all over her parents without disturbing the other passengers too much. It helped that she had a friendly grandpa behind her who never seemed to tire of playing peek-a-boo.

They had a two-hour stop in Toronto and also the benefit of having access to the business lounge. But first, there was some exploring to do. Windflower took Amelia Louise on a tour of the terminal building. She loved the wide-open spaces that seemed perfect for running around in. She also loved pressing her face up against the window and watching the planes come and go. After half an hour of that, they went back to find Sheila who'd been taking a look around the shops.

They went inside the business lounge and had a bowl of soup and some crackers while they waited for their flight. The break was pleasant but not as long as they would have liked, and Amelia Louise kept wandering off to visit some of the other business travellers. Some were very happy to see her; others clearly were not. They went out into the main area and found their gate. Amelia Louise was perfectly content to run around again, and she took full advantage of an empty gate nearby to do so at full speed.

Before they knew it, their flight was called, and they were on the final leg of the day's journey. Their business class seats were large and comfy, and for the third time that day, Sheila planned to use her secret suckling method to calm Amelia Louise, but this time it was not the charm. The little girl fussed and mussed until Sheila gave up and utilized the final weapon in her arsenal.

Neither she nor Windflower were big fans of allowing small children access to screen time, and they strictly limited Amelia Louise's time watching TV and other electronic devices. But today was an emergency, so Sheila took out her iPad and turned on Dora the Explorer for her daughter. She looked at Windflower and shrugged her shoulders. He nodded agreement. Dora and Amelia Louise enjoyed the takeoff immensely, and soon the whole family was enjoying a delicious business class meal.

A couple of hours into the flight, Amelia Louise finally fell asleep again. That allowed Sheila and Windflower to also catch a catnap, which was very much appreciated by both of them. Amelia Louise woke as the pilot announced their descent into Edmonton International Airport, and Sheila was able to pacify her with the last bottle of milk in her bag.

"Looks like we're going to make it," said Sheila.

"What a relief," said Windflower. "She was really good, and of course you had a plan for everything."

"If I weren't so tired, I'd think up a nice quote," said Sheila. "But all I have is 'all's well that ends well.'"

"That's perfect," said Windflower as the plane bumped onto the runway. "Just like you."

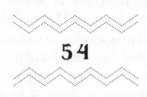
They waited until everyone got off the plane and then went to the luggage area. Windflower got their rental car organized while Sheila watched for their bags. They would stay tonight at the Leduc Inn near the airport and make the two-hour drive to Pink Lake in the morning. Their luggage arrived in good time and in good shape, and the little family soon found themselves in a nice suite at the hotel. Sheila unpacked what they needed for the night while Amelia Louise helped her dad make her bath. After her bath Windflower went down to the lobby to give Sheila a chance to get her down and to call back home.

He called Jones on her cell phone.

"Hey, Sarge, how was your flight?" she asked.

"We made it in one piece," said Windflower. "Actually, it wasn't bad at all. How are you making out with the case?"

"Slow progress," said Jones. "Forensics is coming in the morning, and Smithson is riding shotgun over there until after they're done. We couldn't kick Matthews or the other tenants out of their own house, although I was tempted with him."

"Yeah, he's the kind of guy who's already on the wrong side of the equation, one of the ones that let the bad guys get away with so much stuff."

"Well, at least we know who one of the bad guys is now. Big Con is Conrad Jablonski, affiliated with the Aryan Warriors. Inspector Quigley found him in the international database after the RCMP print search turned up a blank."

"Any sign of him around there?"

"No such luck, sir. Sounds like he's out of our jurisdiction. He was spotted leaving Marystown sometime yesterday, and when

Smithson checked the passenger manifests, he found him on a
flight to Los Angeles via Toronto. He's in California by now. We'll
post his picture around here anyway in case anybody knows him or
saw anything, but not holding out a lot of hope on that."

"Too bad. Anything from Doc Sanjay yet?"

"He confirms that cause of death is blunt force to the head,
with the probable weapon being the iron fence post, since he also
says that is Leo Grandy's blood on the end of it. It also has Big
Con's fingerprints, so we could likely close this case if we could lay
our hands on him."

"Good work," said Windflower. "Sounds like you got everything covered. Anything else going on?"

"Pretty quiet right now," said Jones. "Helps to have Smithson
here though. He's pretty handy, you know."

"I think you've been missing him."

"Just his technical expertise." Then Jones started laughing.
"He's a good cop."

"He is," said Windflower. "Okay, I'm signing off. I'll check back
in tomorrow night."

"Goodnight, Sergeant."

Windflower crept back into the darkened room where Amelia
Louise laid stretched out on one bed with pillows surrounding her
to keep her from falling off. Sheila was sleeping solidly in the other.
Windflower undressed as quietly as he could and slipped in beside
Sheila. He didn't see or hear anything else until their wake-up call
in the morning. After a breakfast of fruit and croissants, they were
on the highway north to Pink Lake before ten o'clock.

The road was busy until they were well outside Edmonton.
Highway 2 was a major route north, and Windflower had travelled
it in both directions many times. An hour and a half in, they turned
west past Athabasca and through the winding side roads to Pink
Lake. Amelia Louise had fallen asleep somewhere along the way
and barely stirred when Windflower stopped at the Cedar Motel,
the only hotel or motel anywhere near Pink Lake. Sheila stayed in
the car while Windflower checked in and brought in their luggage.

Amelia Louise only woke when Windflower lifted her out
of her car seat. He lay her on the bed in their room while Sheila

got their clothes ready for the rest of the day. He was grateful the baby was having a sound sleep as this would be another long day for the whole family. While the motel was only 15 minutes from the reserve, they had to stop to visit with Uncle Frank and pay their respects to Auntie Marie before the funeral, which would be followed by a community feast.

Once the baby stirred again, Windflower dressed in his black suit and Sheila gave her a bath. Then she left Amelia Louise with Windflower to partially get her ready while she changed into her black dress. Her official mourning dress, she called it, because as mayor she had to attend every notable funeral in Grand Bank. And as Grand Bank was an older and aging community, there were a lot of funerals to go to. Windflower did his best and was almost finished when Sheila came in to tie up her daughter's hair in pigtails. Amelia Louise didn't particularly like that, but without some restraints, her hair would soon be everywhere.

Once everyone was appropriately dressed, they drove to the Pink Lake Reserve and stopped at the community lodge where Auntie Marie, like all other elders, were waked before burial. Windflower nodded to the few familiar faces he recognized in the outer room of the lodge and followed the well-worn path to the back area where he found some of his cousins talking to Uncle Frank. Uncle Frank smiled when he saw them and went to Sheila and gave her a hug.

"Welcome," he said to Sheila. He smiled again at little Amelia Louise and tried to pick her up, but she clung to her mother's legs for dear life. "That's okay," said Uncle Frank. "I will still be your great uncle later when you want a treat."

"I am so sorry," said Sheila. "She was such a nice lady, always so kind to me and Amelia Louise."

"It is sad. I cannot lie," said Uncle Frank. "But I have made my peace, and I am ready to let her go. Welcome, Nephew," he said to Windflower.

Windflower thought he would cry if he spoke, so he simply went to his uncle and hugged him. That seemed to help. "It is my honour to be here," he managed to say.

Uncle Frank called one of his nieces over and introduced her to Sheila. "Would you show her where the food is?" he asked. "And if this little girl is very, very good, she may have a treat. Would you like a treat?" he asked Amelia Louise. She still cowered near her mother, but Windflower thought he saw her give a very slight smile.

After they left, Uncle Frank put his arm around Windflower's shoulder and led him into a smaller room off the hallway. The few people who were in there scattered quickly when they saw Uncle Frank. One solitary woman remained in the room. Windflower recognized that she was the keeper today, one of the respected women in the community who kept a round-the-clock watch with a newly deceased. They had been the ones who had washed and dressed Auntie Marie.

As Windflower drew near, he could see that Auntie Marie had sweetgrass in her right hand to help purify her spirit and tobacco on the raised platform where she now lay. Tobacco was used by many Indigenous peoples to aid communications between this world and the other and to connect more directly with Creator. Auntie Marie looked pale and much thinner than when Windflower saw her last, but she was dressed in her ceremonial robe, and he noticed there were new moccasins on her feet. They were likely also made by the women who took care of her after her death.

Windflower touched her hand and, of course, it was cold. That always surprised him a little, and it made him want to pull back, but he stayed, holding her hand, feeling his aunt's spirit still in the room. Despite himself, he started to cry, and Uncle Frank again put his hand on his shoulder.

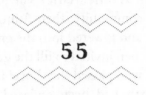

55

It's okay to cry. Sadness is a healing emotion," said Uncle Frank. "Today we cry, and then when she is given back to Mother Earth, we must be strong and let her go. Many people say not to cry on the night of a burial so that the spirit has our blessing and the freedom to leave. Be with her a moment alone, and I will go see how the rest of your family is doing."

Windflower stayed for a few minutes with Auntie Marie and her silent helper, alone and undisturbed in the room. Then he went and found Sheila and Amelia Louise. His daughter had found a bowl of Jell-O and some playmates who were busy circling the room. He stayed to watch while Sheila went with Uncle Frank to say her goodbyes. Windflower picked at a sandwich and watched the kids play, but he was mostly in his own thoughts about Auntie Marie.

They spent another hour at the lodge until the women keepers gathered and said a prayer in the middle of the room surrounded by all the people standing in a circle around them. It was in Cree, and Windflower only knew a few words in his native tongue, but he knew this was in Auntie Marie's honour. After the song he went with Uncle Frank and the keepers to say one final goodbye before Auntie Marie's body was wrapped in a special blanket and placed inside the casket. Both men kissed her on the cheek and the keepers rolled the casket out in front of them and into the waiting hearse.

It was not long to the burial ground, and all of the mourners who could, including Sheila and Windflower carrying Amelia Louise, walked behind the keepers, who were singing, and a drummer, who played a solitary beat to accompany them and the procession. At the gravesite, some of the elders were invited to speak, and they offered prayers for Auntie Marie's safe journey and praise for her many gifts to the community. Then Auntie Marie's casket was draped in her blanket and lowered into the ground. The male relatives and friends were then invited to fill the grave with earth, starting with Uncle Frank who passed the shovel next to Windflower.

When all the earth had been replaced, all the community members gathered in a circle for one more round of prayers and another song for the spirit of Auntie Marie. The drummer, now playing a more vigorous beat and singing as well, led them all back to the lodge where the big hall was filled with a full buffet of traditional and modern foods. As if by magic, all of the sadness and solemnity of the funeral ceremony was gone and people seemed happy and animated and alive as they shared in the food and the company.

There was a ton of food, and Windflower and Sheila walked around with Amelia Louise in tow to take a look. They came back with heaping plates of salads, smoked trout, venison stew and bannock that smelled like it had just come out of the oven, which it probably had. They also had a dessert table with a wide variety of pies. Windflower took a large piece of Saskatoon berry pie and two small pieces of some others. Sheila found a pie that a woman told her was her family's secret recipe pie but had the usual berries along with black and red currants.

Amelia Louise was quite happy with her slice of bannock and sat on her mother's knees as the music and dancing began. There was an air of celebration that Windflower was relieved to find and settle into after the deep sadness he had felt earlier. They ate and enjoyed themselves, and when the music stopped, Uncle Frank made a speech thanking the community for their kindness and love. It was a beautiful and fitting end to a great ceremony.

By this time Amelia Louise was at the end of her enthusiasm, and Sheila took her outside while Windflower said his goodbyes to Uncle Frank. His uncle brought him to a quiet corner of the room and handed him a package wrapped in a blanket. "Your Auntie wanted you to have this," he said.

Windflower unfurled the blanket and nearly cried again when he saw what was inside. It was Auntie Marie's ceremonial pipe.

Windflower admired the long wooden stem and the catlinite bowl. Some people called that pipestone, but he remembered Auntie Marie telling him the correct name for it and how she used it, filled with tobacco, to make her connection with Creator.

"I am very honoured," said Windflower.

"Some people have their pipe buried with them so they can use it on the other side, but your aunt thought you might need it more over here," said Uncle Frank.

"Thank you," said Windflower, holding back his emotions. He wrapped the pipe back up and walked out with his uncle. Uncle Frank hugged Sheila, and Windflower could see him whisper something in her ear. His uncle gave a now drowsy Amelia Louise a kiss on the cheek and hugged Windflower again.

"Come over in the morning. We'll go for a walk in the woods, like old times," said Uncle Frank.

"We'll do that," said Windflower. He helped Sheila get Amelia Louise into the back of the rental car, and they drove to their motel. Along the way Windflower asked what Uncle Frank had whispered.

"It's a secret," said Sheila.

"Okay, then I'm not going to talk to you until you tell me," said Windflower.

"You, the silent treatment? You gotta be kidding me. You wouldn't last five minutes without giving me your opinion about something or other," she said.

Windflower made a sign of locking his lips. When he looked in the mirror, Amelia Louise was doing the same. He laughed out loud.

"What's so funny?" Sheila asked.

Windflower pointed to his lips and mimicked a sorry.

Sheila laughed too. "Okay, I'll tell you. You're such a big baby. Uncle Frank said that I was your only living connection to the spirit of women and that you would be lost without me."

"That's a bit of a stretch," said Windflower. "Not completely lost. I'd still have her," he said, pointing backwards. But when he looked again, she was drooped over in her car seat, solidly asleep.

"Not much help there," said Sheila. "Uncle Frank was talking about female energy and intuition, of which I remind you, you have very little. And what you do have, you don't use."

"Ouch," said Windflower.

"You know it's true. Was there something in that blanket you put in the trunk?"

"Auntie Marie's ceremonial pipe. It's very special."

"Wow. That is quite an honour and a responsibility."

"I know. I feel blessed," said Windflower, suddenly growing quiet. Sheila was quiet, too, all the way back to their motel. Amelia Louise woke when they stopped, and after they got changed from their fancy clothes, Windflower took Amelia Louise out to the little playground where she played in the sandbox and tried the Little Tikes slide. Tiring of that, she got her father to lift her into the toddler swing and push her, again and again and again, and she squealed each and every time she went high in the air—or at least what seemed high to her.

Playtime over, they ordered hamburgers from the restaurant for supper, and Windflower had a bath and book-reading duty while Sheila relaxed for a few minutes. Afterward, Amelia Louise cuddled with her mom, and Windflower went to the lobby to call back to Jones who was on the night shift in Grand Bank.

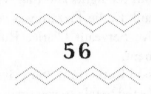

56

Jones answered on his first ring. "Hey, Sarge, glad you called. It appears someone around here knows Jablonski."

"Who?" asked Windflower.

"Tizzard," said Jones. "He saw the picture and recognized him as one of the guys from jail in Las Vegas. He said he had a friend out there that he could call."

"Who would Tizzard know in Las Vegas?" asked Windflower.

"I don't know," said Jones. "But I told him to make the call."

"Very good. Anything else going on?"

"Nope. I think we've had enough excitement for a while. How did everything go out there?"

"It was good. It's always sad to lose someone, but she had a beautiful send off."

"That's good," said Jones.

"Okay, I'll let you go," said Windflower.

He went back inside where Sheila was reading her book and Amelia Louise was curled up in what looked like a very comfortable ball on the other bed. He went and gave her a kiss, lay on the bed beside Sheila and picked up his Richard Wagamese book.

"Everything okay?" she asked.

"Things are good," said Windflower. "But Tizzard appears to know that skinhead guy from Las Vegas we were looking for and has another contact who may be able to help find him."

"Eddie is a very interesting character. You never know what's going to happen to him next."

"That is true."

Windflower started to read his book, but even though it was still early, both of them did not last more than a few more minutes before Sheila turned out the lights and they fell asleep.

Back in Grand Bank Eddie Tizzard was very much awake. He was phoning Detective Sergeant Clarice Rutherford of the Las Vegas Police Department.

"Good evening," said Rutherford. "Surprised to hear from you."

"Well, I never expected to talk to you again either," said Tizzard. "But we need your help. Did you see the picture I sent you?"

"I did," said Rutherford. "He's well known to us. Big Con is a rising leader in the Aryan Warriors. He's out on bail right now waiting to come up on drug and assault charges. Nearly killed a black street dealer."

"We'd like you to find him for us, if you can," said Tizzard.

"Okay," said Rutherford. "But, who's we? I thought you were going freelance."

"I'm back as a special constable with the Mounties 'cause they're short-staffed, and a couple of people have been killed. Drugs. Our own little drug war it seems. And we have evidence that your guy is responsible for one of the deaths."

"Not our guy. But if you have evidence and can get me an official request from the RCMP, I will put a few more officers on it for you. We'd love to get him off the streets permanently, and out of the country would be even better."

"Perfect. You'll get that request tonight from Inspector Ron Quigley. You know, I'm sorry I couldn't help you back then. But this is kind of a way of helping."

"Absolutely," said Rutherford. "If we can get more of these Nazis off the street, it's good for everybody, especially around here."

"Thanks again," said Tizzard, and he hung up with Rutherford and called Quigley.

"Inspector, LVPD will help us find our suspect if we formally request it. The person to send the request to is Detective Sergeant Clarice Rutherford.

"Good work, Eddie," said Quigley. "It's good to have you back. We could use you full-time."

"I'm still working my way through that," said Tizzard.

What Winston Windflower was working his way through was thick bush in Northern Alberta. At least in his dream he was. He had fallen deeply to sleep but not long after had found himself here, surrounded by an ocean of trees and a narrow slit of a path that he was trying to get through. He realized what this path was after a few steps. His grandfather had told him this was a deer trail, and when he looked down, he could see some small, distinctive footprints. He kept pushing through until he saw a clearing.

He walked out into the bright sunlight and saw that this was a different place than his other dreams. There were wildflowers blooming everywhere, and the colours were so bright they almost hurt his eyes. He blinked, and that's when he saw her. It was Auntie Marie, but she looked so young and radiant that he almost didn't recognize her.

"Come, Nephew, and sit beside me," said his aunt.

"You look great," said Windflower. "Younger," he added with some surprise in his voice.

"We get to choose our appearance over here," said Auntie Marie. "I didn't have time to do my hair, so I thought I'd take about 30 years off my age, a few pounds, too." She let out a big belly laugh. "I've come to say my goodbye. Wasn't that a great funeral? I just wish I could have had one more piece of pie."

"It was very nice," said Windflower. "I want to thank you for my gift."

"You are welcome, Nephew. I knew that you would need it more in your world. You can use it to access the power you will require in your life. You have many people depending on you, and more will come to you in the future for guidance. Do not try to do this on your own."

"I understand. I accept the honour and responsibility."

"That is good. You must also listen to the helpers you have been given."

"Who do you mean?"

"The pipe and tobacco will help you from this side, but you have a strong woman, Sheila, who can assist you, if you allow her to. And your daughter may be your greatest teacher of all."

Windflower nodded. "I will miss you, Auntie."

"I will be with you in spirit," said his aunt. "I will be the first sprinkle of sunlight in the morning and the first sparkling star at

night. I will be with Grandmother Moon and watch over you."
Then, Windflower watched as Auntie Marie seemed to come apart
like a jigsaw puzzle, and in seconds all that remained of her was a
red bow from her hair lying on the ground. He picked it up and
held it, and then he woke up in the motel near Pink Lake.

He got up and went to the bathroom. On the way back he
looked out the window and up into the night sky. It was filled with
many, many stars and a full white moon that looked like it took up
half the sky. He whispered a prayer to Grandmother Moon to look
after his Auntie Marie and crawled back into bed where he stayed
until he heard Amelia Louise move around in the morning.

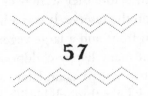

57

Windflower got up and dressed and, as quietly as possible, got Amelia Louise changed and dressed too. He gave her a bottle and turned on the TV to the cartoon station. He prepared the coffee in the small drip coffee maker in the bathroom and sat with his daughter to wait for it to brew.

Soon after Sheila woke up, the three of them went to the motel restaurant for breakfast. Windflower ordered the speciality of the house, buttermilk pancakes. He opted for the large stack, whereas Sheila took the regular version and placed a kid's order for Amelia Louise. Windflower was lost for a few moments in pancake bliss, or maybe it was a maple syrup high. He snapped out of it, though, as Amelia Louise grabbed at the syrup jug and lifted it toward her mouth.

"That was close," said Sheila.

"It sure would have kept her going full throttle all morning," said Windflower. "This is going to be another long day. I'm glad we're going to spend a few minutes with Uncle Frank in the woods. It will be good for all of us."

"Yes, I agree," said Sheila. "Driving to Edmonton and then flying to Toronto to change flights for St. John's could really turn into a nightmare for us. But we survived on the way up, so I suppose we'll be okay on the way back."

"As long as we don't get delayed too much, I think we'll be fine," said Windflower. "But this one needs a facecloth to get the syrup off her face right now."

He took a squealing Amelia Louise out of her high chair and passed her to Sheila so she could wipe the baby's face and hands. Windflower paid the bill and followed them back to their room.

It took about an hour for everyone to get cleaned up, dressed for the day and packed before they were back in the car driving to Uncle Frank's house on the reserve. It was a little bungalow with a well-tended garden in front and a large vegetable patch out back. Windflower had spent many happy childhood days here with his mom and aunt, and then visited again later as an adult. Whenever he had returned to Pink Lake through his life, he would visit Auntie Marie and Uncle Frank here, which was where he first learned and then honed his dream-weaving skills.

He was still very much a novice, but Auntie Marie had been well-recognized in the community as a master dream weaver, and she had given Windflower a solid base upon which to build his own abilities. That was one of the first things that Uncle Frank reminded him of as they started their walk through the forest behind the reserve. Sheila and Amelia Louise stopped to look at a giant mush-room on the path while the two men walked ahead, talking about the love they shared for the woman they had just lost.

"Your aunt will be watching to see that you keep practicing dream weaving and our other traditions," said Uncle Frank.

"I have learned so much from her and from you," said Wind-flower. "I will do my best."

"Do your best with her, too," said Uncle Frank as he scooped up Amelia Louise who had run towards them.

"That's the easy part," said Windflower.

"What's easy?" asked Sheila as she caught up.

"Doing our best for her," said Windflower. He took Amelia Louise in his arms and held her high above his head. When he tried to put her down, she screamed for more. Ten times later, he could finally let her go. She ran to her mother.

"What will you do now?" Sheila asked Uncle Frank.

"It will be too lonely here," he said. "I was thinking about taking a trip to Newfoundland. I had that planned before Bill Ford got shot. I was going to stay with him, but that's off now. I hear he's doing better, though."

"He was recovering when I saw him," said Windflower. "But he's still got a long way to go."

"I figured as much," said Uncle Frank. "But I still might go. Jarge said I could stay with him. He said I should retire there, put my name in for the old folks' home. Crazy, eh?"

"That's not as crazy as you think," said Sheila. "Coming back to

Grand Bank might be good for you, and if you came, you could help us look after the B & B."

"You mean like a job?" asked Uncle Frank.

"More like a caretaker," said Windflower. "Levi Parsons is running the place now, but you could help out if you'd like."

"I think I'd really like that," said Uncle Frank. "Let me think some more about it. I might even ask her, too," he said, pointing up to the sky.

"Good idea," said Windflower. "Now, we'll see who's the fastest runner." He put Amelia Louise on his shoulders and ran as quickly as he could. The other two caught up, and everyone then walked along a path that came to the side of the lake. There was a clearing near the water and a number of large boulders in a circle.

"This was my swimming hole when I was a kid," said Windflower. "It was cold, but boy did we have fun here."

"There's some great fish in here, too," said Uncle Frank.

"What kind of fish?" asked Sheila as she tried to hold Amelia Louise because she was squiggling to try to get into the water.

"Lots of trout and big walleye," said Windflower. He grabbed Amelia Louise but let her put her fingers in the water. She pulled back.

"It's cold, isn't it?" he said.

"Ish cold," said Amelia Louise, who then decided to seek comfort from her mother.

"It was his hideout, too," said Uncle Frank. "He and his buddies would sneak some beer off of one of their dads and come down here for a fire and a party."

"Tell me more about the bad boys," said Sheila.

"Let's head back," said Windflower. "We've got to get going."

But it was too late to escape completely unscathed. All the way back, Uncle Frank and Sheila chatted and laughed about Windflower's childhood antics, and Amelia Louise joined in the fun with a singsong of "bad boy, bad boy, bad boy."

"It was so nice to see you, Uncle," said Windflower. "I hope we will see you soon."

"Yes, please come," said Sheila.

Uncle Frank hugged them both and kissed Amelia Louise on both cheeks. He waved as they drove off down the road that would bring them to the highway to Edmonton.

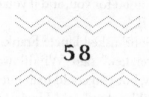

58

Amelia Louise fell asleep almost as soon as the wheels hit the highway, and Sheila took her into the terminal to give her a bottle while Windflower returned the car and loaded the luggage onto a cart. They were almost right on time and breezed through security and into the business cabin where they again got a great meal. Amelia Louise watched A Bug's Life for most of the flight. She only got upset when they started their descent into Toronto, but Sheila knew how to fix that.

They had a couple of hours to kill in Toronto, and Amelia Louise spent the first one running up and down the long corridors. Then Windflower found the little play area, and before she could get upset again, they were back on the plane for the last leg of the day. Luckily, all that running around had tired her out, and she fell asleep shortly after takeoff. There were a few frantic moments after she woke, but one more bottle saved the day. Finally, the seat belt lights came on, and they dropped into St. John's.

It was a short trip to the hotel where they were spending the night near the airport. A tired and grumpy Amelia Louise had a little food and a very short bath and then was out like a light. Sheila was not far behind her. Even though it was getting late, Windflower decided to phone into the office for an update.

"Hey, Sarge. You're up late. Where are you?" asked Jones.

"Just got into St. John's. You're on overnight again?" asked Windflower.

"Yes, my turn," she said. "But I never mind the night shift here. It's almost always a calm, reflective time. I'll miss that when I leave."

"Not too late to change your mind," said Windflower. "Anything new?"

"Not too much. Forensics left us with bags of stuff that we put in storage, and it looks like Matthews was more heavily involved than we thought. Tizzard found a guy who says that Matthews was an informal 2IC for Leo Grandy."

"Squeeze Matthews again. See what else you can get out of him, and then we'll throw the book at him. People like him help the scum get a foothold." Windflower paused. He could feel himself getting upset. Maybe he was just tired. A cross-country flight can do that.

"Tizzard talked to his person in Las Vegas," said Jones. "Turns out it's a detective with the Las Vegas Police Department. He said he put her in touch with Inspector Quigley. He's hoping they might know where Jablonski is."

"Thanks for the update," said Windflower. "I'll give the inspector a call in the morning."

Windflower quietly slipped back into the hotel room, undressed and got into bed. He started thinking about work, the people in his crew, Inspector Quigley and what might happen next. But it all felt like a jumbled-up mess. He was grateful that his tiredness soon took over, and he conked out solid, just like the rest of his family.

When Windflower woke, Sheila and Amelia Louise were playing on the floor. He got up and made the coffee and sat down beside them.

"Good morning, my love," he said to Sheila.

"Good morning, sweetheart," she said back.

"Mornin, mornin," said Amelia Louise.

"I'll get everything organized while you're having your shower," said Sheila.

After Windflower's shower, they went downstairs for a breakfast of cereal, sliced banana, juice and a toasted bagel. Later they were back in the car and on the road to Grand Bank with a stop along the way in Goobies.

As Sheila drove, Windflower was sitting in the back doing his best to keep Amelia Louise amused when his cell phone rang.

"Good morning, Ron," said Windflower. "We're on our way back. Just left St. John's."

"Everything go okay?" asked Quigley.

"So far, so good," said Windflower. "Uncle Frank may be coming down for a visit. Might even stay longer."

"Would be nice to see him," said Quigley. "How's he holding up?"

"He's okay. Sad, but okay. I think he might miss Auntie Marie too much if he stayed out there. He was asking about Bill Ford. How's he doing?"

"He's really improving. They've moved him into a regular room, and the next move might be to St. John's at the Miller Centre."

"That's where both Sheila and Tizzard had their rehabs. Great programs and excellent staff." Sheila looked in the rear-view mirror and gave Windflower a thumbs up.

"Speaking of Tizzard, he made a connection with the LVPD," said Quigley. "A woman detective called me, Detective Sergeant Clarice Rutherford. They've been trying to nail that Big Con creep for years. He's part of the Aryan Warriors and causing them a big problem out there. She's going to check around for us."

"Great," said Windflower as Amelia Louise started to wrestle his cell phone out of his hands. "I gotta go, but I'll check in later."

Windflower passed Amelia Louise his keys, keeping her amused at least temporarily while he tried to enjoy the scenery. But that was rapidly sinking into a bank of fog that was creeping lower and lower to the ground. By the time they reached Goobies, the fog was so thick, they couldn't see their own hands in front of them.

Windflower filled the car with gas while Sheila and Amelia Louise went inside to go to the bathroom and to get some lunch for the drive home. Windflower followed and then carried Amelia Louise over to their car. They had planned to have a bit of a picnic, but that was pretty hard to do with the blanket of thick, damp fog covering everything.

"We'll have an inside-the-car picnic," said Sheila, and she handed Amelia Louise a piece of cheese and an apple-berry squeeze pouch. "This is the last of these," she said to Windflower. "They're super convenient, but she doesn't need them anymore."

"She'll eat just about anything right now," said Windflower as she made an unsuccessful grab for his turkey sandwich. "But she loves bread," he added, handing her a small piece of his sandwich.

She seemed to agree since she stuffed that in her mouth and held out her hand for more.

After lunch Windflower took over driving and slowly and carefully navigated their way down the highway through Swift Current and Marystown and into their driveway at home. Amelia Louise had a little catnap along the way, but Sheila had managed to mostly keep her awake. She had drifted off again just before they pulled into the driveway, but Windflower was able to get her into the house and her crib without waking her up.

He kissed Sheila goodbye and jumped in his Jeep to head over to the RCMP office. Betsy was happy to see him and so were Smithson and Evanchuk. He got their updates and checked his messages and email. One from St. John's RCMP caught his eye. It was headed Re: Community Outreach. He clicked and opened it. He assumed it was simply an acknowledgement of his application. But it was more than that. It was inviting him to an interview and suggested several dates for the following week.

He closed the email and shut down his computer. He needed a little time to think. He drove out to the highway and turned down the road to the T at L'Anse au Loup. The T was a magical place for Windflower and a special one for many of the local residents. The T itself was a narrow strip of land that was crossed by a little peninsula forming the distinct shape that gave the place its name. What gave it magic was the quiet and solitude of being so close to the ocean and watching the tide change the physical environment right before your eyes.

Windflower parked his Jeep near the large beach rocks at the end of the bumpy and unpaved road and started to walk along the shoreline. As was the case many other days, he was the only human present. There were many different kinds of birds swooping and singing, and further on there was a place where a roving pack of seals came to bask in whatever sunlight and warmth remained in the fall air. But Windflower was the lone human, and he liked that.

He tried to think of nothing as he walked along. It was his form of walking meditation. If he could push out his thoughts and fears, it often opened up enough space for him to let new and fresh ideas in. As thoughts of work or his family or community came up, he tried to note them and let them go. After about 15 minutes his mind felt clear and calm. Now he could think about the job application and the possibility of uprooting and leaving for St. John's. He sat on the end of the beach and watched the water flow in and out. He saw the seals playing in the surf, occasionally climbing onto a large rock near the shore and fighting off all comers for the prized perch. That's how life was some days, he thought, although the seals knew claiming the space was just a game and one that many people took far too seriously.

Windflower weighed the pros and cons of a move, including Sheila's desire to go back to school and her strong wish, although she would not demand it, that he leave the Force. He made himself dig deep and ask the real question. What did he want? This was tough, he thought. But he stayed with it until the beginnings of an answer started to form in his brain and, more importantly, in his heart. He walked back to his Jeep and headed home.

59

Soon after he arrived home, he was back out again. Sheila suggested, and he wholeheartedly agreed with, fish and chips for dinner. She called ahead, and he picked up their order shortly afterward. There was a large, two-piece fish and chips dinner with tartar sauce and coleslaw for him and another to be split between Sheila and Amelia Louise. The smell of the freshly cooked chips in the bag nearly drove him crazy, and he could barely breathe until his order was dumped on a plate and he applied the requisite salt and malt vinegar.

Amelia Louise was quite content to stuff one french fry in her mouth and gnaw on another one while Sheila and Windflower enjoyed their meal.

"Anything new at the office?" asked Sheila.

Windflower put down his fork and looked at her. "I got a reply to my application. They want me to come in for an interview next week."

"What did you tell them?"

"I didn't reply yet. I wanted to talk with you. Let's finish our dinner and have a walk. We can talk along the way. It makes me feel less tense."

"Me too," said Sheila.

"Me too, me too," said Amelia Louise, who, having thrown her last piece of french fry overboard, was trying to grab for more.

Windflower handed one over as Lady scooped up the one that fell under her chair. "I bet you'll be happy, too," said Windflower to Lady, who perhaps would be, but at that very moment was more focused on getting some more of those delicious chips from Amelia Louise.

After dinner, cleanup was a breeze with plates and forks in the dishwasher, and then Lady led the way out the door and down the walkway with Amelia Louise running not far behind. She didn't like it when Windflower put her in the stroller, but Lady stayed by her side when he leashed her up. The fog was thinning out quite a bit, and by the time they got down to the wharf, they could see it drifting out to sea.

"We're supposed to get a couple of fine days," said Sheila.

"That'll be nice," said Windflower. "Maybe we can go for a little hike on the weekend."

"Maybe you should try another walk first," said Sheila.

"I'm good," he said, but he did notice that the more he walked, the more strain he felt on his ankle. But he sure wasn't going to tell Sheila that.

Sheila said hello to a couple who were out for their evening stroll and then sat on a bench overlooking the water. Windflower pulled Amelia Louise up next to her and then sat down.

"Do you want to go to St. John's?" he asked.

"I want to go to school," said Sheila. "I can do that remotely or in class, depending on where we're living."

"So, you're saying it's up to me about St. John's."

"I think you should decide about your own career. But remember, you did give me a voice."

"I did and I still do. So, let me tell you my thinking, and then you give me your opinion."

"Okay," said Sheila, picking up a restless Amelia Louise out of her stroller and holding her in her arms.

"I think the St. John's move might be a temporary one," said Windflower. "But it feels like if I start moving in that direction, I am leaving the RCMP, sooner or later."

"It does feel like that to me, too," said Sheila. "Are you okay with that?"

"I think so. It's time we had more of a normal life. I'm ready to give it a try. If you'll help me."

"Wow, asking for my advice and my help? Absolutely. Why don't you try the job in St. John's and see how it goes?"

"Okay. That's assuming they'll give it to me."

"Go to the interview and see what happens," said Sheila. "One thing I've realized is that when we are healthy and thinking clearly, there are only good choices in front of us. That's what you have now. We have a good life, and we'll continue to have a good life."

"A great life," said Windflower.

"Grate, grate, grate," said Amelia Louise all the way home.

They were hoping to get Amelia Louise settled down early, but all of the excitement and change in routine in the previous days made that impossible. She was just too wired up. So after bath time and three stories, they took her back downstairs and let her run around until she finally exhausted herself. She was trying to stay awake on the couch next to her mom, but slowly and then with a thump, she simply fell over. Windflower carried her upstairs and tucked her in while Sheila went to have her bath.

He went downstairs and was starting to finally relax himself when his cell phone rang. It was Tizzard.

"Hey, Eddie. What's up?" asked Windflower.

"We got 'im," said Tizzard.

"We got who?" asked Windflower.

"Big Con, Jablonski. Well, we didn't get him. Clarice, I mean Detective Sergeant Rutherford and the LVPD, got him. But they're shipping him back to us."

"That's good news. Are they sending him to Halifax or Toronto?" Those were the most likely destinations for a dangerous criminal like Jablonski.

"I think they're sending him to Marystown," said Tizzard. "That's what the inspector said."

"I'll call him and see what's going on," said Windflower. "Anything else?"

"Yeah, we've been tracking back on Gerald Matthews. We picked up all kinds of stuff at his apartment, and his fingerprints are all over weapons and scales and things. And I've got a few guys who are willing to talk about him. They want immunity, of course, but I think we might be able to lay a few heavy-duty charges on him."

"That is good. Keep on it. I'll be back in tomorrow."

After hanging up with Tizzard, Windflower phoned Ron Quigley.

"Inspector, I hear congratulations are in order," he said. "Although I think luck might have had something to do with it, that and the Las Vegas Police Department.

"Maybe they had luck," said Quigley. "But I would have you know that 'diligence is the mother of good luck.'"

"I know that one," said Windflower. "Benjamin Franklin. I hear our bad guy is getting shipped back over there. I'm surprised. I thought the brass would want him."

"Oh, they do," said Quigley. "We get him for 24 hours. He gets escorted into Marystown, and then we ship him over to you in Grand Bank for arraignment."

"Over here? Why?"

"They want us to make a show of parading Jablonski into court. It's one of their new strategies. It's designed to make the community more aware of the damage that these guys are doing and to discourage people from getting involved with them."

"I like it. When do you think this will happen?"

"Probably on Monday, although he will likely be in Marystown on Sunday night. Can you have someone come over to escort him? They'll be sending their guys from HQ down, but it would be good to have as much local content as possible."

"No problem," said Windflower. "I know the perfect team to send along."

"'Have no fear of perfection—you'll never reach it.'"

"Salvador Dali," said Windflower, but it was too late. Quigley was gone, probably laughing to himself at getting the last word, thought Windflower. He'd get him next time. Now he was ready for bed.

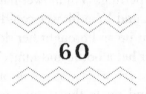

60

Windflower woke early and snuck out of bed and downstairs before anyone else was stirring. He put on the coffee and grabbed his RCMP hoodie and his smudging kit. He got by everyone except Lady, who insisted on coming outside with him. It was a glorious morning, and the sky was just turning pink in the east. It was a magical and mystical time of day as the world shrugged itself awake.

Windflower took out his medicines and put a little of each in the bowl. Then, he remembered he'd forgotten something and went back inside. When he came out, he unwrapped the pipe that Auntie Marie had given him and laid that beside him. He lit the mixture and smudged all over his body and over his head. After he was finished, he felt both calm and clean. That was the spirit he wanted to be in as he examined the pipe again.

He rolled it between his fingers and near to his heart. He could feel his own heart beating, but he could also hear something else. It sounded like a drumming, and he realized it must be his Auntie Marie connecting with him. He listened very carefully now, and it was almost as if she was standing in front of him. As if in a dream she spoke to him.

"Blessings, Nephew. All is well with me. I am with my family, your family. I am proud of you for being honest and brave and most of all for asking for help. Sometimes that is the bravest act we can do, asking for help. I love you."

Then she was gone, leaving Windflower sitting in a daze on his back porch with Lady looking at him like he was no longer there. "It's okay, girl," said Windflower. "It's just my Auntie come to visit." That explanation was fine with Lady who took it as an invitation to come closer for some petting. Windflower happily obliged.

They went inside, and Windflower could hear Amelia Louise start to wake. He went up and brought her down with him to give Sheila a break. He got her a bottle and himself a cup of coffee and turned on the news to see what was going on in the world. Soon after Sheila got up and made them some oatmeal while Windflower got cleaned up for work.

"Thank you, Sheila," said Windflower as he was leaving.

"For what?" asked Sheila.

"For just being you," said Windflower.

"That's nice," said Sheila. "Are you sure there's nothing you want?"

"Well, that's a different matter. I want everything, but for now I'm just grateful to have you." Windflower wiped Amelia Louise's face and hands and laid her on the floor where she quickly scampered off. "I have to go into the office for an hour or so, but the good news is that I'll be off the rest of the day," he said.

"I know the drill," said Sheila. "What's the bad news? I can see it on your face. 'Your eyes are the window to your soul.'"

Windflower feigned shock. "Ah, Sheila, you 'seek to quench the fire of love with words.'"

She went closer to him and gave him a playful punch in the ribs. "You think you're 'sharper than a serpent's tooth,' but I want the truth, Sergeant."

"I have to work tomorrow. We've managed to catch the person who killed Leo Grandy, and he's being shipped over here for processing on Monday. I don't have all the details yet, but it looks like all the cases around here are connected, and the guy we're bringing back is part of a gang—white supremacists—who were trying to take over the drug market around here."

"Are there many locals involved, besides Leo Grandy?"

"There's a few, including Gerald Matthews."

"He's been trouble for years," said Sheila. "He's got that property on Evans Street and another one on Hickman Street that he's been running into the ground, even as he rents them out."

"Well it appears he was a close associate of some of them," said Windflower. "We're trying to put together a solid case against him.

Maybe we should charge him the same day if we can. I'll talk to Tizzard and see where he is on this. You should talk to Ron Quigley."

"That's good. I'll give him a call. Anything we can do to slow this whole drug mess down would be positive for our community."

"Great. I'm going into the office. Why don't you meet me at the Mug-Up later for por' cakes and pea soup? And afterward we can go on a hike up Farmer's Hill."

"See you later," said Sheila as Windflower was walking out the door.

Amelia Louise came running behind him. "See ya, see ya," she cried.

Windflower picked her up and twirled her in the air above his head. He kissed her and handed her off to her mother. "'Parting is such sweet sorrow,'" said Windflower.

"Go," said Sheila. "Call me when you're heading to the café."

When Windflower got to the office, Tizzard's car was parked out front, and he was sitting in the lunchroom, having a snack.

"Still eating?" asked Windflower.

"I try to never stop," said Tizzard. "I'm just waiting for Carrie to come back from her highway run, and we're going to my dad's for breakfast."

"You're going to eat again?"

"Just a small bit. I have to save myself for por' cakes later."

"I'm going to talk to Jones and suggest that she and you pick up Jablonski in Marystown tomorrow. What's going on with Matthews? Do we have enough to charge him?"

"I left the file on your desk. There's a list of all the evidence with his prints. And I've got statements from two people who'll testify against him. I think it's good to go to the Crown."

"Excellent," said Windflower. "Enjoy your food. But remember, 'There is a difference between eating and drinking for strength and from mere gluttony.'"

"I'm eating for strength," said Tizzard.

Windflower laughed, got a coffee and went back to his office. Evanchuk came by and picked up Tizzard a few minutes later. Windflower was happy to have the office to himself for a while. He read Tizzard's file and agreed with his recommendation. There was plenty to move on. He called Assistant Crown Attorney Lauren Bartlett and left a message on her cell phone.

Then he opened the email from St. John's about his application. He thought about it one more time and then typed in that he was available for an interview next week and that he was looking forward it. The last part might have been a bit of a fib, but he left it, and hit send.

He was about to pack up for the day when Jones came into the office.

"Hey," he said. "I thought this was your day off."

"It is," said Jones. "But I had a bit of paperwork to clean up. Didn't realize how much you have to do when they put you in charge."

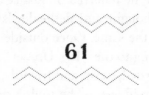
Yeah, I get it. There's lots to keep up with, especially the paper-work," said Windflower. "I think you did a pretty good job. Thanks for filling in."

"No worries," said Jones. "I kinda liked it, to be honest."

"I'll make sure to note this assignment in your file," said Wind-flower. "You'll get another chance at promotion, I'm sure. I do have another job for you, though. Not quite as glamorous as acting corporal."

"What's that?"

"You heard that they caught Jablonski and they're shipping him back?"

"Yeah, he's going to Marystown."

"He is. But we've been asked to arraign him here, in Grand Bank. Sort of a signal to the community. And I don't know if you've seen this." Windflower handed Jones the file that Tizzard had prepared. "We're going to do Gerald Matthews on Monday as well," said Windflower.

Jones ran through the file. "This is good," she said. "Have you talked to the Crown?"

"Just left a message. Anyway, I want you and Tizzard to go pick Jablonski up in Marystown and bring him back. And I want you to come with me to the courthouse on Monday."

Jones smiled broadly. "I like it," she said. "A black RCMP officer bringing a white supremacist to justice. Wow. Thank you so much."

"You're welcome," said Windflower. "Now if you'll excuse me, I have a date with por' cakes and pea soup, and my family, of course."

"Enjoy your day, Sergeant."

As Windflower walked away, he could see that Jones was still smiling to herself, and he reflected on justice and karma. Hell may indeed be empty, he thought, and all the devils here, but it looks like justice is possible all the same. Once outside he called Sheila and told her he was heading to the Mug-Up.

The café was crowded, warm and friendly, and everyone smiled and said hello to Windflower as he took a seat in the corner and grabbed the high chair for Amelia Louise. He had a cup of coffee and chatted with people while he waited for Sheila and their daughter to arrive. When they did, Amelia Louise quickly became the centre of attention.

"She has more friends than you," said Moira Stoodley, who had come by to say hello to Windflower.

Sheila was chasing her daughter around the café as she visited with everyone, until she finally nabbed her and brought her squiggling back and handed her to Windflower. He put her in the high chair and strapped her in, but she was still waving to everyone she'd just said hi to.

"She's very social," said Windflower.

"Busy this morning?" asked Sheila to Moira.

"About the usual," said Moira. "I don't mind because I made up all the por' cakes last night, and Herb got the soup going. This is my morning to visit."

Windflower ordered their soup and por' cakes and got a few crackers from Herb to keep Amelia Louise amused while Sheila and Moira caught up. When their food arrived, Windflower tied a bib around Amelia Louise and cut up a por' cake for her and put it on her plate. Then he poured a large dollop of molasses on the side of her plate, and Amelia Louise did what she always did. She took her fingers and dipped them in the molasses. "Ummmm," she said.

"Is it good?" asked Windflower.

"Sum good," said Amelia Louise.

"Spoken like a true Newfoundlander," said Moira. "I should go and see how Herb is making out." She left, and Windflower and Sheila enjoyed their Saturday lunch special. Letting Sheila and Amelia Louise finish up, Windflower went to the cash to pay just as Tizzard and Evanchuk showed up.

"I hope you left some for us," said Tizzard.

"There may never be enough for you," said Windflower. "Go say hello to Sheila, and I'll be right over. Windflower watched Tizzard creep up on Amelia Louise, and then her shrieks of 'unca, unca, unca' could be heard all over the café.

"I suggested that Carrie and Eddie come over for dinner tonight," said Sheila. "Hope that's okay."

"Perfect," said Windflower.

"I have to work later, but it will be nice to have a visit," said Evanchuk.

"How have you been feeling?" asked Windflower.

"Mornings are not my best time," said Evanchuk. "But I'm hoping that will pass as I head into the next trimester."

"It's awful," said Tizzard. "Some mornings she can't eat breakfast at all. I would die if I couldn't have my breakfast."

"Or your lunch or supper," said Sheila, laughing.

"Or your snacks," said Windflower, joining in the fun. "We'll see you tonight. Come by whenever you want. We're going for a walk."

Windflower followed Sheila in his Jeep, and they parked behind the clinic where the trail that led up Farmer's Hill began. They got out of their cars, and while Windflower had planned to put Amelia Louise in her carrier and on his back, she had other ideas. As soon as she was released from her car seat, she took off down the pathway towards the brook, followed very closely by Lady who had also managed to escape the back of Sheila's car.

Windflower ran after them to make sure that Amelia Louise didn't fall in the water, but Lady seemed to have positioned herself between the brook and the little girl. "Good girl," said Windflower as he reached to put on her leash. "Sorry," he added. "We have to put your leash on in case there's anyone else on the path."

Sheila caught up, and soon the three of them and Lady were moving along the pathway towards the dam. Near the dam Amelia Louise decided she'd had enough exercise for one day and was whining to be picked up. Windflower put her in the carrier and strapped her to his back. They passed a couple of fellow travellers, but the foot traffic thinned out the further they went up the trail.

Windflower took the leash off Lady, and she happily went off to sniff and snarf her way through the underbrush. They took the fork in the road that led to Farmer's Hill, but Windflower felt his ankle start to throb a little and suggested they settle for a shorter walk today. Sheila gave him one of her 'I told you so' looks but, gratefully for Windflower, stayed silent.

Both Windflower and Sheila were ready for a little break, so they stopped at the main lookout. Amelia Louise needed a break, too, apparently because she was out cold in the carrier.

Windflower took it off and laid her on the ground near them. Sheila took out a bottle of water and offered it to him. He took a drink and handed it back. He stood and walked to the edge of the raised platform and looked down into Grand Bank.

"I love this little town," said Windflower. "It's so calm and peaceful and perfect, despite its imperfections."

"I agree," said Sheila. "It will be hard to leave, even for a year if that's what it is."

"I think we'll be back. Maybe it'll be just to visit, but it doesn't feel like we're at the end of our time in Grand Bank."

"For sure. 'Often when you think you're at the end of something, you're at the beginning of something else.'"

"That's very wise. Some great philosopher?"

"Yes," said Sheila. "Mister Rogers."

Amelia Louise started to stir in the carrier. "Let's go back down," said Windflower.

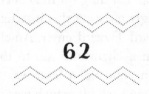

62

I thought we could have scallops for appetizers, and maybe you could fry up some fish," said Sheila. "One of the staff gave me a few fillets from their food fishery catch."

"I love that idea of the food fishery," said Windflower.

"Well, we needed that after they shut down the inshore cod fishery," said Sheila. "Newfoundlanders would die without their fish."

"Herb keeps asking me to go with him, and I never seem to have the time. But scallops with cod fish sounds delicious," said Windflower.

"Great. I was going to try to make Coquilles Saint-Jacques."

"Wow. I'm impressed."

"The important word is try."

"Take your time. It'll be great. 'To climb steep hills requires slow pace at first.' I'll look after the monster while you get that ready. The fish is simple."

Windflower took Amelia Louise to the living room and Sheila started getting everything ready. She pulled out a package of cleaned shells to put the finished product in and laid them on the shelf. She mixed up some flour, salt, curry powder and cayenne pepper in a large bowl and then tossed the scallops in the mixture.

Next, she sautéed the scallops in melted butter until they were golden brown. After that she added some mushrooms and onions and finished that part off by putting in a little white cooking wine and scraping the bottom of the pan to get all the browned bits into her sauce. Once that was ready, she spooned the mixture into the shells and topped each with some breadcrumbs and Emmental cheese. That part done she went out to the living room and waited with the others for their guests to arrive.

Amelia Louise was standing on the couch trying to play with Molly, who was strongly resisting this interference in her personal place. When they heard Tizzard enter, Amelia Louise began her now famous 'unca, unca' chant and ran to the door. She tried to jump in Tizzard's arms, and he at least was able to shield Evanchuk from the near-flying assault, which was a very important task because she held a mysterious white cardboard box.

"You brought dessert," said Sheila. "You shouldn't have, but we thank you, Carrie."

"Thanks," said Windflower. "What is it?"

Both women looked at him like he'd just broken Sheila's best china, but Tizzard was happy to help him out. "It's a lemon meringue pie. We got the last one at Lake's Bakery in Fortune. Did you hear they were closing down?"

"It's pretty sad," said Sheila. "We've been eating baked goods from Lake's all our lives in Grand Bank. But I guess the owners are getting older and their young ones don't want to take it over."

"That is super sad," said Tizzard.

Windflower got the adults, except Evanchuk, a glass of wine, and they had a pleasant chat about babies and the weather, and even a little about work, too, until it was time to get dinner going. Windflower had already cut up his pork fatback and put it on medium heat to fry up. While that was happening, he sprinkled some flour on a plate and added a generous measure of black pepper and a dash of salt. Once the fat had melted, he pushed the fried pork to one side, dipped the cod in the flour and placed the fish in the pan. About five minutes later, he turned the fish.

Sheila came in and put the scallops under the broiler, and as soon as Windflower finished, he placed the fish in the oven to keep warm. Sheila put on some green beans with butter and garlic and called everybody to supper. The Coquilles Saint-Jacques was a great hit, as was the fish—with the pork fat scrunchions sprinkled over the top—and the garlicky green beans.

Over dinner the conversation turned to the future and what lay ahead.

"What are you going to do, Eddie?" asked Sheila.

Tizzard looked at Evanchuk, and she nodded to go ahead. "I'm going to come back, but mostly to give us some cushion when it comes to leave and stuff. Carrie's going to take off her full maternity leave, and I'll take paternity when she's done. Then, we'll figure out what happens next."

"That's pretty good," said Windflower. "You can make up your mind along the way whether you want to stay or leave the Force."

"What about you guys?" asked Evanchuk. "There's a rumour that you might be going to St. John's."

This time Sheila looked at Windflower, and he smiled to go ahead. "I think we're going to play it by ear, too," she said. "I want to go back to school, and it might be possible to do that full-time in St. John's. More will be revealed."

"Time to reveal that pie," said Windflower. Everybody, including Amelia Louise, liked that idea.

After dessert and cleanup Tizzard went for a walk with Windflower and Lady while Sheila and Evanchuk gave Amelia Louise her bath. It was a fine night, and the two men walked along full and happy as Lady showed them off to all her Grand Bank canine friends. When they got back, Tizzard read the bedtime story, and the foursome had a game of cards before Evanchuk had to go to work.

Goodbyes and hugs were a great way to end the evening, and Windflower felt particularly grateful as he turned off the lights and said good night to his four-legged friends. He paused and looked up at the sky before heading upstairs. The moon was a bright white orb, and he thought about his Auntie Marie and wished her a good night, too. He could almost feel her smile back at him. With that warm feeling inside he went up and climbed into bed with an already-sleeping Sheila.

Sunday morning dawned bright and beautiful, and it was Windflower's turn to not only get up with Amelia Louise but to look after her all morning. Sheila got to sleep in and later to go to church. In a few years she would take her daughter, but a few failed attempts had turned them both off the experience for now. That was all okay with Windflower. He liked a little father-daughter time.

First up was Pop-Tarts and a few cartoons for Amelia Louise and a large coffee for Windflower. This was the unhealthiest breakfast ever, and Windflower did his best to hide the evidence. He also would try and make up for it by making scratch waffles with strawberries later on. But for now everyone, including Lady who had got about a quarter of Amelia Louise's Pop-Tart, was happy.

When Sheila came down, she watched Amelia Louise while Windflower had his Sunday morning spiritual time. He went outside with his smudging kit and sat on the back porch with Lady by his side. She was used to this ritual and seemed to even be attracted to it. Sometimes Windflower, like on this morning, would try and smudge her, but the smoke chased her away. "I guess you like praying more than smudging," said Windflower. Lady skulked off and went to the furthest part of the yard, pretending not to notice him.

Windflower laughed out loud at his dog's antics and continued his smudge in silence. He said his prayers afterward with a special one for his Uncle Frank and another for Tizzard, Evanchuk and their baby that was on the way. It reminded him of how deliri-ously happy and totally anxious he had been all at the same time when Amelia Louise's birth grew nearer. He ended his prayers with a wish for his Auntie Marie and another to Grandmother Moon to watch over him and all members of his family, two-legged and four-legged alike. As if she could hear him finish up, Lady came running back so she'd be there with him when he decided it was time to go back inside.

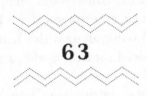

63

Sheila went to have her shower while Amelia Louise helped Windflower make the waffle mixture. Her version of helping was to spread doughy goo all over herself, her high chair and anything within a five-foot radius. Windflower managed to clean her up and then get the waffle iron hot while he sliced up a bowl of strawberries and took out the maple syrup and whipped cream.

As soon as she saw the whipped cream can, Amelia Louise opened her mouth wide and held it open. "You are going to get me into so much trouble," said Windflower. But he still turned the can towards her and sprayed a small amount into her mouth. 'Mmmmm," she said.

"What tastes so good?" asked Sheila as she came into the kitchen. "Strawberries," said Windflower, and he handed Amelia Louise a freshly cut piece. "Shushhhh," he mimed to Amelia Louise. "Shushhhh," she said as loudly as she could back to him. He started to wag his finger at her, but Sheila stopped him by giving him half of the first waffle and Amelia Louise the second. Sheila poured syrup and put a tiny portion of whipped cream atop some strawberries on each half.

"God, I love a man who can cook," said Sheila.

After waffles, Sheila got ready for church, and Windflower cleaned and dressed Amelia Louise for the day. Normally on Sunday morning Windflower would go for a run with Amelia Louise on his back and Lady by their side, and Lady was waiting impatiently for her Sunday morning run. "Sorry, girl, said Windflower. "It will have to be a walk this morning. But maybe we'll go see the ducks."

"Ducks, ducks, ducks," said Amelia Louise.

"Yeah, we're going to feed the ducks," said Windflower. He

grabbed the carrier in the hallway and dumped out the contents on the floor—a juice box, an extra sweater, a bib, a fruit cup and a spoon, all for Amelia Louise, along with a half-empty water bottle. Then Windflower noticed something else, a red bow lying in the middle of the jumbled-up mess.

"Sheila, when did you get this bow?" he asked, showing it to his wife.

"I've never seen it before," said Sheila. "Where did you find it?"

"In here," said Windflower, pointing to the carrier.

"We must have picked it up somewhere," said Sheila. "It looks brand new. Why don't you put it on Amelia Louise to keep the hair out of her face?" She kissed Amelia Louise and gave Windflower a quick peck on the cheek and was gone before her daughter could kick up a fuss.

Windflower stood holding the bow in his hand. It couldn't be, he thought. But maybe it is, he thought again. It looked like the red bow from the dream he had in the motel just outside Pink Lake, the red bow that Auntie Marie had left behind. Could it really be the same one? Maybe Auntie Marie wanted to protect him and his family and had sent him this gift. Sheila had said to put it in Amelia Louise's hair, so he did.

Windflower didn't have much more time to puzzle over the ribbon's origins as Lady was scratching at his leg and Amelia Louise tugging at it. "Okay, okay, let's go," he said.

He packed some stale bread and a bottle of water in the side of the carrier, put Amelia Louise in and on his back, put the leash on Lady, and off they went down through town, past the Mug-Up café where people were having their Sunday morning breakfast, past the wharf and all the seagulls and then over to the brook.

As soon as the ducks saw Windflower standing beside the water, they came swimming towards him. The bigger ones came first, followed by the flying seagulls, with the mother and baby ducks pulling up the rear. Amelia Louise was dancing now as she threw small pieces of bread into the water and watched the ducks scramble and dive for their share. Windflower threw some, too, but he had to hold Lady back from jumping in the water after both bread and birds. They had several minutes of pure excitement and energy, and all of them were all invigorated when it was over. He picked up Amelia Louise and carried her as she continued to wave goodbye to her duck friends all the way home.

Windflower got everyone inside and relatively cleaned up. He made himself and Amelia Louise a peanut butter sandwich and half a banana for lunch, which she promptly shared with Lady. Even Molly, who had not been part of the excursion, got a portion, which she snagged before Lady could get to it. The collie considered fighting for it, but after the cat hissed at a rather feeble attempt, that was the end of that battle.

"Law of the jungle," said Windflower to Lady as he witnessed the recent skirmish.

"What law?" asked Sheila as she came in from church. "And who are you talking to?"

Rather than admit he'd been talking to the dog, he switched direction. "I'm going to the office for the afternoon. How about hamburgers on the barbeque for dinner?"

"That sounds good," said Sheila. "I'll make us some veggies and a salad."

"Perfect," said Windflower. "See you later." He kissed Amelia Louise, not quite succeeding at avoiding the peanut butter all over her face. Sheila wiped him off and gave him a kiss to send him on his way.

Tizzard, Jones, Evanchuk and Smithson were all at the office when he got there.

"What are you all doing here?" asked Windflower.

"I'm just going home," said Evanchuk. "I was saying goodbye to Eddie before I left."

"I'm just coming on," said Smithson. "I helped Tizzard bring in Matthews."

"We brought him in last night," said Tizzard. "Jones figured it would be better to have him in here before we brought over Jablonski."

"I'm here to go to Marystown, whenever we get the call," said Jones.

"Okay," said Windflower. "I'll call the inspector for an update. Before I call, can I talk to you for a sec?" he asked Jones.

The other officers went to the back, and Jones followed him into his office.

"Are you sure you want to do this?" asked Windflower. "You don't have to. I can get Smithson to go with Tizzard."

"You mean because he's a white supremacist and I'm black?" asked Jones. "I want to go, sir. I think it's important that I do and be seen as doing it."

"I don't disagree, Constable," said Windflower. "But he won't be happy, and he will let you know it. He will likely say some hurtful things."

"Thank you for your concern, Sergeant," said Jones. "I fully expect that he will. But his words have very little impact on me. He won't say anything that I haven't heard before. But I will never allow any person, black or white, man or woman, to hurt me in that way ever again. This feels like justice, sir, and I very much would like to be part of it."

"Very well," said Windflower. "Let me call Inspector Quigley."

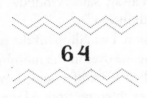

64

Quigley told Windflower they would be ready to have the prisoner picked up at three o'clock. Other officers would also be escorting in two additional vehicles and would remain with the prisoner until their return to Marystown after the court appearance. The following day, Monday, Grand Bank detachment would be responsible for transport to and from the courthouse. They would also be responsible for maintaining a security perimeter around the detachment and then again around the courthouse.

Windflower gave his team directions after the call. He and Smithson would take care of the security perimeter right away, and he sent Smithson out to start putting up the barriers. Jones and Tizzard were dispatched to Marystown to be ready when the green light was given for the prisoner escort. Evanchuk would hold the fort until everything got organized and would then go home to get a break. She would be back later to do the regular patrol and to relieve Smithson.

Once Jones and Tizzard had left, Windflower took a run to the Mug-Up. He wanted another coffee and maybe a treat. This could be a long day. But he also wanted to order a tray of sandwiches for the night and to get Herb and Moira to make him a dozen breakfast sandwiches for his crew in the morning.

Windflower had a pleasant visit and a partridgeberry muffin with his coffee. He also got to visit briefly with Herb Stoodley who was thinking about applying for a moose licence and was wondering if Windflower wanted to be part of his crew.

"It's tough to get the moose out. That's assuming I'm lucky enough to get one. I'm too old for that stuff. 'But age with his stealing steps hath clawed me in his clutch,'" said Herb.

"I'll see if I can get away," said Windflower. "But I'd say you still have some salt of youth in you."

"Thank you, Winston. I will drop off the sandwich tray tonight, and you can send someone over in the morning for the rest."

Windflower finished his coffee and drove back to the office to wait for the prisoner to come from Marystown. Smithson was standing outside a wooden barrier well away from the detachment when Windflower arrived. He moved the barrier back and Windflower went into the building. He sent Evanchuk home and passed the time by going through a new stack of paperwork that Betsy must have delivered when he wasn't paying attention.

He heard the company arrive before he saw them. He looked out the window and saw the two RCMP vans and Tizzard pushing a very agitated Jablonski ahead of him. Jones went first and opened the door. Windflower could hear the prisoner screaming at her, using language that would curl anybody's ears, almost all of it racist, sexist and degrading. Unperturbed, Jones pushed on down the hallway and opened a jail cell. Tizzard manhandled Jablonski, still screaming, into his cell.

"That was a rough ride," said Tizzard as they came back to Windflower.

"Are you okay?" Windflower asked Jones.

"I'll be fine after I wash the filth off me," she said. "Is it okay if I take a break?"

"Sure. We got this. Here comes the cavalry," he said as the four other Mounties who were in the vans came in. "See you in the morning."

Jones left, and Windflower and Tizzard walked to the back with the guys from Marystown. They walked past a still scowling Jablonski and a much more subdued Gerald Matthews in the cell at the very end of the hall. "You won't let him get me, will you?" asked Matthews.

Windflower put his finger to his lips and whispered. "You don't want him to know that you're in here." And then he walked away.

Tizzard made a fresh pot of coffee and opened the sandwich tray. The Marystown guys agreed to split the overnight shift with two always being here and the others at the motel not far away.

Smithson and then Evanchuk would ensure that the perimeter was protected. Tizzard would do the overnight patrol, so he left to get some sleep before coming back in at midnight. Windflower would be on call all the way through and would cover off the evening shift after he had dinner.

Windflower called Quigley to let him know that everything was set and secure in Grand Bank and drove home for dinner. Sheila had taken the hamburger patties out of the freezer and laid them on the counter to thaw. They were Windflower's homemade spicy hamburgers with curry powder, hot mustard powder, garlic and Worcestershire sauce.

He gave Sheila and Amelia Louise a peck on the cheek, got changed and was outside with Lady in a few minutes. Sheila already had the salad on the table and was steaming some carrots and vegetables. All they needed now was the meat. He fired up the grill and cleaned it when it was hot. Then he put the four burgers on the hot grill. Six minutes later with several turns in between, the burgers were hot and juicy and done.

Amelia Louise got a chopped-up burger with half a bun and veggies. Sheila and Windflower had the other burgers along with the salad and a heaping helping of the remaining vegetables. There was a lot of eating and little talk as Windflower felt he had to get back as soon as possible to oversee the operation at the detachment.

Sheila cleaned up, and Windflower headed back to work. Despite his anxiety, there was very little going on at the office. Smithson maintained his lonely vigil outside while the two Marystown officers played cards in the back. Windflower shuffled his papers for a bit and then settled into the quiet for the next couple of hours. He was falling asleep in his chair when Evanchuk came in and surprised him. He wished her a good night, and not long after he was home and in bed.

Despite his late night he woke early. He managed to get out of bed without waking Sheila. Once downstairs, he took Lady for a quick spin around the block and dropped her back at home. He wrote a note for Sheila and drove to work.

Evanchuk was on duty at the barrier, and he waved as he went by. Inside, Tizzard was telling the two Marystown officers about his Las Vegas escapades. They didn't really believe him, but Tizzard was having great fun just by telling them. He asked Windflower to verify his story, but Windflower declined.

"I'm not involved. I wasn't there. All I care about is a cup of coffee right now," said Windflower.

"Freshly made," said one of the Marystown guys. "But I am getting a bit hungry."

"Can you check the Mug-Up?" Windflower asked Tizzard as he poured himself a coffee.

Tizzard got up and was back in five minutes with a brown paper bag.

"You asked the right guy," said Tizzard, causing all the other Mounties to laugh. "Fresh breakfast sandwiches from the best café in town."

All the Mounties dug in, and Windflower went to his office to check in with Quigley.

"I'm on my way over there," said Quigley. "I also spoke with Lauren Bartlett. They're all ready to go, and the media will be out in full force. Might even get some national coverage."

"Good stuff," said Windflower. "We're all good here. If you get here soon you might even get a breakfast sandwich. Then again, Tizzard is here, so you may not."

Quigley laughed. "Pull rank and save me one," he said and hung up.

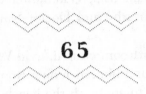

65

The rest of the morning flew by until it was time to go to the courthouse. Windflower got Matthews out the back door and over to the courthouse first, before the real action started. He was part of the story but only playing a bit role today. The star of the show was Jablonski, but Windflower hoped that Jones would be too. He staged the departures so that Jones went out first, followed by Tizzard with Jablonski and then the Marystown Mounties, providing what he called a 'dishonour guard'. The media were lined up outside the courthouse and captured the whole thing.

Inside the courtroom Gerald Matthews sat cowering on one side of the prisoner area as Jablonski was led in. The Marystown officers took off Jablonski's handcuffs and leg chains. He rubbed his hands together and stared first at Jones and then glared at Matthews who seemed to sink in his chair.

The judge asked Assistant Crown Attorney Bartlett to speak. She rose and read the charges against Jablonski into the record.

"How do you plead?" asked the judge.

Jablonski was pushed to his feet and started a long and winding rant about blacks and Jews and women and Latinos and the new world order that was coming. The judge was banging on his gavel to get him to stop. Then he did. He stopped talking. And he fell to the ground clutching his chest. Most of the crowd gasped and were frozen to the spot, but every police officer in the place jumped and ran towards Jablonski. Jones was the closest. "He's not breathing, no pulse," she said.

"Do CPR," said Windflower, who was the nearest to Jones. Jones looked at him for a second, and the irony of a black woman trying to save a white supremacist was not lost on either of them.

As Jones bent over Jablonski, Windflower called the paramedic station at the clinic nearby, and Doctor Sanjay, who was almost always on call.

"Let's get the courtroom cleared," said Windflower quietly to the other officers around him, including Ron Quigley. But before anyone had a chance to approach the bench, the judge made the necessary announcement.

"Ladies and gentlemen, there's been an incident, nothing for you to worry about. The officers will help you get out in an orderly fashion," said the judge. Inspector Quigley nodded at the judge and organized the officers to ensure that everyone was filing out of the courtroom calmly.

Windflower approached Tizzard. "Get Matthews back into lock-up right away and stay with him," he said.

The paramedics were fast, and before the courtroom was even emptied, they had their gurney rolled in and were connecting Jablonski to the paddles. They shocked him once, twice, three times, but there was no movement. They looked at Windflower and shook their heads. Doctor Sanjay got there shortly afterward, confirmed their diagnosis and instructed them to bring Jablonski to the clinic. He, too, shook his head at Windflower as he left with the paramedics.

Windflower and Quigley moved apart from the other Mounties.

"Well, that was a surprise," said Quigley. "Not quite the show we had planned but spectacular nonetheless. What do we tell them?" he asked, pointing outside. "They look like hungry wolves looking for something to eat."

"I guess we give them the truth," said Windflower. "I think it's about the community. Let's talk to the mayor. Is Mayor Hillier outside?" he asked Evanchuk. "Can you see if you can find her?"

Evanchuk came back with Sheila. She, Windflower and Quigley talked about how they would deal with the media together. Windflower would talk about the impact that drugs and gangs were having in Grand Bank, Quigley would speak in bigger terms about the regional impact, and Sheila would ask for community support to stop the spread of drugs and violence and how everyone had to work together.

"Ready?" asked Windflower. Sheila and Quigley nodded, and the three walked out into the mob of waiting media.

Later that evening, Sheila and Windflower were watching the news and complimented each other on the job they'd done.

"I loved your line about 'we're not here to protect the community. We're here to help the community protect itself,'" said Sheila.

"That's not really my line. It's from a very wise woman who was advising a big city police department about how to get the community on their side," said Windflower. "But I loved when you called on everybody to be a leader in their own way—in their families and neighbourhoods and in Grand Bank. That was powerful."

"Yeah, we're just grand, aren't we?" said Sheila.

"I'd say we're not too shabby b'y," said Windflower. "Let's go to bed."

ONE MONTH LATER...

Windflower was sitting on his back porch, watching some of the first snow of the season fall gently into his garden. Lady was oblivious to the snow as she continued to try to find interesting things, dead and alive, under the leaves.

Windflower smudged the pipe first as he'd seen Auntie Marie do. Then, he placed a small amount of sacred tobacco that he'd been given in Pink Lake into the pipe. He puffed on it to light the tobacco and then watched the smoke float all around him. As he watched the smoke and the snow, even Lady and the backyard seemed to fade away until all that was left was a grey haze.

He could almost make out activity within this dusky scene, but he also heard a voice talking to him. It was not out loud, but it came from inside him. Listen, the voice said. Feel and try not to see.

He took a deep breath and followed that advice as best he could. The quieter he sat, and the more he calmed his mind, the more he started to feel. At first it was like the wind, blowing softly through his hair. Then, he could feel the presence of one, then many, touching him somehow, although they were not physically there. Finally, he started to sense and feel that his Auntie Marie was sitting right there beside him. He felt her smile like sunshine on his face, and then he felt her love like an overwhelming tide of comfort that he could have fallen asleep into.

In fact, he almost did, and Lady was staring at him when he nearly fell over from where he was sitting. Lady was giving him that 'are you okay?' look, so he patted her on the head. "I'm fine, Lady. In fact, I feel great."

Windflower went back inside where Sheila was getting Amelia Louise her breakfast. "There's some bacon in the oven if you want to make yourself an egg," said Sheila. "I'd do it, but I have to go over to the town office."

"Oh, yeah, it's your last day," said Windflower. "After today you'll be a free woman."

"Not really," said Sheila. "Just a change in roles. I'm going from being mayor to being a full-time student and a mother of two."

"Well, it'll just be one until after Christmas when our foster daughter arrives."

"I'm excited about Stella coming to live with us. It's just a lot of change. You'll have a new job, and we'll be in St. John's. Maybe it's too much all of a sudden."

"I could give you a quote, but I'd rather not die this morning," said Windflower, buttering his toast. "Besides, my new job as public outreach coordinator will mean I'll be home every night."

"That is good," said Sheila. "And we'll close up the B & B this weekend, so that's another worry gone."

"Maybe Uncle Frank will come in the spring to help us open up," said Windflower.

"That would be nice," said Sheila. "Okay, I'm going to get her ready."

Windflower finished his breakfast and cleaned up. He yelled goodbye to Sheila and drove to work. Windflower said good morning to Betsy and started to work on cleaning up his desk when Ron Quigley called him.

"Good morning, Sergeant. How are you on this foul weather day? 'Barren winter with his wrathful nipping cold' awaits us."

"It's a grand day, despite the weather," said Windflower. "Besides, 'there is no such thing as bad weather, only different kinds of good weather.' What can I do for you?"

"I'm trying to fill the holes that you've created," said Quigley.

"Not just me," said Windflower. "Jones is taking her own initiative. And I don't have to remind you that you already took Smithson."

"You're right. Don't remind me. But the more that happens around here the less likely it is that I'll get to Ottawa."

"True, but Ottawa could be worse than Marystown. And you'll still have Evanchuk and Tizzard over here.

"That's true, and I got some good news on that front. Tizzard's reinstatement came through."

"He'll be happy with that," said Windflower. "If you get them someone solid as part of their team, they should be okay."

"That's what I'm thinking, too," said Quigley. "Oh, Gerald Matthews got a deal, by the way. He serves a year at the pen in St. John's in return for testimony. He'll have to be in protective custody, but he's a survivor."

"Another cockroach. The interesting thing is what happens when he gets back here. I think people will treat him like a pariah. He certainly deserves it."

"It seems strange how everything ended, don't you think? Most of the really bad guys, including Jablonski, either died or have been put away for a long time."

"I heard someone once say that you have to wait for the next world to get true justice. All we have here is the law. But it did turn out pretty well, although I'm not sure how much we had to do with it," said Windflower.

"Doesn't matter," said Quigley. "'All's well that ends well.' And given how it started, this certainly ended well, at least for the good guys."

"Bye Ron," said Windflower.

After Quigley hung up, Windflower sat in his office, which for the first time in a long time was quiet and calm. After all of the excitement of the last month or so, things were finally getting back to normal. That's when Windflower realized how much he would miss after he left the Grand Bank detachment—not the hurly-burly of crime and criminals, but the peace of feeling like you were finally at home.

"Penny for your thoughts, Sarge?" asked Tizzard as he interrupted Windflower's reverie.

"I was just thinking how grateful I am to just be here today," he replied.

"I get ya," said Tizzard. "I was hugging Carrie this morning, and I think I actually felt the baby kick, although she said she probably just had gas."

Windflower laughed. "Doesn't really matter, does it?" he said.

"I don't think so," said Tizzard. "My dad always says that happiness is what's inside your head. So be careful what you feed it."

"Good advice. Any other pearls of wisdom you want to pass along?"

"Never think on an empty stomach. So we should go to the Mug-Up to get a muffin."

"I like that idea," said Windflower. "I like that idea a lot."

THE END

BEFORE THE STORM . . .

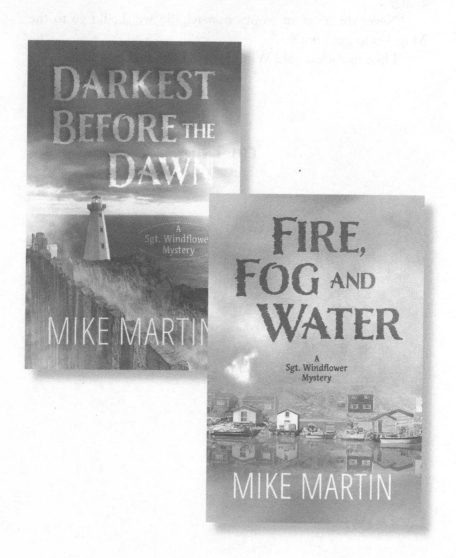

CHRISTMAS WITH WINDFLOWER

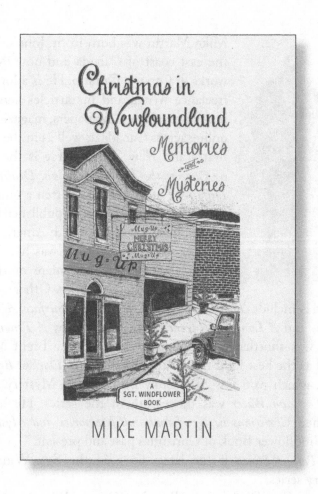

OttawaPressAndPublishing.com

ABOUT THE AUTHOR

Mike Martin was born in St. John's, NL, on the east coast of Canada and now lives and works in Ottawa, Ontario. He is a long-time freelance writer, and his articles and essays have appeared in newspapers, magazines and online across Canada as well as in the United States and New Zealand. He is the author of *Change the Things You Can: Dealing with Difficult People* and has written a number of short stories that have been published in various publications across North America.

The Walker on the Cape was his first full fiction book and the premiere of the Sgt. Windflower Mystery Series. Other books in the series include *The Body on the T, Beneath the Surface, A Twist of Fortune* and *A Long Ways from Home,* followed by *A Tangled Web,* which was shortlisted for the 2017 Bony Blithe Light Mystery Award as the best light mystery of the year, and *Darkest Before the Dawn,* which won the 2019 Bony Blithe Light Mystery Award. *Fire, Fog and Water* was the eighth in the series. He has also published *Christmas in Newfoundland: Memories and Mysteries,* a Sgt. Windflower Book of Christmas past and present.

A Perfect Storm is the latest book in the Sgt. Windflower Mystery series.

He is Past Chair of the Board of Crime Writers of Canada, a national organization promoting Canadian crime and mystery writing, and a member of the Newfoundland Writing Guild and Ottawa Independent Writers.

You can follow the Sgt. Windflower Mysteries on Facebook at https://www.facebook.com/TheWalkerOnTheCapeReviewsAnd-More/